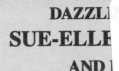

ONLY FOR A KNIGHT

more . . .

"As usual, Welfonder gives her many fans another memorable historical read."
—ReadertoReader.com

"Such a sensually romantic read . . . enticing."
—HistoricalRomanceWriters.com

WEDDING FOR A KNIGHT

"TOP PICK! You couldn't ask for a more joyous, loving, smile-inducing read . . . Will win your heart!"
—*Romantic Times BOOKclub Magazine*

"With history and beautiful details of Scotland, this book provides romance, spunk, mystery, and courtship . . . a must-read!"
—*Rendezvous*

"A very romantic story . . . extremely sexy. I recommend this book to anyone who loves the era and Scotland."
—TheBestReviews.com

MASTER OF THE HIGHLANDS

"Welfonder does it again, bringing readers another powerful, emotional, highly romantic medieval that steals your heart and keeps you turning the pages."
—*Romantic Times BOOKclub Magazine*

"Vastly entertaining and deeply sensual medieval romance . . . for those of us who like our heroes moody, *ultrahot*, and *sexy* . . . this is the one for you!"
—HistoricalRomanceWriters.com

"Yet another bonny Scottish romance to snuggle up with and inspire pleasantly sinful dreams . . . a sweetly compelling love story . . . [with a] super-abundance of sexual tension."

—*Heartstrings*

BRIDE OF THE BEAST

"Larger-than-life characters and a scenic setting . . . Welfonder pens some steamy scenes."

—*Publishers Weekly*

"A wonderful story . . . well-told . . . a delightful mix of characters."

—**RomanticReviews.com**

"Thrilling . . . so sensual at times, it gives you goose bumps . . . Welfonder spins pure magic with her vibrant characters."

—**ReaderToReader.com**

"Four-and-a-half stars! . . . A top pick . . . powerful emotions, strong and believable characters, snappy dialogue, and some humorous moments add depth to the plotline and make this a nonstop read. Ms. Welfonder is on her way to stardom."

—*Romantic Times BOOKclub Magazine*

KNIGHT IN MY BED

"Exciting, action-packed . . . a strong tale that thoroughly entertains."

—*Midwest Book Review*

more . . .

Until The Knight Comes

ALSO BY SUE-ELLEN WELFONDER

Devil in a Kilt

Knight in My Bed

Bride of the Beast

Master of the Highlands

Wedding for a Knight

Only for a Knight

Until The Knight Comes

Sue-Ellen Welfonder

WARNER FOREVER

NEW YORK   BOSTON

Cover design by Diane Luger
Cover illustration by Craig White
Typography by Ron Zinn
Book design by Giorgetta Bell McRee

Warner Books
Hachette Book Group USA
1271 Avenue of the Americas
New York, NY 10020

Printed in the United States of America

First Printing: July 2006

10 9 8 7 6 5 4 3 2 1

For Roberta M. Brown,
for all that you are.
Friend of immeasurable worth,
supportive agent, and fellow dog lover.
My most trusted confidante.
You've shone light onto my darkest hours
and guided me through the worst kind of cold.
A thousand blessings on you, my forever friend.
I'd be lost without you.

Acknowledgments

Scotland is my inspiration and passion, where I go to replenish my soul. So much more than hills, mist, and heather, whisky and kilted men, Scotland casts long shadows that reach deep into the hearts of many.

My own heart is irrevocably given and when there, it is always the wild places that call me. No place stirs me more than Scotland's remote far north, but I am very fond of Nairn, a small Highland town on the Moray Firth.

Many of my most precious memories belong to the shining waters of a small loch not far from Nairn, and the ruins of a stronghold that stand proud on a tiny island in the middle of that loch.

The spirit of the real Mariota dwells there, I am sure, for the stronghold was once her home. I know I have felt her there. And the great man who loved her with a passion so fierce he defied his world and times to keep her.

She inspired this book—even though Alexander Stewart never betrayed her. Far from it, their love was boundless and still lingers on that tiny, loch-girt isle. The real Mariota possessed a bold spirit, much strength, and a generous, loving heart. I have been wanting to honor her with a book for some while. This story is hers—and the Wolf's.

Special thanks as always to my editor, Karen Kostolnyik, for her skilled eye and gentle guidance. She understands my heart and always knows just how to refine my stories. And to Michele Bidelspach, a true gem, for being there.

And as ever, endless appreciation to my very handsome husband, Manfred, my real-life knight, for shielding me from dragons and dark winds. He makes it possible for me to dream. And, of course, for wee Em, Keeper of all my happiness. His canine devotion is my entire strength.

Until The Knight Comes

The Legacy of the Bastard Stone

❧

Long ago, in one of the darkest periods of Scotland's history, but not so distant that time has blurred the memory, a great MacKenzie chieftain prided himself on his strong character and strict uprightness. An indomitable warrior, he was known to fame as Ranald the Redoubtable, his name commanding respect far beyond the Highland fastnesses of his own rugged Kintail.

A masterful man well able to maintain peace in this vast country of darkling hills and shadowed glens, he had but two disturbing weaknesses: a thread of greed that at times vied with the goodness of his heart and a distinct tendency to loftiness.

Susceptibilities that were to prove calamitous when a low-born by-blow of the clan lost his heart to the daughter of a neighboring chieftain. A mere cowherd, Cormac by name, the young man's physical prowess and skill rivaled even the fittest of Ranald the Redoubtable's sons, much to the puissant laird's annoyance.

Cormac's claim that the lass, a maid much-prized for

her beauty and high spirits, wanted him with equal fervor only ensured that fate was to go against him. Indeed, when he approached his chieftain for help in amassing a suitable bride price, false hopes were given, empty promises cast to the fickle winds.

On a day of rain and strong winds, he was to journey to the farthest reaches of Kintail, the dark shores of Loch Hourn, to climb to the highest point of the sea cliffs where a certain outcropping of rock resembles a giant door.

If upon positioning himself atop this natural-made arch, he is able to balance on one foot, he will be deemed worthy to claim any chieftain's daughter as his bride.

And to celebrate his daring and agility, he will be rewarded with double the bride price he'd desired.

Regrettably, as the *seannchies* so poignantly extol, just as Cormac completed his incredible feat and began the climb down, his foot caught on the edge of the door-like outcropping and he plunged to his death, never to know whether his liege-laird would have kept his word or no.

Only Ranald the Redoubtable knew, and over time his guilt overrode his greed and his pride, the true goodness of his heart triumphing to banish his darker side for the rest of his days.

In young Cormac's honor, the rock formation was dubbed The Bastard Stone and in its shadow, a mighty stronghold was raised: Cuidrach Castle, place of the forceful and determined.

And since these earliest times, Cuidrach stands as the proud inheritance reserved by Clan MacKenzie for the most valiant warriors amongst the clan's by-blows. One such stalwart in each generation is raised from his lowborn status and granted the style of Keeper of Cuidrach.

A tradition upheld all down the centuries until one such favored bastard turned so black-hearted that the villainy of his deeds left the clan little choice but to withdraw the privilege, the sad forfeiture leaving Cuidrach to stand untended for decades.

But now a new Keeper of Cuidrach has been named.

A braw young clansman of the same strong character and strict uprightness as his long-passed forebear, Ranald the Redoubtable.

And if along Kintail's wild coastal headlands, the windswept hills could stir, they'd surely be restless, the wind eddying about the rocks perhaps whispering of an ancient wrong.

And pleading it be righted at last.

Chapter One

❦

DRUMODYN CASTLE
SCOTLAND, THE FAR NORTH
AUTUMN 1344

*H*ugh *the Bastard.*

The three words dealt Mariota Macnicol a smiting blow, each one lodging in her throat like searing lumps of hot-burning coal as she stood on the threshold of the tower bedchamber and stared at the man she loved more than life itself.

Certainly more than her own, for she'd willingly suffered the pains of scandal and ruin to be his lady, turning her back on her well-comforted existence to pave him the way to his dreams.

His lofty ambitions.

And now Hugh Alesone, Bastard of Drumodyn, was dead.

Or soon would be, for the twinkling blue eyes that had e'er besotted her were now full-glazed and bulging, the horror on his handsome face as he caught sight of her, an unmistakable recognition of his imminent end.

Aye, Mariota's golden giant of a Highland lover was about to die naked in his bed.

Naked in the arms of an equally unclothed whore.

Shivering, Mariota stared, not trusting her eyes. Shock and disbelief crashed over her, stealing her breath until her anguish rose in a tide of fury, and the welling pain burst free.

"No-o-o," she cried, agony ripping her soul. "By the living God! *Hugh. . . .*"

" 'Tis m-my heart," he gasped, his eyes widening.

Her own heart pounding furiously, Mariota bit down on her lip as he broke away from the sweat-dampened bawd straddling him and pressed both hands against his chest, its well-muscled planes, resplendent with a smattering of golden hairs, proving as drenched and heaving as his whore's fleshy, over-generous breasts.

His penis glistened as well, highlighted almost obscenely by the glow of the night candle. Flaccid now, and surprisingly small for such a great stirk of a Highlandman, the dangling appendage was clearly wet from vigorous love play.

A truth underscored by the disarray of the bed coverings, the flagon of wine and two half-emptied goblets on a fireside table, and the trail of discarded clothing littering the rush-strewn floor.

That, and the reek of passion sated still hanging so heavily in the chill air.

"Saints have mercy!" Mariota clapped her hands to her face, the only movement she could manage for her legs felt leaden, her feet as roots of stone.

The other woman suffered no such loss of agility, scrambling off the bed so swiftly her ungainly efforts to extract herself would have been comical if her very presence didn't feel like a vise around Mariota's heart.

All but spitting and snarling, the bawd flung the last of the bed coverlets from her naked body, knocking over the flagon of wine in her clumsiness, the blood-red libations splashing onto the floor rushes.

Watching her exodus, Mariota curled her hands into fists. The back of her neck throbbed, its tender skin blazing as her gaze lit on the spilled wine, some still-coherent part of her seeing a reflection of Hugh's ignoble demise in the quickly spreading stain.

An irony the Bastard of Drumodyn would miss for he'd collapsed onto the bedsheets, lay staring at her from blank, unseeing eyes.

And just looking at them sent a bitter, piercing cold sluicing through her. "Dear sweet saints," she gasped, more to herself than the woman still looming so naked beside the bed. "He's dying. . . ."

But Hugh Alesone was already gone, having left to join his forebears, breathing his inglorious last without a further word spoken.

And with his departure, a great gusting wind rushed into the room, guttering candles and sweeping across a worktable strewn with parchments, the icy blast scattering his treasured writings to every corner of the room.

Love sonnets, the most of them, and composed for Mariota, but also painstakingly gathered accountings of the ancient line from which Hugh claimed descent—even if his bastardy had constrained him to subsist on little more than his own silvered words and broth of limpets and milk.

Good enough fare until Mariota's munificence enabled the would-be bard to indulge his higher tastes and live as befitted one who believed to carry the blood of kings.

Scarce able to believe him dead, she swayed, almost reeled into the other woman. But she backed away as quickly, something about the woman's moist red lips and the slant of her eyes, prickling Mariota's nape.

"You!" she cried, awareness slamming into her. "You are—"

"Elizabeth Paterson," the whore supplied, her gray eyes cold and glittery as a winter dawn.

In numbed shock, Mariota recognized her with surety now. If not by name, then by reputation, for the woman was none other than the notorious alewife of Assynt.

Widowed and slightly older than Hugh, Elizabeth Paterson ran the Burning Bush, an establishment of less than noble repute where the high-spirited widow was rumored to offer wayfarers much more than victuals and simple lodgings.

The air around Mariota grew colder. "You are the alewife," she said, the acknowledgment sounding far-away, her voice a stranger's.

"And that surprises you?" Nowise inhibited, the bawd made no attempt to cover her spurious charms. "Did you not know Hugh had dark, *lusty* tastes? Needs he could only quench with someone like me?"

Mariota gritted her teeth, her world splitting open to become a yawning void filled with naught but Hugh's naked, inert form and the triumphant little sneer playing about the alewife's generous, love-swollen lips.

"Be gone from here." Mariota flicked a hand at the crumpled clothes on the floor. "Dress, and take yourself from my sight."

The bawd ignored that and lifted her chin. "A pity you returned sooner than expected, Lady Mariota," she said, her throaty voice taunting. "You might have been left to your illusions had it been otherwise."

Mariota stiffened, something inside her cracking, turning her to stone.

"I turned back before even nearing Dunach," she admitted, the name of her home bitter on her tongue. "Praise God I did not plead my father's beneficence yet again—"

The alewife sniffed. "I told Hugh he'd seen the last of Archibald Macnicol's coin. Word of your puissant father's spleen with you is widespread."

Sliding a hand down her belly, the bawd let her fingers hover above the dark tangle of her nether hair. "See you, Mariota of Dunach, Hugh knew you might return early, but he did not want to forego our *amusements*."

Mariota's eyes began to sting, hot gall rising in her throat. Equally damning, she seemed unable to lift her gaze from the other woman's abdomen.

Elizabeth Paterson's decidedly swollen abdomen.

Her emotions churning, Mariota dug her hands into her skirts. "It would seem the two of you indulged often enough."

The other shrugged. "That may be, but 'tis not Hugh's child I carry. Not that he cared. Truth be told, he took great relish in hearing of my *encounters* at the alehouse."

Mariota starcd at her, wordless.

The alewife's lips quirked. "If you would know the whole of it," she said, reaching to trail her fingers across Mariota's stomach, "he gloried in my swelling form, even likened my sweetness to a ripening plum. His get, or no."

Recoiling from the woman's touch as well as her

words, it took Mariota a moment to notice the multi-colored bursts of light suddenly flashing about the alewife's fingers, and yet another to recognize the bawd's true purpose in putting her hand to Mariota's waist.

"My dirk!" Mariota's heart slammed against her ribs at the sight of her bejeweled lady's dagger in the other's hand.

She fumbled at her skirts, her cold fingers finding the blade's empty sheath, the discovery sending chills down her spine.

"You've stolen my dirk!"

"Say you?" The alewife feigned astonishment. "Och, nay, my lady, 'tis not stealing it I am—only borrowing."

"Borrowing?"

The alewife nodded, her mouth curving in a satisfied smile as she returned to the bed and, with the dirk's blade, swept several of Hugh's windblown parchments onto the floor.

Spearing one that yet clung to the edge of the mattress, she waved the thing at Mariota. "See you, lady, to your face he called you his minx but behind your back he named you a fool," she said, her tone steeped in derision. "I was neither. Ours was an understanding of mutual fulfillment and I meant to use him as boldly as he used me."

Her eyes flashing, she yanked the scroll off the dagger and tossed it at Hugh's body, her mouth twisting in another mirthless smile when the parchment landed on his shriveled manhood.

But, as quickly, her attention flickered to the half-opened window shutters across the room, and something about the glint in her eyes iced Mariota's blood.

"Did you know that your precious Hugh carved footholds in the outer wall of this tower?" She spoke softly, her fingers playing over the gemstones in the dagger's hilt. "He cut them there to allow such as me to win in and out of this chamber discreetly."

"Indeed?" Mariota raised a brow. "I see nary a shred of discretion on you."

The odd look in Elizabeth Paterson's eyes intensified, her expression hardening. "The need for suchlike is past, would you not agree?"

Mariota held her rival's stare and hoped her own features appeared as cold. Drawing a deep breath, she strove to ignore the tight edges of fear beginning to beat through her, the rapid hammering of her heart.

"Tcha, my lady, all that remains is my need for revenge." The woman's contemptuous glance slid over Mariota. "Aye, vengeance will be mine and served on you!" she hissed, hauling out to slap Mariota full across the face.

Mariota gasped, the smashing blow sending her reeling. She flung up an arm to stave off further blows, but her knees gave out and she sank to the floor.

"Not so proud now, are you?" The whore's face darkened with malice.

Mariota blinked, tried not to gag on the blood filling her mouth as Elizabeth Paterson's menace and her own pain slipped over her like a sheet of cloaking ice.

"Fie, but you have lost your wits, eh?" The alewife leaned close, spite pouring off her. "You'd best gather them, for when I climb out yon window, your life will be worth less than these floor rushes," she vowed, scooping up a handful and letting them drift onto Mariota's head.

"A meet revenge, Mariota of Dunach, for with your untimely return, you have ruined my life!"

Mariota stared at her, the woman's gall restoring her tongue if not her strength. "'Tis you who—"

"'Tis I who could have made Hugh a master at barderie," the other boasted, waving the dagger for emphasis.

"You come of a long line of fighting men, warrior lairds who live by the sword," she went on, her eyes blazing. "I have the blood of poets, and a sufficiency of influence in bardic circles to have seen him on his way. So soon as he'd amassed enough coin for us to journey forth from this bog-ridden land of dark hills and desolation."

"Sweet Jesu, you are mad," Mariota breathed, her cheek still burning like a brand. "Hugh would ne'er—"

"Hugh would as he pleased, and he ne'er intended to make you his wife," the other flashed, bringing the blade dangerously close to Mariota's face. "But if it soothes your mind, I had no use for him beyond his promise to settle me with a new alehouse—a fine establishment to serve a better lot than frequent the Burning Bush."

Mariota struggled to her knees, silently cursing the light-headedness that kept her from standing. She did turn a blistering stare on the woman. "And now you, like I, have nothing."

"Not so," Elizabeth Paterson disagreed, whirling back to the bed, a *whooshing* streak of steel revealing her intent.

"No-o-o!" Mariota's eyes flew wide as the dagger plunged into Hugh the Bastard's chest. "In sweet mercy's name!"

"Not mercy, revenge." Her tone chilling, the ghastly

deed done, the alewife calmly retrieved her gown from the parchment-littered floor and crossed to the windows.

Heedless of her nakedness and with her flaunting wealth of hair swirling around her, she tossed her gown into the dark night beyond, hoisted herself onto the broad stone ledge.

"Be warned. Hugh's men will have heard the ruckus," she said, looking pleased. "When they come, your dirk will be raging from the Bastard's heart. You will be thought to have murdered him. Vengeance will be mine."

And then she was gone, her parting words echoing in the empty chamber, the threat behind them giving Mariota the strength to clamber to her feet.

She staggered forward, intent on reclaiming her dagger however mean the task, but the moment her fingers curled around the blade's jeweled hilt, the sudden clamor of pounding feet stayed her hand. Harsh male voices, raised in outrage and disbelief.

Hugh's men.

A half score of them pushed into the room, ready anger flaring on their bearded faces, hot fury thrumming along every inch of their brawny, plaid-hung bodies.

Her own body chilled to ice, Mariota faced them. "God as my witness, I did not kill him. 'Twas—"

"Whore! See whose blade pierced his heart!" The nearest man pointed at the dagger hilt thrusting from Hugh's chest. The dirk's jewels sparkled, each colored stone screaming her guilt. "Think you we do not have eyes?"

"And lo! See the handprint on her cheek," another yelled, seizing her arm. "They fought and she slew him in his sleep!"

A third man spat on the floor.

"Hear me, you err . . ." Mariota protested, but her tongue proved too thick, the agony in her head and arm too laming.

With the last of her strength, she jerked free and threw a glance at the window. But nothing stirred save a thin smirr of rain.

Elizabeth Paterson may well have been a moonbeam—a figment of Mariota's imagination.

But the blade lodged in Hugh the Bastard's heart was real.

And it was hers—as all at Drumodyn knew.

She knew she was innocent. And that Hugh the Bastard was a bastard in more ways than one.

A murrain on the man and all his perfidy!

Her peace so won, she offered her arm to the guard who'd seized her only moments before, let the fire in her eyes dare him into escorting her from the chamber.

Mariota of Dunach, proud if misguided daughter of the far-famed Archibald Macnicol, would be double damned if she'd tremble and cower before any man.

And she'd be thrice cursed, and gladly, if ever she fell prey to love again.

"Pigs will sing from trees the day I take a wife."

His mind spoken, Kenneth MacKenzie glanced around the dais table of Eilean Creag Castle's great hall, looking for understanding. Perhaps a sympathetic nod or, at the very least, a companionable grunt to acknowledge the wisdom of his views.

He received neither.

Worse, he was almost certain he'd caught one or two looks of pity.

Having none of that, he fixed his gaze on the high, vaulted ceiling. Just long enough to swallow the snort rising in his throat. Dear to him or nay, the menfolk of Clan MacKenzie had addled wits when it came to the lasses.

He knew the dangers.

Not that he ne'er appreciated the amiable sweetness of soft, well-rounded and acquiescing females. Their warm loveliness and other such intoxicating accoutrements.

He relished suchlike indeed.

But only with a good measure of caution and when mutual need and satisfaction could be assured, hearts and emotions unfettered.

A wife was a wholly different matter.

And utterly out of the question.

"Singing pigs? And in trees?" Elspeth, Eilean Creag's female seneschal shook her gray head as she plunked down a platter of oatcakes in front of him. "Tut, tut, laddie, here is no way to talk."

The only woman in the hall this early of a morn, and the most free-spoken one at that, she dusted her hands on her skirts and looked at him, her merry eyes displaying how little she thought of his declaration.

Her certainty that he'd unsay the words.

But Kenneth made no reply.

Nor did he regret the sentiment.

Indeed, were it not for the respected old woman's bustling presence, he would have spoken more boldly. Told every gog-eyed, woman-crazed fool who called the loch-girt castle their home exactly what he thought of their jabber. As it was, he simply pressed his lips together and reached for an oatcake.

Not that the sternest look he could muster or even stuffing his mouth with Eilean Creag's finest baked delicacies might spare him the seneschal's keen-eyed perusal.

Or her opinion.

"Stranger things than singing pigs have been known to roost in these hills," she said, proving it. Leaning close, she topped his ale cup. "A wise man is prudent with his vows."

"And a wise woman knows when to curb her tongue," Duncan MacKenzie, the Black Stag of Kintail, declared from his laird's chair at the head of the high table. "She knows, too, when men wish to be left alone."

That last, Kenneth's uncle put to the woman with a level, narrow-eyed stare. Taking the hint, she nodded and withdrew. But not before flashing the MacKenzie chieftain a smug look of her own.

"Stranger things, indeed," she mumbled as she hastened away.

"Pay her no heed," the kinsman to Kenneth's left advised, casting a glance at her receding back. "She would have us believe creatures of legend yet haunt our shores."

"And do they not?" Another man slapped his hand on the table. "I once saw an *uraisg* creeping along the lochside not ten paces from where I stood. Half-human, half-goat, he was, with a wild mane of hair blowing in the wind and long teeth and claws a-flashing in the moonlight."

Kenneth frowned. "It matters naught to me what lurks in Kintail's woods," he said, tightening his fingers around his ale cup. "So long as I am left in peace."

Peace well earned, he allowed to himself, not wanting

to bicker with his kinsmen only a few short months after they'd welcomed him into their fold, naming him the new Keeper of Cuidrach.

His heart welling at the honor, he reached to smooth the folds of the blue-and-green plaid slung ever so casually over his shoulder.

The MacKenzie plaid . . . the very same weave and style worn by nigh every man presently crowding Eilean Creag's cavernous great hall. But to Kenneth, a forever reminder of the dastard who'd sired him.

A blackguard who'd allowed his mother, God rest her soul, to give him the name even though the reputed skirt-chaser ne'er bothered to lessen her shame by wedding her.

At the memory, his jaw tightened.

As did his resistance to having a wife thrust upon him, however well-meaning his kinsmen.

For all their goodwill, they had not shared his troublous years at sea. Rough years spent chasing the dreams of wealthier men, risking his life for their greed. He alone had slept on the frigid decks of wave-tossed galleys, wrapped in his plaid and with naught but the comfort of its wool and the tight-pressed body heat of other slumbering seamen to keep him warm.

That, and his memories of home.

His longing to return.

Lifting his ale cup, he took a pull of the frothy brew. "Trust me," he began, careful to catch the eye of each kinsmen still gawking at him, "I crave Cuidrach's solitude and shall glory in its quiet."

"So you say," Duncan MacKenzie fired back. "But it is that very stillness that concerns us. The long and dark winter nights, soon to break upon the land."

Leaning forward, the MacKenzie chief maneuvered Kenneth right into the corner he'd been striving to avoid.

"See you," he pressed, pinning Kenneth with a piercing stare, "it is not the sad tale of the Bastard Stone or some henwife's prattle about legendary beasts that weighs on us. 'Tis the emptiness of Cuidrach itself that we would see filled for you."

Kenneth said nothing.

A reply wasn't needed. Every man present knew what the MacKenzie chief meant by filled.

He wanted Kenneth wed.

As did the others, judging by the enthusiastic bobbing of heads to be seen throughout the hall.

"Cuidrach is a lonely place," a new voice said into the hush. "The hold would be much better if enlivened by the good company of women, their lightness and warmth."

Kenneth arched a brow at the speaker, Sir Lachlan Macrae. His own chosen garrison captain. A man a full score of years older than Kenneth, and widowed. Kenneth had deemed him a fair choice to head up Cuidrach's guard, thinking he'd savor the holding's isolation.

Its lack of women.

But Sir Lachlan, like the others, stared at him as if he'd grown the devil's own horns.

"It *is* peace I crave," Kenneth insisted, pushing to his feet. "Precious solitude unmarred by female skirlings and chatter. Wifely or otherwise."

But as he strode away, the seed of an echo followed him. Dim, distant, and alluring, its tendrils wound through him, fragmented images of hopes long extinguished, annoying remnants of shut-away dreams.

Nonsense he would not let plague him.

Foolery he had no intention of heeding.

And one thing he knew with surety—he would ride for Cuidrach sooner than planned. Nary a pig had crossed his path in recent days, but he did not want to press his good fortune.

He was, after all, a prudent man.

Chapter Two

⚜

Deep in Drumodyn's dungeon, Mariota shifted on her lumpy pallet, her splitting head not keeping her from wondering whate'er foolery had possessed her to think Hugh's men would listen to reason. A false hope it'd been, and one that mocked her now, firing her indignation and calling her back from the merciful oblivion she'd been whiling in for the saints knew how long.

But waking only plunged her into a black mood the likes of which hadn't plagued her since the day her father had disowned and banished her, sending her from their home at Dunach Castle for consorting with Hugh the Bastard.

A man Archibald Macnicol had deemed an up-jumped swellhead, an insolent cur unworthy to sweep the ground beneath his only daughter's feet.

Wincing at a pain that went deeper than the pounding at her temples, Mariota swiveled her head to the side and opened her eyes.

Not that much could be seen in the murk greeting her.

Damp walls and shadow pressed near, the small stone cell proving dark save for the glow of a tiny coal-burning brazier. The only stretch of comfort she could distinguish before swirling black mist closed about her again.

Mist and, amazingly, the faint strains of the most beautiful music she'd ever heard. A lute or harp if she could trust her dulled perception. And such sweet singing. . . .

Almost angelic.

At once, icy chills swept her. Sainted holy hosts or nay, she wanted naught to do with angels. Weakened, shivering, and hungry she might be, she was nowise ready to exit this world.

The angel, however beguiling her song, could return whence she'd come. Or seek out someone more amenable to her visit.

That decided, Mariota raised herself on an elbow and tilted her head toward the distant music.

Or what she'd thought had been music.

For now, even straining her ears, she heard only the rushing of her own blood.

No other sounds reached her, apart from the snoring of her guard and, through the high slit in the wall that served as a window, the light patter of rain.

Night sounds by no means as enchanting as angelic song, but infinitely sweeter for their normalcy. Stinging heat pricked the backs of her eyes then, the grimness of her surrounds hitting her like a hard-toed kick in ribs.

Equally distressing, the wretched little cell began to spin again, a great wave of weariness washing over her, urging her to let the darkness reclaim her.

The darkness and . . . *furtive sounds.*

Awake again at once, she heard a scuffle and a thud,

hurried fumblings at the iron bar of the door. An overloud *creak* as the door swung open and a figure appeared in the torch-lit doorway. Soberly garbed and generous of girth, the woman bore no trace of misty glitter or gauzy wings.

But she did look familiar.

"Nessa!" Mariota's brows shot upward, her nose recognizing her friend despite the unaccustomed ampleness of the other's form.

And for all her big-heartedness and charm, Nessa Mackay smelled.

Not unappetizingly, but . . . distinctly.

Of peat smoke and salted herring, the good rich earth and the sea.

Widowed some years now, she plied her late husband's trade, drying what fish and eel kindly valiants brought her, and tending her small farmery as best she could.

Such served her well, Nessa was wont to say, claiming her wants were few.

"Nessa . . . ," Mariota repeated, near choking on her astonishment. "Is it yourself?"

"Even as you can see!" Nessa's hands went to her hips, her gaze sweeping the cell. "This is worse than I'd feared. A plague on the miscreants for bringing you here."

"But how did *you* get here?" Mariota shook her head, her mind still flailing. "Hugh is dead. His men think I—"

"Och, I ken what the louts are saying. Why else would I be here, in this guise?" Nessa patted her somewhat lopsided hips. "Someone must help you out of this tangle!"

Coming closer, she whipped open her cloak, revealing the sacks of provender hanging about her waist. "Word travels fast in these hills. I came prepared. I've even secured two garrons. They stand waiting in the birch-wood beyond the stables."

Mariota's heart began to pound. "Saints praise you, but there is more—"

"Ooh, no doubt, my lady. Even much that you do not know." Nessa wagged a finger. "Aye, there is much amiss. We must be away from here this night."

But Mariota sat still, her brow furrowing. "I cannot leave until my name is cleared," she said, her resolve firm however strained her voice. "My good repute might be tarnished, but I will not be named a murderess—"

"Not you, but I may now bear such a stain in truth." Nessa flicked a glance at the guardsman.

No longer snoring, nor moving at all, the man lay sprawled on the stone floor just outside the door.

Nessa's face hardened. "That one cared more for the plump flesh he supposed about my hips than the respect usually accorded a castle guest," she said, readjusting her cloak. "He lunged for me when, in my guise as traveling bardess, I sought a word with you. I shoved him away, but deep in his cups as he was, he stumbled and knocked his head on the drawbar. I would ne'er have desired it, but I fear he is dead. . . ."

"Mercy!" Mariota's gaze narrowed on the man, the dark red stain spreading from beneath his head.

Heat, rapid and pulsing, spread up her throat and flooded her face. "Aye, we must be gone," she agreed, pushing to her feet.

She eyed the dead man, praying her words would not be misunderstood. "Like as not, I am in this cell, foul as it is, because I am well born. Hugh's men will release me once they come to their senses." She paused, moistened her lips.

"You would be dealt with more severely, met at once by the sharp end of a sword. And that I cannot allow—"

"Faugh!" Nessa waved a dismissive hand. "You, my lady, will have naught to say of my fate or your own if we do not make haste." She grabbed Mariota's arm and pulled her from the cell. "It is your very station dooming you! At first light they mean to take you to the River Inver, at the far end of the loch—"

"What are you saying?" Something inside Mariota stirred, a memory hovering just outside her grasp. "Why would they take me there?"

Nessa shot her a glance. "Have you forgotten the Each Uisge said to dwell near the river mouth? The most dread water-horse in all Assynt?"

Mariota shuddered. "Every man, woman, and bairn hereabouts has heard the tales."

And even if she hadn't, of late, the glens had been ablaze with prattle about the river-dwelling monster, a creature able to assume a bonnie man's form and, so disguised, lure fetching lasses to watery ends.

But the Each Uisge of River Inver hadn't ravished a woman in ten years. Tongue-waggers claimed he'd made a pact with the good folk of Assynt, that every tenth year he'd be delivered a living sacrifice so long as he bided beneath the river's surface.

And, Mariota recalled with a sinking heart, the time for a new sacrifice was at hand.

Her eyes flew wide. "You are not saying they mean to offer me to the water-horse?"

"That is the way of it, aye." Nessa flicked a finger at Mariota's heavy braid. " 'Tis said the beast favors comely wenches with reams of coppery red hair."

Mariota glanced at her plait, feeling ill.

Even in the dimly lit passage, her hair gleamed a bright shimmering bronze.

Some might even say *coppery red*.

"I do not believe in the Each Uisge," she said, lowering her voice because they were nearing the stairs leading up to the great hall. "Such foolery is good for naught but entertaining gullibles on cold, fire-lit nights."

"It scarce matters what you believe . . . *they* believe." Nessa tossed a glance up the darkened stairwell as they hastened past. "And, may the fiend roast their toes, they think the water-horse will find you a particularly pleasing sweetmeat because you are a lady!"

"They've run mad." Mariota bit back an oath when her foot collided with a stack of charcoal baskets and empty braziers heaped against the wall. "Full addled."

Nessa huffed. "That, too, will make nary a whit of difference when you are trussed up and sinking like a stone."

Mariota quickened her step, her pulse racing now that a little-used door to the bailey loomed before them. "Ne'er would they dare such a deed."

"Mayhap not when you were their leader's lady love," Nessa countered, already fiddling with the door latch. "But now, and with the death of the alewife—"

Mariota drew a sharp breath. "The alewife of Assynt?"

Nessa nodded and flung open the door. "The very one," she confirmed. "Found dead beside the River Inver a few nights ago, she was. Word is the Each Uisge had his way with her. But whatever caused her end, her demise has folk clamoring for a new sacrifice."

"Dear saints," Mariota gasped, her stomach roiling.

Outwardly calm, but inwardly shaking, she followed

her friend into the bailey and braced herself against the night's wind and rain, the long road before her.

A new life she wouldn't begin to contemplate until Drumodyn and all its darkness lay far behind her.

A fortnight later, Sir Kenneth MacKenzie, newly styled Keeper of Cuidrach, reined in atop a high gorse-covered ridge and surveyed the wide expanse of hill and sea spread before him. The evening air held a wet chill, but neither the cold nor the deepening twilight dampened his spirits.

Swallowing hard, he drew a hand across his brow, hoped the gesture would hide his emotion from the men pulling up beside him.

Not that his handpicked array of companions shouldn't understand, for this was Kintail at its finest. And this lonely corner of Kintail was his heritage—a landscape he'd carried etched across his heart during every one of his years at sea.

A legacy he'd ne'er dreamt to claim.

Remembering that ache, he breathed deeply of the damp, earth-rich air, his blood quickening.

In the distance, flurries of wind played across the dark waters of Loch Hourn and on its high, precipitous cliff rose the great arch of the Bastard Stone, and, not far from its shadow, the silent ruin of Cuidrach Castle.

"Yonder she lies!" One of his men pointed to the abandoned stronghold. "But I vow Cuidrach is not so empty as we were led to believe."

At once, all eyes turned on the speaker, young Jamie the Small, a great strapping lad, all high spirits and cheer. He was known and heckled for his unmanageable shock of auburn hair and, amongst the men bold enough to tease him, the astounding size of his most manly accoutrement.

He was also amongst the youngest of Kenneth's stalwarts and possessed of excellent vision.

Certainly better than Kenneth's for *he* saw naught but the emptiness of the land, a few notable gaps in Cuidrach's walling, and the gathering dusk.

But Jamie was looking round, eyes bright. "There, a faint drift of smoke," he insisted, still pointing. "Someone has lit and stirred a fire to blaze. And in the tower!"

"Havers, lad, 'tis cloud and mist you see," an older man challenged, tut-tutting into his beard. "Naught else."

Unfazed, Jamie lowered his arm. "Wayfarer, broken men, a wandering friar, I know not. But someone whiles there," he said, and with entire authority. "I'll eat a brick of peat for my supper if I am wrong!"

"And I shall consume double your portion if you are right," Kenneth took him up, with equal conviction. "We shall find naught at Cuidrach but our own shadows—and a good night's rest!"

But, of a sudden, something charged the air with all the crackling intensity of an approaching thunderstorm. Saints, he could even feel gooseflesh rising on his nape, the shimmer of awareness pulsing through his bones!

He cleared his throat, ignoring the sensation. "And lest we wish to linger on this hill until we are hoary and gray, I say we make haste. Let us be away home!"

The words no sooner left his lips than he sent his mount plunging into the autumn evening, his men having little choice but to spur after him.

But when, at last, they drew up before Cuidrach's walls, a great hoot of laughter came from young Jamie.

Blue threads of peat smoke *did* curl from the keep.

And pale yellow light glimmered in one of the upper-most windows.

Reining in not far from the gates, Kenneth stared upward, disbelief washing over him.

"Heigh-ho!" Jamie cried, his voice bursting with all the exuberance of having been proved right. "I told you I saw smoke!"

"Aye," Kenneth admitted, scanning the parapet walk, his narrow-eyed gaze searching for further signs of intrusion. "And the worse for whoe'er dares come at me with a handful of peat—"

"Holy Saint Columba!" one of the men crowed then, gesturing wildly toward the tower. "An angel!"

Snapping his own gaze back to the lit window, Kenneth saw not an angel but a woman.

Clearly in the full blossom of her beauty, her silhouette appeared only for a fleeting moment, just long enough for the fiery-haired siren to close the shutters. And give the men below a good view of her curvaceous form.

Even, Kenneth would have sworn, a quick glimpse of thrusting, chill-tightened nipples!

A certain part of himself beginning to tighten in response, he frowned, imagined icy water sluicing over his male parts as he raked a hand through his hair and blew out a stunned breath.

"By the Rood," he muttered, staring at the window.

A window now soundly shuttered, its flickering golden light no longer so easy to see.

Not that it mattered. He'd already seen enough. And now he knew why he'd experienced such prickling urgency on the hill.

There could be no doubt.

Cuidrach was anything but empty.

A woman had claimed the castle and that wasn't even the worst of it. Setting his jaw, he ran a finger beneath the neck opening of his tunic, his dark mood complete.

Nay, the worst of it was, the woman he'd glimpsed had not been just any woman.

She'd been a naked woman.

Chapter Three

✠

"God's bones!" Mariota spun from the window, one hand pressed to her wet, naked breasts. "There are men below," she said, her heart thundering. "A whole party of them, drawn up before the gates!"

"Hah!" An equally unclothed Nessa sprang to her feet in the same wooden bathing tub Mariota had vacated moments before. "And you gape at me in disbelief?" she challenged, jamming her fists against her well-rounded hips. "Did I not say tempting the Devil would bring him a-calling?"

Mariota made an impatient gesture. "I ken right enough what you said," she admitted, her stomach already clenched in knots. "But it scarce matters now."

Snatching a drying cloth, she began rubbing the rivulets of water from her chilled body. "Dear, sweet Christ," she breathed, her cheeks flaming despite the cold air biting into her nakedness. "Who would venture so deep into this forlorn corner of nowhere?"

In agitation, she flicked a hand at the limed walls, bare

of even the simplest hangings. The chamber, too, noble only in its spaciousness, bore little furnishings save the two bracken-stuffed pallets and scratchy old plaiding the women used for bedding.

The meager light of a few candles and a poorly burning cresset lamp illuminated the remains of their supper: a half-eaten round of coarse brown bread and a rind of moldy cheese, and the shiny opened hulls of fresh black mussels, gathered only hours before. Simple fare, washed down with spring water.

Testament enough to Cuidrach's dearth of comforts.

A lacking she hoped would work in their favor.

"Even if someone wished to come here," she ventured, "on such a night of mist and rain they'd need a hawk's vision to find us."

Nessa clucked her tongue and twisted water from the long coil of her dark hair. "They do be saying the Devil's eyes are well peeled. He—"

"The Fiend is not below, only a company of men," Mariota disclaimed, ignoring how her heart thumped. "They will be travelers," she asserted, wishing her damp palms did not say otherwise. "Simple wayfarers."

Nessa snorted. "Whate'er their purpose, if you'd heeded my warning about throwing open the shutters, like as not, they would have ridden on, thinking this an abandoned shell." She stepped from the tub, stood dripping. "Now they will have seen the candle glow, ken we are here."

"Oooh, to be sure." Mariota's stomach gave a lurch. Chances were, they'd seen much more than the flickering light of a few tallow candles.

Wincing at the thought, she crossed the room, handed

her friend the drying cloth. "No matter, we will greet them as we discussed. So soon as we stand before them, I am lady of this castle. Dutiful wife to my absent husband, the present Keeper of Cuidrach."

Nessa raised a brow, her expression more eloquent than words.

Secretly agreeing with her, Mariota pulled on her gown, not even bothering with a camise, though she did attempt to plait her still damp hair into some semblance of decency.

"They are only passing through—you shall see," she declared again, willing it so. She waited until her friend scrabbled into her own clothes, then added, "Once they see we can offer them scarce more than slaked oats and water, they shall be eager enough to leave."

But the foolery no sooner left her tongue before a great clamor sounded from below. The champing of horses' bits and the *clop-clopping* of hooves, the unmistakable *clink* of steel . . . a cacophony well recognizable to Mariota.

The undeniable sounds of the arrival of knights.

A great many knights and with the ruckus they caused rising up from *within* the curtain-walled bailey.

Her stomach churning, Mariota grabbed a candle from the room's small table and hurried for the door. "Come you," she said, urging Nessa into the darkened corridor. "Let us intercept them before they ride their presumptuousness right into our hall."

A feat of boldness already in full progress as the two women hastened down the winding turnpike stairs.

An invasion straight from the depths of Mariota's blackest nightmares, for *he* was no longer contained safely in his grave in distant Assynt, but stood grinning at her from the middle of the great hall.

Hugh Alesone in all his golden splendor.

"Oho!" he cried, his voice ringing with mirth. "Not one angel, but two!"

Another man, older and well-bearded, plunked down a heavy-looking travel coffer and stared. "Mercy me—and to think we didna expect to meet up with anyone save old Ranald or a few wood pigeons!"

Hugh just peered owlishly at her, his good humor scarce contained.

Mariota set down her candle, too stunned for words.

She drew back her shoulders, readying herself for a confrontation. But then torchlight flickered across the man, revealing not just his amused grin and brawn, but also his youth.

That, and the astonishingly large bulge at his groin.

She swallowed, her error obvious. Whoever this knight was, he was *not* Hugh Alesone.

But he was standing in Cuidrach's hall and more of his rain-splattered ilk were streaming in behind him. Several of these wind-tossed souls also bore good-sized travel chests and what looked to be assorted knightly accoutrements of the highest quality.

The kind of gear her warrior laird father would have examined with a gleam in his eye, his tongue clicking in hearty approval.

She clenched her fists in her cloak, strove for composure. "We are not wood pigeons or angels," she said, her pulse racing. "Merely women—"

"That we can see," said another man, his voice a shade deeper and carrying none of the others' levity. "Indeed, I doubt an angel has graced these walls in longer than man can remember. And with surety, not two."

Stepping from the shadows, he narrowed dark eyes at her. "Celestial beings can surely find more amenable haunts to grace with their hallowed presence. Do you not agree, my lady?"

"Not necessarily." Mariota lifted her chin at his arrogant menace. "Mayhap it would depend on what conditions such a being found amenable?"

"Or," he said, arching a raven brow, "perhaps what conditions drove the . . . *angel* to such a place as this?"

"And you, good sir?" Mariota returned, struggling against the urge to squirm beneath his midnight gaze. "Devils are known to seek such places as well. What brings *you* here this dark and rainy night?"

To her surprise, the corners of his mouth lifted in a smile . . . a sensual-looking smile but without warmth.

He said nothing.

Nor did he need words.

Faith, she could *feel* him all over her, sliding round and inside her, his all-possessing power so palpable, for one crazy-mad moment she imagined him seizing her, pulling her close for a deep, bruising kiss that would blot out her past and banish her cares and hurts in one shattering, decadent moment.

A lightning-quick impulse that would make her forget, possibly even love again.

Certainly desire.

But the coldness of his stare restored sanity and Mariota raised her chin a notch higher, puffed a wayward strand of hair off her forehead. "I asked you a question," she prodded, some not-to-be-repressed part of her femininity still taking his measure. "Why are you here?"

"You cannot guess?" He stepped backward, held up his hands, as if inviting her to examine him.

And she did, her blood heating more with each slow-beating *thump* of her heart.

Tall, raven-haired, and powerfully built, he *was* a man to inflame a woman's . . . interest. Much to her discomfiture. Indeed, the sheer male dominance of his presence brought a hot flush to her cheeks and, worse, smashed any remaining vestiges of her hope that he and his men might be simple wayfarers-in-passing.

These were men with a purpose.

And judging from the number of them moving about in the thin curtain of rain visible beyond the hall's open door arch, there were enough of them to garrison a much larger holding than these ruinous walls.

And how she wished this dark-frowning specimen of maleness had taken his men and his business to one of those other, more commodious keeps.

Instead he loomed far too near, the rain-fresh, out-doorsy scent of him and the heat of his large, masculine body, filling the small space between them. Befuddling her wits and making her shiver.

And that was just the beginning of it.

In truth, everything about him made it increasingly difficult for her to breathe.

And next to impossible to feign calm.

As if he sensed her ill ease and meant to seize advantage, he stepped even closer, his stare burning her, displeasure and something else—something infinitely more unsettling—pouring off him until she had to lock her knees to keep from swaying beneath his stare.

A measuring, all-seeing perusal that, she was certain, pierced clear through her cloak and gown to her nakedness beneath.

She returned the look, damning propriety to glare right back at him, straight into the deepest, darkest blue eyes she'd ever seen. And what she saw made her breath catch, all but choked her.

Without question, *he* led the men still pouring into Cuidrach's hall. Marked as a knight by the flash of his spurs and the glint of mail showing beneath his plaid, his arrogant stance, and the cold, assessing look in his eyes revealed his status.

Even more telling, three vertical scars marred his left cheek. Thin, barely-there lines, but prominent enough to warn that he was a man battle-probed and hard.

One who weathered his storms and would not be disposed to make light of falsehoods.

Or fall easy prey to contrived feminine intrigues.

Proving it, he boldly touched her hair, smoothing back the errant strand she'd been trying to puff out of her face. And the instant his fingers lit on her cheek, another dangerous-looking half-smile curved his attractive mouth.

Mariota stepped back from his reach, tried in vain to ignore the disturbing *intimacy* of his stare.

The intimacy of everything about him.

"You are here alone?" he spoke again, his deep voice provocative.

Softly Highland, seductively smooth, but undeniably . . . challenging.

Mariota bristled, found her steel in the shaming way his mere voice undid her. "What is the meaning of this?" She made a sweeping gesture, indicating the men tramping about, shouldering goods or dashing rain from their hair and beards. Some even lighting wall torches and setting up trestle tables.

Almost laying claim to Cuidrach.

Acting as if they belonged here.

Her mouth going dry at the notion, she glanced at Nessa, noted what could only be called grim humor twitching that one's lips.

Mariota frowned.

She saw nothing amusing in their plight.

She looked back at *him*, hoped her cheeks weren't as bright a red as she suspected. "I warn you, sirrah, if my friend and I are but two this e'en, we shall not be so few in number much longer," she lied, wishing he didn't make her feel like a sparrow caught in the talons of a hawk. "My husband's return is imminent."

"Indeed?" The knight arched a brow. "And who might this paladin be?" he inquired, his tone indicating he hadn't missed the ravages wrought upon the hall by years of disuse. "I wonder at a man who'd leave his lady unguarded in such a comfortless keep."

"And where is *your* lady this cold, inhospitable night?" Mariota shot back, her words edged. "Safe, dry, and well-cosseted—or no?"

"I do not have a lady," he said, giving her another penetrating stare. "But if I did, you can be assured she would not be dwelling here unguarded."

"An ill matter, aye," a stout-bellied man chimed in as

he bustled past, red-faced and puffing under the weight of the iron-bound coffer hoisted upon his shoulder.

"Ne'er seen the like," another agreed, stroking his great bush of a sandy-colored beard. "Master of the house leaving two fine-looking women to fend for themselves in this remote upland bit of nowhere."

Ignoring the Nordic-looking beard-puller, Mariota kept her focus on the dark, lady-less knight. "If you find these walls without succor, sir, then I ask you again, why are you here?"

She tilted her head to study him, her perusal gaining her a moment to compose herself before yet another untruth passed her lips.

Before his searing gaze could fluster her into forgetting who she was supposed to be.

In especial, when that all-knowing gaze seemed so wont to settle on things she'd rather he'd not notice.

Like her mouth.

Her damp braids.

And worse, the chill-tightened nipples she knew were thrusting hard against the soft drape of her cloak.

Things that might reveal the lusty, hearty woman she'd once been. The stranger who now slept inside her and best not be wakened. Not even in the familiar guise of a well-loved laird's daughter, accustomed from birth to give a warm welcome to the weary traveler.

Any weary traveler.

However disturbing.

Tensing, she touched a finger to the fine silver brooch fastened at the neck of her cloak. Norse in design, the exquisitely wrought piece was one of the few remembrances she had of her once-doting sire.

Her privileged existence as Mariota of Dunach.

Her life before Hugh Alesone.

Taking strength from that past now, she straightened her shoulders and held the knight's stare. "Do you not have a name?" she demanded, one hand on her hip as she eyed him, all verve and feminine spirit. "Or is it your style to seek shelter from the rain without the courtesy of an introduction?"

"Och, I am well-used to the rain," Kenneth evaded, his tone more arched than he would have liked. "Such a mischance is not why I am here."

She raised doubting brows. "Then why are you—if you will not reveal your style?"

I do not have a style, he almost blurted, so off-balanced by the proud toss of her head and her flashing-eyed stare he failed to recall that he now did bear a title, and one he'd sworn to carry with dignity and pride.

He would have done, too.

Could he not still see her silhouetted in the tower window, her full, rounded breasts bared and beckoning, their generous swells luminous in the candle glow. Even now, her nipples taunted him, jutting prominently beneath the soft folds of her cloak.

A once-but-no-more-fine excuse for a mantle that clung to her womanliness, its threadbare wool revealing as much as it concealed, and, saints save him, carrying the scent of her recent ablutions.

An enticing scent, dark and alluring, its musky warmth all too distracting.

Frowning, he scooped his hands through his hair and stared at her, almost wishing her pock-faced and crooked of limb. "I am Sir Kenneth . . ." he began only to break off, near choking on the strangeness of putting *sir* before his name.

Rightfully bestowed or no, he still felt out of place in the world of such niceties—all manners and good graces.

The beauty before him exhibited no such discomfiture, every assured and vehement inch of her proclaiming her a lady. Indeed, he'd wager the morrow on her lineage.

Truth be told, if blood counted for aught, this woman's was rich—despite her intriguing state of dishabille and her unexpected presence at Cuidrach.

In *his* hall.

Irritation knifing through him, he folded his arms, drew a deep breath and tried again. "I am Sir Kenneth MacK—"

" 'Tis *her* name, I'd be keen to hear," Jamie proclaimed then, striding forward, his beaming smile and shining-eyed exuberance making it impossible to be wroth at his thoughtless intrusion. "Hers, and her friend's."

"I am Nessa," the dark one said, a dimple deepening her cheek as she smiled at Jamie. "Tiring woman to my lady."

"No mere serving maid—that I vow!" Clearly drawn by their voluptuous sensuality, all damp-haired and musky-scented as they were, Kenneth's youngest knight swept the two women a deep bow. "I am Jamie the Small," he announced, straightening. "Of Clan Macpherson, but—"

"Too young to ken when to hold his flapping tongue," the stout-bellied man declared, joining them. Relieved of the strongbox, he clapped a hand on the younger man's shoulder. "Jamie's nine older brothers ne'er gave him leave to say his mind. A slight the lad now addresses by filling *our* ears every blessed hour o' the day and night."

To Kenneth's surprise, a wistful look touched the beauty's eyes and some of the reserve slipped from her face. "I know something of older brothers," she said, holding out her hand to Jamie. "And younger ones."

"And those brothers have nary a concern that you dwell here alone?" Kenneth shot an annoyed look at Jamie as that one took her hand and raised it to his lips. "Brothers are known to be protective."

"Some of mine are dead," she said, her tone flat. "And others who may have cared are no more."

Kenneth lifted a brow, more disturbed by the revelation than was good for him. "There is no one?"

Mariota drew a deep breath. "Of those who remain, suffice it to say, they are not . . . troubled."

A few of the men glanced askance at her. The dark knight, *Sir Kenneth,* simply locked his gaze on hers, the look in his eyes intensifying until she almost feared he could see straight into her heart.

That he could sense her pain.

Mayhap even sympathize with her.

A possibility that struck a much too dangerous nerve as her father's ne'er forgotten words tore through her, spiraling back to rip open her wounds and remind her of how poorly she'd judged.

How easily she'd succumbed.

Any man who professes to love you for naught but the sweetness of your smile and the bliss of your arms, is about to lead you down a sorrow-fraught path—straight to where'er he suspects your well-filled coffers!

Anger pulsing through her, Mariota pushed the

prophetic observation from her mind and welcomed the cold numbness she knew would soon sweep her.

"I am Lady Mariota," she said then, uncaring if the chill in her voice made her appear shrewish. "As lady of this castle, I can offer little hot food, nor even ale to quench your thirst, but you are welcome to what comforts are here."

Something flashed in the knight's eyes, a glint of annoyance or perhaps dark bemusement. "You are kind," he said, his features disturbingly handsome in the torch-light. "*Lady* of Cuidrach."

Well aware of the flush in her cheeks, Mariota gestured to the hearth where tendrils of steam still rose from the great iron cauldron suspended above the fire.

"Some heated water yet remains," she offered, her voice firm. "Mayhap attending your ablutions will compensate for our other lackings."

"Fair lady, I see no lackings save an honest explanation for your presence," he returned, his stare darker, more probing than ever.

"An honest explanation?" Her face flaming, Mariota indicated the hall's hard-packed earth floor, its bare-swept coldness yet showing remnants of ash and lye.

An unavoidable annoyance to be endured until she and Nessa could gather and strew a new layer of fresh rushes and sweet-smelling herbs—a necessity she hoped might now lend substance to the lies already spilling from her lips.

"You think yourself deceived, good sir?" She hardened her face as best she could, tried to breathe past the tightness in her chest. "Then know that we would not have troubled ourselves sweeping out the old floor rushes and tossing them onto the dung heap did we not desire to ready the hall for my lord's imminent arrival."

To her surprise, a faint gleam of amusement sparked in his eyes again. "Then I ought thank you, to be sure," he said, nodding approval when an as-yet-unseen companion strode past with a large dog basket and a clutch of tatty, moth-eaten plaids.

"Thank me?" Mariota blinked, her mind whirling.

"Indeed," the knight concurred, stepping aside to allow the passage of an ancient-looking hound. "For ensuring—"

"Nay, do not say it." She lifted a hand and took a deep breath, a sinking feeling spreading through her.

"See you, in all my years functioning as lady-of-the-keep for my father, I saw to the needs of quite a few knightly guests, making certain their bellies were filled and their throats adequately quenched. I spent hours assuring the lordly ones received orderly lodgings, their beds kept warmed and their bathing water hot.

But ne'er once have I seen a wayfaring knight escort a lame-hipped, aging dog across my hall and then settle the beast in his own bed beside the hearth fire."

She paused, drew a breath. "Until now."

And the implication made her shudder.

She shot a glance at Nessa, but that one was already threading her way toward the hall's main door arch, her purposeful stride showing that she, too, had guessed their visitors' intent.

Leaving *him* to follow her or nay, Mariota hastened after Nessa only to discover chaos in Cuidrach's rain-splattered bailey.

The courtyard hummed with activity, its broken cobbles wet and gleaming in the spluttering torchlight, restless horses and weary-looking, pannier-burdened pack ponies . . . everywhere.

And baggage carts, a good half dozen.

Sturdy contrivances piled high with household goods. The personal possessions and pride of a well-pursed and landed knight.

Including, she noted with a jolt, the unmistakable framework of his dismantled bed!

Suspicion biting deep, she spun around, not at all surprised to find him already upon her. He loomed tall before her, his piercing stare pinning her in place, shattering her composure.

I should have told you straight away . . . she thought she heard him say, but the words hung in the crackling air between them, their meaning lost in the sharp patter of the rain, the thudding of her heart.

And whate'er he'd held back, plague take her, *she* ought not lie.

Already, she'd told too many.

But her palms were damping and his tight, wry smile lamed her tongue.

She flashed a look at the most incriminating of his baggage carts—the one groaning beneath the weight of his massive, ill-winded bed frame.

He stood motionless, watching the slant of her gaze, a slight twitch beneath his left eye the only visible indication of his own perturbation.

That, and the faint whitening of the three thread-like scars seaming his cheek.

Her nerves fraying, Mariota did her best to ignore how her world seemed to spin and contract around her, the whole of it narrowing until little remained save the intensity of his stare and the heat pulsing up and down the back of her neck.

Ill ease compounded by the two knights hefting parts of the dismantled bed onto their shoulders. Their air of purpose as they strode past her, into the hall, sent an odd giddiness coiling through her belly.

And with the giddiness came knowledge.

She turned a sharp look on *him*, the dark-eyed knight watching her so closely. "Good sir, you do not mean to make this your home?"

"With surety, nay," he returned, his deep voice devilish. "This holding already *is* my home. See you, I am Sir Kenneth MacKenzie."

Mariota blinked at him, her heart sinking. "Sir Kenneth MacKenzie?"

"Indeed, fair lady." He sketched her a bow. "The new Keeper of Cuidrach."

Chapter Four

✤

The new Keeper of Cuidrach.

Mariota flinched but kept her chin lifted, her gaze steady on the darkly handsome knight watching her so intently. A sinuous, deep-seeing look that made her tingle and burn, his intense perusal sparking flames she'd thought forever extinguished. Far from it, he stoked feelings that stunned her. Especially when his midnight eyes deepened in hue and he stepped closer. Almost as if he meant to reach for her, pull her skin-to-skin close, nuzzle his face against her neck, then stroke her hair and kiss her, whisper love words in her ear.

Beguile and woo her, pay court to her heart.

Win her trust as her body melted against him.

Instead, he merely reached to adjust her cloak when it caught and flapped in the wind.

But he'd come so near that his warmth and clean, manly scent engulfed her, the masculine headiness of him teasing her senses and weakening her knees.

Much to her embarrassment for the heat in his eyes came from irritation, not passion.

"Your plight is regrettable, lady, but I came here to live quietly," he said, proving it. "Quietly and . . . alone."

Her face flaming, Mariota swallowed, the intensity of him and her own guilt beating through her. Hot waves of mortification that robbed her wits and struck at every vulnerability she possessed.

"You have nothing to say?" His voice was low and dark, might even have been seductive if not for his skeptically arched brow. "You needn't fear me—I assure you."

"Fear you?" Something inside Mariota twisted. Shame, she was sure, for he unsettled her in ways that could only be called unseemly. And, too, because until very recently, she'd never told a falsehood in her life.

But rather than take them back, she found herself peering at him, the next lie already on her lips. "I am not plagued by some regrettable plight," she denied, clutching her cloak against the cold. "And, for certes, I am not afraid of you."

He folded his arms, doubt all over him. "What then, my lady?"

Mariota swallowed, keenly aware of his men bustling about the bailey. "I simply thought to dwell here in solitude—like you," she said, trying hard not to fidget. "It was ne'er my intent to deceive you. For truth, I sought these walls because I believed you did not exist!"

A glint of amusement lit his eyes. "Then I vow we share more than one might venture, since I find the existence of a *wife* equally astonishing."

He paused and the gleam turned cynical. "Aye, not to

be believed. And nigh as inexplicable as why a woman of gentle birth would hie herself into such a dark glen as this?"

"Why, indeed?" Mariota quipped, nervousness edging her voice. "There are reasons aplenty, do not doubt it."

"Even so, do you not fear broken men, my lady?" He towered over her, the wind whipping his plaid, tossing his hair. "Caterans who skulk through empty lands such as these? Burning and pillaging as they go?"

"Are *you* such a man?"

Surprising her, he laughed, and the brief glimpse of warmth proved . . . devastating. "I have told you who I am," he said, serious again. "'Tis who *you* are, that I would know."

"I am Mariota of Dunach," she admitted, her heart clenching on the name. "And I was raised to fear little, though I am wise enough to avoid the notice of such marauders as you described."

"And how?" His brow shot upward. "By hiding away and claiming to be lady of this keep?"

"I will not deny that . . . deception," she owned, guilt pinching her again. "Cloaking myself with what I believed to be an empty title seemed harmless. In especial, if doing so might warn off unwanted . . . attentions."

Kenneth looked at her, admiring her spirit even as he strove not to be swayed by the fetching gold flecks in her enormous, sea-green eyes.

Something about her summoned images of hot, tumbled bedding and rich, satisfying sensual sport.

Worse, a trace of vulnerability that made him want to protect her.

Frowning, he forced himself to recall other green eyes.

Ones not near so luminous and vulnerable as Lady Mariota's, but potent enough to chill his blood and banish unwanted bestirrings.

"So-o-o, Mariota of Dunach," he began, "whose bothersome attentions drove you here?"

She drew a deep breath. "I misspoke," she admitted. "'Twas not unwanted attentions that brought me here, but . . . wrath and superstition. I was to be sacrificed—given in offering to the Each Uisge of River Inver. Some might scoff at water-horses and other such mythical beasts, but those who believe fear them mightily. I escaped only because Nessa took great hazards to rescue me."

"I see," Kenneth said, the weight of his knightly spurs suddenly tremendous.

Not that it mattered.

He'd just stepped into a whirl of chaos and honor demanded he dwell there.

The ancient code of Highland hospitality fettered him, binding him to grant her sanctuary. As did his newly bestowed knighthood. That, and his inability to walk past a woman in need.

A compulsion that had often caused him more than his share of grief.

So he blew out a frustrated breath that felt uncomfortably like resignation. "The effort it took you to come here was trouble well spent," he heard himself saying, his voice sounding like a stranger's. "You will be safe at Cuidrach, I promise you."

But she didn't seem to hear him, her gaze sliding past him into the hall where some of his men had stripped to the waist and were taking turns at the steaming cauldron.

Sir Lachlan, the contented-looking loon, was already full submerged in a hastily readied bathing tub.

A rickety-looking contrivance set discreetly in a darkened alcove and clearly meant for his own bathing pleasure as well as his captain's.

"You needn't offer to bathe me," he said, noting her flush. "I will leave such niceties to my captain. A dipped bucket from the castle well will suit me fine."

"I thank you, then—and for everything," she said, the color in her cheeks deepening. "But your men, will they not look askance at me after I've . . . now that I've—"

"Named yourself lady of the keep?" he supplied, his gaze on the band of white skin at the base of the third finger of her left hand.

A revelation that sent heat pouring into his loins.

"Och, nay, they willna mind," he said, certain of it. "They'll relish your presence, my lady or no."

He took her arm then, guiding her back into the hall, a scene now rife with warmth and domesticity, the very air gilded by the bare-bottomed brawn and muscled flesh of his weary but grinning men.

"Oh!" Her eyes widened on Jamie. Full naked and beaming, he was accepting a drying cloth from Nessa's outstretched hand. "He is—"

"Aye, that he is," Kenneth agreed, smiling for the first time since glimpsing *her* nakedness limned so seductively in the tower window.

A vision still tormenting and rousing him.

"Tell me," he began, stopping to adjust the fall of his plaid, "did those poltroons in Assynt choose you as their Each Uisge's victim because you are widowed?"

She blinked. "Widowed?"

He glanced at her hand, indicated the place where, until her flight from Drumodyn, Hugh the Bastard's ring had adorned her finger.

Mariota swallowed, cast about for an explanation. One that wouldn't brand her as a light-skirt. But then men began gathering at the fireside, flagons of ale in their hands, sweet ballads on their lips.

"Come you," urged the new Keeper of Cuidrach, dragging her toward the merrymakers, "we shall speak of your travails later—for the nonce, my men will entertain us."

But Mariota held him back, tugged on his arm. "Your men? Do you not sing then?"

"Me?" He flashed her a disarming smile. "Fair lady, I could not compose verse if my life depended on it. The moon would sooner tumble from the heavens."

Mariota eyed him, her pulse holding still. "Most knights are well skilled in spinning poignant song, seducing with their words."

"Not this knight," he assured her. "You will see I am less practiced in the usual chivalric niceties." He paused, cocking a brow. "Does my lack of a silvered tongue bother you, Lady Mariota?"

"Bother me?" She shook her head, her pulse now racing. "Nay, I am glad. Indeed, I say it a boon."

A blessing that both relieved and unsettled her.

Several hours later, even as long, rough swells broke upon the rocks below the Bastard Stone and lashing rain swept Cuidrach's cliff-girt shore, a gentler night curled round distant Drumodyn Castle. The soft mist drifting past its thick walls and stout towers at stark contrast to the turmoil gathering within.

And at the center of that storm, one man, Ewan the Witty, held court, his scowls sharp as the razor-edged steel of a sword, his deep voice booming.

"*A red fox?*" he snorted, no trace of humor on his rough-hewn features. "Och, saints alive—I do not trust my own ears!"

Garrison captain to the recently murdered Hugh Alesone, he fisted his hands and frowned—as did every other bearded, plaid-hung follower and erstwhile companion-in-arms of the late, great Bastard of Drumodyn.

His still-faithful minions crowded the smoky, black-raftered great hall, their dark stares and fury aimed at one hapless member of their number.

Wee Finlay—the unfortunate soul whose supposedly light task it'd been to watch over a simple lute.

Albeit a priceless one.

A gold and gem-encrusted instrument of untold worth, come only shortly into their hands. Left behind, or forgotten in haste, when its owner, the conniving bardess who'd brought them such grief, had used its lure to bedazzle them long enough for her to free and abscond with their leader's murderess.

Extinguishing the life of an innocent guardsman in the sordid process!

"A fox—bah!" Ewan fumed again, his eyes blazing.

"Aye, a fox, I'm a-telling you," Wee Finlay shot back, his own glare equally hot. "And a cheeky creature he was, bold as the morrow." He paused to wag a finger. "No one else set foot in this hall while the rest of you were away to Dunach looking for the Lady Mariota—for naught, I might add!"

"Hell's afire!" Ewan roared at the top of his lung

power, his face purpling. "You'd have us believe a fox stole in here and secreted the lute from yon iron-bound coffer? Spirited the treasure out from beneath your sniveling nose when you'd vowed to guard it with your life?"

Finlay thrust out his jaw and shrugged. "Foxes are cunning—would any amongst you deny it?"

"Mayhap 'twas a fine, sweet thatch of some *other* kind of reddish fur that caught Finlay's eye?" another called out, sounding well pleased with his suggestion. "We all ken he has a soft spot for the lasses. . . ."

"I wouldn't exactly say *soft*," a barrel-chested man flung into the fray, his bawdy jest quickly followed by a burst of hoots, ayes and noddings.

Only Ewan the Witty didn't share in their mirth.

His ill humor still rolled off him in great, angry waves.

"A drooling dotard would have proved a sounder safe-guard for our treasure," he owned, beginning to pace before the high table. "With Hugh the Bastard dead, we had sore need of that lute!"

Halting, he stared round the smoky gloom, his fierce gaze raking each man present.

"Myself, I think *she* came back to fetch the thing." Going toe-to-toe with Finlay, he jabbed a meaty finger in the smaller man's chest. "Like as not, she and her friend hid in the wood, knowing we'd ride straight to her father at Dunach, looking for her. Then, so soon as they saw us do just that, they crept in here, found you snoring on your pallet, and helped themselves to the lute!"

"I ne'er snored a day in my life," Finlay objected. "And the sun won't rise again if I slept at all while you were off on a fool's mission."

"A fool's mission?" Ewan jerked his brows. "Aye, mayhap it was since the lady's father insists he hasn't seen her. And if she can't be found, mayhap we ought just leave her be and sacrifice *you* to the Each Uisge?"

Wee Finlay glared at him. "You'll ne'er see your precious lute again if you do!"

"Och, say you?" Ewan took a step closer. "How so? By all the powers of heaven, I am burning to know."

"Because," Finlay began, seeming to grow in stature as he spoke, "only I can recognize the fox that stole the lute."

"'Recognize the fox'?" someone scoffed from the shadows. "By his scent or by that red pelt that so bewitched you?"

"By his eyes," Finlay returned, undaunted. "The creature had queer eyes. *Magic eyes.*"

A hush fell over the hall then, all bluster and chortles silenced.

Ewan caught himself first. "Here is odd talk," he said, glowering at the little man. "God's mercy on you if you are lying."

"I ne'er spoke more true words," Finlay insisted. "Find the fox that looked at me as if he could see to the back of my soul and you'll have your lute."

"The lute, and those two scheming women," Ewan asserted, looking and sounding becalmed at last. "I can feel it in my bones."

Later still, closer to the smallest hours of the night, Nessa slipped along Cuidrach's stone-slabbed parapet, taking shelter in a tiny cap house at the far end of the deserted and silent wall walk.

Corbelled out over the crenellated walling and lit by

the cold light of the moon, the turret-like room proved the perfect retreat for one such as she, a warm-blooded woman possessed of a wise head and a stout heart . . . at times weakened by cravings of the flesh.

Fool yearnings of the soul.

Aches and longings she oft wondered might ne'er lessen.

Even so, she pressed her hands against her breast and inhaled deeply of the chill night air, willing the return of her usual calm.

Instead, she caught faint strains of music drifting up from the hall and, stout hearted or no, something inside her stirred, for even after some years of widowhood, she hadn't adjusted to being alone.

Her heart thumping, she glanced around the empty little room, imagining a pallet bed against one of the walls with two naked bodies writhing there. Intimately entwined, so close not the smallest sliver of space separated them, their sinuous movements silvered by moon glow, incredible pleasure sating them.

Almost feeling her phantom lover's breath warm against her cheek, she steeled herself, banished her dreams back whence they'd come.

Like as not from too much of Sir Kenneth's wine—an indulgence that now set her senses spinning.

Sure of it, she stepped deeper into the room's shadows, out of the wind and rain, and sighed, drawing her cloak tighter around her shoulders.

She squared them, too, for just as this was not a night to spin pointless dreams, neither was it a prudent hour to peer into the past.

Hers, or Cuidrach's.

Even if from this high vantage point, the ill-famed Bastard Stone could be seen thrusting its blackness into the heavens, its foam-girdled rocks shrouded in mist yet keeping constant, unsleeping watch.

A vigil Nessa understood but chose not to let darken her spirits.

She meant Cuidrach and its ghosts no harm.

She'd only wished to seize what remained of the night's magic, the warmth she'd caught in a certain knight's appraising eye.

A twinkling interest she'd surely imagined.

Just as she now would almost swear she heard a certain old woman's strange words hushing past her ear, echoing in the room's moon-filled emptiness.

In the fullness of time, there e'er comes a reckoning and all things right themselves.

"Lady."

Nessa started as her reckoning stepped through the door. The calm she'd almost managed to reclaim slid away as swiftly as the remembered words of a diminutive black-garbed crone she'd seen but once in her life.

The knight, Sir Kenneth's garrison captain, Sir Lachlan Macrae, she'd seen but once, too. Seen, and *bathed* him, the memories of that particular intimacy now making all of her senses snap to attention.

"You were missed in the hall," he said, his deep voice melting her, every tall, mail-glinting inch of him shattering her composure.

Making her . . . want.

She met his gaze, knowing herself lost even before his mouth curved in a slow, provocative smile that did deliciously rousing things to the pit of her belly.

Her already tingling female places.

Reactions she knew the handsome, bold-eyed knight surely inspired in any female he chose to make the recipient of his charm.

He came closer and the barest hint of a dimple deepened in his left cheek. "Did you weary of our fireside storytelling, my lady? Our music and song?"

"Sir?" Nessa took a step backward, away from the heady intoxication of him.

As smoothly, he closed the space between them. "I saw you leaning forward to watch and listen. Did I misjudge your interest? Or has your path been so fraught that you've lost the ability to see the magic and romance of these high hills we call home?"

Nessa shifted, her mind returning to the scene in the hall. Sir Kenneth's men strumming lutes and extolling the blue of sea and hill and sky, singing praise of the noblest valor and battles won, but also of black treachery and heartache, their every honeyed word going to her head like wine.

Each sweet turn of verse a dream and a . . . nightmare.

"Ach, I ken the magic, the legend and wonder. I see it every day—even in this wild and forlorn place," she admitted, choosing her words carefully. "'Twas the *romance* that sent me up here, naught else."

"The romance?" He touched her hair, the barely there contact sending shivers all over her. "How so?"

Holding his gaze, Nessa drew on the strength of harsh years and even harder victories, small though they might have been. "I am a herring widow," she said, more proud than shamed by her humble heritage. "I am not accustomed to the fineries of courtly song and airs. But I understand the heart—and the body. Having been well-loved once, I ache to know such bliss again. Your men's songs brought back painful memories."

The knight lifted a brow. "And the magic? How do you see that?"

"As potent and real as when the world was new," she said, meaning every word. "To be sure, and I believe in magic. *Highland magic.* In especial since rescuing my lady from the dungeon at Drumodyn Castle—a tale you heard this very e'en."

She looked down. "Most of it, anyway."

"And what did I not hear?"

Nessa swallowed. "You are a knight," she said, not quite sure how to put her hesitation into words. "You live, breathe, and think in a different world than mine. You might not understand."

"Mayhap you ought tell me and see?" A glimmer of admiration lit his eyes. "I already know that you went to great trouble and risk to spirit your lady out of a dungeon cell. No ordinary woman could master such a feat. I would hear how you did it?"

"O-o-oh, I did have help," she said, telling him true. "The help of greed, Sir Knight. The lust of men for all that sparkles and glitters."

Sir Lachlan crossed his arms. "I see," he said, clearly not seeing at all.

"The whole of it is a long tale." Nessa moistened her lips, uncomfortably aware of his doubt. "But there can be no question that greed allowed me to hasten my lady from Drumodyn Castle. As proof, I say you that when we fled the dungeon, every man abovestairs was clustered around the high table examining a golden lute I'd left there, their every other thought surrendered to the shine of gold, the dazzle of gemstones. . . ."

Surprise widened the knight's eyes. "And where did you—a professed herring wife—obtain such a treasure?"

"A black-garbed old woman left it in my possession. A *cailleach* she was, nigh ancient, but with sharp, almost twinkling eyes."

"And this crone simply left the lute in your keeping?"

Nessa nodded. "So I have said—and so it was. I am Highlander enough not to question such things."

He touched her face then, his caress encouraging her, loosening her tongue.

"The *cailleach* claimed to be a traveling wise woman," she explained, her breath catching as his fingers strayed to her neck. "She ne'er told me her name, just came to my door asking if I had any pains in need of healing—in exchange for fresh milk or a sack of dried herring."

"And for that she gave you the lute?"

Nessa shrugged. "I promised her the provender, inviting her to warm herself at my hearth while I gathered the milk and herring, but when I returned, she was gone, the lute resting upon my table."

"Ah, well . . ." He lifted her braid, appeared to study its dark gloss in the slant of the moonlight. "Did she say how she happened across such a fine instrument?"

"To be sure," Nessa said, the intimacy of watching him watch his thumb slide over the thickness of her braid, making her heart pound.

"Well?" he pressed, looming before her like some mythic Fingalian giant.

"She said a wandering bard had given it to her in appreciation for healing him of the ague."

"Such a gift for curing the ague seems . . . over-generous."

"Who is to question the doings of wise women? And that she was, I am sure. Thanks to her, my lady lives and breathes, will greet all her morrows." Nessa scarce heard the words, so strong was the sensual drag pulling between them, hazing her wits, melting her. "So, aye, sir, I believe in magic."

"In all kinds of magic, my lady?"

"What other kind do you mean, Sir Knight?" she voiced the expected response.

The one she knew would land her on the cold stone of the little guardroom floor.

See her unravel in sweet, needy release.

"My name is Lachlan, not 'Sir Knight.'" He came closer, reached for the edges of her cloak.

"And the magic I mean," he said, as the cloak slipped from her shoulders, "is the kind that burns between a man and a woman—then, when they both desire such flames to sear and consume them."

"I . . ." Nessa bit her lip, the words dry in her throat.

He clutched her to him, held fast. "The kind of magic that flared between us when you bathed me—and still does. Even now. This moment."

Nessa drew a trembling breath, any pretense of resistance spinning away in a dark wind of want, need, and incredible urgency as the little room and its chilly moonlight blurred into nothingness, leaving only him and the awareness beating between them.

He set her from him and looked deep into her eyes. "You do not deny it?"

Nessa lifted her chin. "I will deny nothing—so long as

you assure me there is no reason we shouldn't assuage certain . . . hungers."

"No reason exists," he vowed, the rough edge to his voice underscoring the truth of his words. "Not since my lady wife passed on some years ago."

"Then let us find solace," Nessa agreed, all the world stopping for her as she lifted her hands to the stays of her gown, swiftly loosing them.

Freeing herself to the first stirrings of pleasure she'd known in countless empty nights.

And, were she honest, to this degree, mayhap ever.

Chapter Five

✦

"What do you mean you will no longer be sleeping here?"

Mariota stared at Nessa, watching her move about the bedchamber, calmly gathering her belongings. A silver-backed hairbrush Mariota had given her two summers ago, her best gown, and even her needlework. Everything went into the wicker basket strategically placed on a settle by the door.

As if she were serious, had indeed lost her heart to the dark-visaged knight, Sir Lachlan Macrae. Truly thought to become his . . . paramour.

Mariota's eyes widened, amazement stealing her breath when her friend paused to pour a cup of ale and flashed her a smug-looking smile.

A dreamy, wholly besotted smile.

"Well?" Mariota prodded, still disbelieving.

Nessa shrugged. "Och, then—I meant just what I said. As of this night, I will take my bed . . . elsewhere."

"On the spread pallet of a man you scarce—"

"I ken him well enough." A soft gleam entered Nessa's dark eyes.

Seeing it, Mariota threw a glance at the tall white candles burning on a chest of fine carved wood. Knightly appointments the plenishings were, newly installed in the chamber. "This is madness," she said, sliding one of the heavy silver candlesticks across the chest top. "And there is no need for you to take such measures. Sir Kenneth has made this room a haven. For the two of us—"

"Tush! Do you not understand? I *want* to be with Sir Lachlan." Nessa smiled again, waved a dismissive hand. "As for this chamber, did you not hear your Keeper tell his men he wished the room swiftly dressed for your comfort?"

"He is not my anything, and he said *our* comfort—yours and mine."

Nessa sniffed. "I would think you might welcome . . . this chance? Truth tell, I vow it best that you sleep here alone," she owned, her eyes alight with merriment. "In time you might even thank me."

Mariota flushed. "If you think to foist me into the Keeper of Cuidrach's arms just because you have found ready succor, you are sorely mistaken."

Even so, she couldn't help imagining herself in the handsome knight's embrace.

Breathless and naked, his mouth devouring hers as his hands explored her, their passion hot and tempestuous.

Nor could she forget his gentle and caring touch. How, in the bailey on that first fateful night, he'd reached to adjust her cloak, then moved so that his back shielded her from the wind.

Hugh Alesone had never shown such thoughtfulness—she'd always been the one to see to *his* comfort.

Mariota looked at her friend, saw the other woman's misty-eyed happiness and bit her lip, trying not to put too much weight on one thoughtful gesture.

Or think too deeply about why her breath caught each time Kenneth MacKenzie turned that deep, dark gaze on her.

Instead, she swallowed and nudged at the floor rushes. "Leaving me alone here will avail nothing—if you believe your absence will hasten matters I have no interest in pursuing," she said, the tingling weightiness in her belly making a mockery of her words.

The sudden spill of warmth in her heart scaring her.

She ignored the sensations, lifted her chin. "Sir Kenneth is as desirous of keeping to himself as I am. He told me so."

Nessa shot her an amused glance. "Did he now?"

"You know he did." Mariota fussed at her skirts, avoiding her friend's eye. "He made quite clear he was not pleased to find us here. In especial, me . . . posing as lady of this keep!"

"That was a surprise, to be sure," Nessa allowed. "But I've seen how he watches you, the ravenous look in his eyes." She tilted her head. "He is a lusty man, I'll wager. And, I am thinking, too long without a woman's attentions."

Mariota looked away. "There are worse things."

"He'd make a fine bedmate, I say you," Nessa decided. "Perhaps it would benefit you both to slake a mutual thirst? Pure need sated. No other . . . *concerns* between you?"

Mariota opened her mouth and shut it as quickly.

A fine bedmate.

Sated need.

"You've lost your wits." She stared at the other woman. "Is your memory so short? Have you forgotten all that happened at Drumodyn? Why we are even here?"

"It is Drumodyn that moves me. And should move you!" Nessa shot back. "O-o-oh, my lady, I do not think you know what is good for you."

"I know what is good for landed knights, newly come to their holdings." Mariota blew a wisp of hair off her brow. "Heed my words—Sir Kenneth will soon claim the comforts of his bedchamber. Think you he will be content sleeping below, on a pallet, when his bed and all its trappings stand waiting in this room?"

Nessa shrugged, the mischief in her eye answer enough.

Disregarding her, Mariota huffed and turned away . . . and almost tripped over Cuillin, the ancient hound claimed by the strapping young knight, Jamie the Small.

"So you've found your way in here, too, have you, laddie?" She reached down to tousle the dog's ears and when she straightened, Nessa was gone.

No doubt into the arms of her knightly lover.

Wishing she could pursue her desires as easily, Mariota stepped into the nearest window embrasure and let the chill air cool her cheeks. She stared into the streaming rain, drew a deep breath. To be sure, she understood her friend's . . . need.

Her passion.

Hers was another matter.

A danger to be squelched before it could bloom.

She tightened her jaw, determined to do just that, but then *his* scent surrounded her. Clean and invigorating, its freshness swept away memories, claiming its own place and filling her with hope.

Hope and moon-slanted shadows, the wet gleam of night-darkened stone.

Recognizing her mistake, she shivered and clutched the cold damp of the window ledge.

His scent hadn't beguiled her at all. It was just the wind gusting past the tower.

Her senses had fooled her.

Disappointed her.

And they continued to mock her when she turned back to the room, for the only scents greeting her were the smoky bite of melted candle wax and the pungent odor of sleeping dog.

Sleeping, old dog.

And looking at him, his stiff legs stretched straight out before him, his fluting snores loud in the silence, her heart dipped and an almost-smile touched her lips.

In a long ago time, she would have smiled even more, found at least some humor in her predicament.

But now, with candlelight flickering on tapestried walls and a certain dashing knight's newly assembled bed winking at her from the shadows, she only found herself . . . trapped. And yearning for the simplicity enjoyed by those who slept on pallets, sheltered by roofs thatched with bracken.

The freedom of choice allowed to women who called themselves herring wives and not . . . ladies.

A world without heartache, lies, and unwise longings.

A bliss that seemed about as attainable as believing the old fireside tale that Cailleach Mhor, the great Hag of the Ridges, created Scotland by dropping a creel of peat and rock into sea!

Or that the silhouette she suddenly caught a glimpse of in the doorway was not a deeper shadow, but *him*.

She blinked, supposing the splatter of rain and the wind must've kept her from hearing his approach. Or his stealth had been deliberate. But he was there now, there could be no denying.

The Keeper of Cuidrach in all his solemn magnificence, the power of his presence palpable and unsettling, and stealing around her like a swirled cloak that both warmed and engulfed.

"Oh!" Mariota gasped, her heart thumping slow and hard.

She stared at him, as keenly aware of his dark sensuality as if their bodies touched, full naked, their breath already mingling.

He didn't move.

He simply stood there, filling the doorway, his plaid slung over one shoulder, his richly tooled knight's belt low on his hips, his expression unreadable.

And, saints help her, the intensity of him unleashed a trickling anticipation that spilled all through her, making her blood run thick and rich.

Hot.

And in ways she'd never thought to experience again.

"I did not hear you. How long have you been standing there?" She placed a hand on her breast, amazed she could speak past the dryness in her throat. "Surely not . . . overlong?"

"Shall we just say that I did not come to claim the comforts of this chamber, but rather to ask of yours?" He took a step forward, the very shadows seeming to draw back from him. "I am indeed content sleeping below, on a pallet of heather, aye."

Heat scalded Mariota's cheeks. "You mistake," she said, embarrassment tightening her chest. "I did not mean—"

"Come, my lady." He stepped closer, pausing near a slanting moonbeam. "Do not demean your spirit by unsaying your words. Or what you wished them to reveal."

"Then . . ." Mariota cleared her throat and met his gaze. "What I said was not meant as a slur to you—only that I wish to be left alone. I made my own fate, see you. And much of it . . . soured, if you would know the truth of it."

"Say no more, lady. I suspected as much, and"—he took her hand and kissed her fingers—"I would not see you distressed."

She pulled away, moving to the window. "Nay, my pardon. 'Tis I who ought apologize—for being here, and for intruding on your peace."

"Peace?" He made a sound that could have passed for a laugh. "Would you know me better, you'd know that true peace has e'er been as remote as the moon for me," he said, watching her. "But I do not mind waiting a while longer for its arrival. So long as it comes at all, I shall be content."

She looked at him, her eyes doubtful. "And you have faith that it will?"

"One must always have faith, my lady. And there is much to rejoice in . . . meantime." He joined her at the window, looked out at the wet darkness. "See you, these very hills bring me solace. And joy. They are my home.

The place I yearned to return to through more years than you would wish to know."

He paused, thinking not of distant sea cliffs, cold and inhospitable, their treacherous heights teeming with screaming seabirds, but of fine, sun-chased days, washed with summer green and scented with broom. And the deep glens, so sweet and quiet, that had e'er been the saving of him.

Savored bliss that even now filled him with a warm gladness.

He drew a breath, glanced at her. "Kintail is peace, my lady. The soft Highland air and the blue mist on the braes. Such can lift my spirits in a trice, and does."

"And that is enough for you?"

"It is."

"Then you are a man content with little."

"Nay, I am a man surrounded by more glories than I can wonder at in a thousand lifetimes," Kenneth amended, his heart swelling with a longing no Highlander would deny. "Nights of crystal stars. Cloud shadows on the moorland slopes—a whiff of peat on a chill afternoon. The soul of the heather pulsing in one's blood. . . ."

He stepped behind her, dipping his head to brush a light kiss to her nape. "Such a world is round and full," he said, resting his hands on her shoulders. "I do not want for more."

"And you needn't with the finery in this chamber," she countered, moving away from him to pace about the room.

"Think you?" Kenneth's brow lifted.

She nodded.

He almost snorted.

She'd not heard a word he'd said, hadn't compre-hended that his idea of comfort encompassed something much deeper and far more lasting than fine bedding and a welter of furs and frothy pillows.

She picked up just such a pillow from the window seat. "I have seldom seen such splendor, even in my father's house," she said, smoothing her fingers over the pillow's embroidered surface. "You have made so many changes. I cannot help but think of your forebear, Ranald the Redoubtable. The tales your men recounted of him in the hall the other night. He would be proud if he knew what you've done here—what you are doing."

And I would rather know poor Cormac at peace.

Kenneth tensed thinking of the sad fate of the long-dead cowherd.

A romantic young fool who, like himself, had once trusted with his all and lost everything.

Frowning, he took the cushion from the pretend Lady of Cuidrach and tossed it back onto the bench. "If old Ranald is pleased, he must say his thanks to my uncle, Duncan MacKenzie. He supplied most of the goods in this chamber, not I."

"Duncan MacKenzie?" Her eyes widened. "I have heard of him. My father knew him . . . fleetingly."

"Then you know he is the Black Stag of Kintail, a powerful man in these parts?"

She nodded. "My father says he is a man of great valor."

"That he is—and generous," Kenneth agreed, speaking from the heart. "He wished to know me well settled, hence his gifts of provender and household plenishings."

She lifted a brow at that and moved to the hearth table, her fingers going to a silver chalice sitting there. Truly magnificent and encrusted with pearls, it gleamed in the candlelight. "Such riches are beyond mere household goods."

Kenneth glanced at the chalice, bit back a smile. "A gift from Sir Marmaduke, my uncle's friend, and the finest Sassunach champion to e'er make these hills his home—if his taste runs a bit to the extravagant."

"And your taste?"

Warm curves and feminine softness.

The unspoken words rang in Kenneth's ears, each one dredging up his deepest wants and desires, flinging them at her feet.

A full woman, generous in spirit, good of heart, and at ease with her sensuality.

And unafraid of his.

Sharply aware of that sensuality now, this moment, he shifted against the heat surging into his groin, half certain his need stood emblazoned across his forehead.

Or that if she looked too closely, she'd see the power she wielded. The uncomfortable *stirring* roused from the simple pleasure of looking at her, inhaling her heady, female scent.

The mistake he'd made by sampling the smooth warmth of her skin—and finding it much to his liking!

He frowned.

She came closer.

As if she knew how fiercely his body reacted to her, how much he desired her.

He bit back a groan, his gaze slipping to her full, well-rounded breasts. The notable thrust of hard nipples against the linen bodice of her gown.

A gown with a top piece that dipped far too low and clung much too provocatively.

She moistened her lips, something in her eyes telling him that she recognized his . . . discomfiture. "Well? What *are* your tastes?" she asked again. "What do you find pleasing?"

"Things that ought not be distracting me," he blurted, curling his hands around his sword belt to keep from reaching for her.

To keep from questioning what he was about to propose and shield him from how easily a few sweet words could make him forget his reasons for wishing her safely elsewhere!

She touched a hand to his chest, the innocent contact making him hard. "And what do you find so distracting?"

"*You* are distracting," he vowed, a muscle working in his jaw. "But never you mind. Of greater import is that I have a . . . proposal for you."

"A proposal?"

He nodded. "See you, just as my uncle's name is not strange to you, so do several of my men believe they know of your father—a puissant warrior laird of the north. Archibald Macnicol?"

She gasped, but caught herself as quickly. "Your men know him but you do not?"

"Och, lass, but I have told you—I am anything but a court-bred knight." Kenneth tightened his grip on his belt, struggling anew to ignore how provocatively her bodice strained across her breasts.

Breasts he just knew would be soft, warm, and plump in his hands. Deliciously sweet beneath his lips.

He swallowed, struggled even harder against a certain *discomfort.*

"See you," he began again, speaking in a rush, "ask me of the people of this glen and I can tell you who their great-grandfathers' grandfathers were, and who they married. But"—he shook his head—"I am no man to ken the names of the titled and privileged."

He frowned, wished she weren't standing so close. "Is this great man of the north, this Archibald Macnicol, your father? Do my men tell me true?"

"Why do you speak of him?" she flashed, the hot lights in her eyes answer enough. "He would sooner cut out his tongue than utter my name."

"That, my lady, I can scarce believe, but I've not forgotten that you said your family is wroth with you." He reached out, captured her chin when she tried to look away. "Surely it is not that grim?"

She pressed her lips into a hard, tight line and shook her head, her eyes glittering.

Frustrated, Kenneth blew out a breath. "Ach, see you, I'd thought to please you by offering you safe escort to your father's holding, Dunach Castle. Thought Dunach's stout walls and your father's own formidable reputation might prove a more secure refuge for you."

"My father . . . *was* formidable," she said, her voice sounding distant, someone else's. "He no longer is. Now, he is ailing. A broken man—a shadow of his former self."

"Then mayhap you ought return indeed? To comfort and care for him?" He let go of her chin, smoothed a strand of hair behind her ear. "If he is ill, he will surely welcome you."

She drew a deep breath. "You do not understand. I am the reason he fares so poorly. To take me there would only worsen his condition, and that is a burden I do not wish to add to the ones I already carry."

"But—"

"No, you must believe me," she said, her voice edged with finality. "You thought and are thinking wrong. I cannot return to Dunach."

He touched her cheek, letting his fingers glide close to the corner of her mouth. "And if I would help you make things right?"

She stiffened. "You cannot—unless you can undo the past."

"No one can work such a wonder, my lady." He quirked a brow at her, attempted a smile. "But if it is impossible to forget the past, mayhap I can help you to look forward?"

She glanced aside, said nothing.

He frowned.

And grew increasingly alarmed by the depth of his concern for her.

Alarmed enough to resort to his alternative plan.

He cleared his throat and ran a hand through his hair. "If you do not wish to be returned to your father," he began, rushing the words before his tongue refused to form them, "I can perhaps find a suitable husband for you. A man of good standing who'd welcome a widowed gentlewom—"

"I do not wish a husband, either. Indeed, that is the *last* thing I desire." She bristled, pinning him with a piercing stare, the gold flecks in her irises glinting in the firelight.

Glinting, and changing color, the startling illusion

giving the impression that her eyes were of purest, liquid amber and not the disturbingly familiar jewel-green of another woman's eyes.

Lying eyes.

Narrowing on him from his own past and chilling him, their treacherous depths prickling his nape and sending shudders down his spine. Icy shivers to mind him of old mistakes and follies and warn him to be wary.

To guard his heart and ignore the hunger *this* green-eyed minx roused in him.

The fierce urge to touch, taste, and have her.

And most disturbing of all, the absurd notion that she among all women might be different.

Chapter Six

❧

Not quite a sennight later, Kenneth accepted defeat.

The futility of fighting his attraction to Lady Mariota, the foolhardiness of thinking he could guard his heart.

Truth was, his store of inventive reasons for avoiding her was near depleted. Not that a single one had worked well in the first place. Indeed, no matter what task he'd sought or what corner of the castle he'd made his own, she'd found him.

Or, far more galling, he'd found himself looking for her.

And then suffered heart pangs and other unmention-able *ailments* so soon as he caught sight of her.

Even now, this gathering of his men, arranged a full ungodly hour before cockcrow, only proved the severity of his predicament. And an earnest meeting it was— called to discuss procuring cattle.

Yet rather than focus on the matter at hand, he'd barely downed his first cup of morning ale before he began scanning the shadows and peering about the torch-lit great hall, hoping to spot a flash of bright, coppery hair.

Or unexpectedly breathe in her perfume, an intoxicatingly fresh scent that always seemed to float on the air, heralding her arrival a split second before she came into view.

But this morning he only smelled ale, somewhat stale bannocks, and . . . the sharp edge of young Jamie's nervousness.

Saints, but the lad was crowding him!

"To be sure, sir," the youth was saying just now, his eyes bright with eagerness, "such is a well-trusted remedy. The reason my da has the finest cattle in the land."

Kenneth frowned and reached for his ale cup, taking a moment to thrust aside any wayward thought that might make his heart hammer and his blood . . . thicken.

Young James of the Heather, tenth son of a lesser Macpherson chieftain, but most times called Jamie the Small, sat beside him at the high table, scratching Cuillin's shaggy head, and hoping his liege laird's darkening brow didn't mean he'd taken offense.

Jamie's throat went a bit dry at the possibility. He hadn't meant to press his suit quite so urgently.

But certain aches rode him hard and encouraging the new Keeper to purchase Macpherson cattle would go a long way in raising Jamie's worth in the eyes of a father who scarce recalled his existence.

Kenneth MacKenzie, at least, noted his presence and kept an open ear.

"Ha—what you do not say, Jamie lad," he finally spoke, his brow clearing. " 'Tis true enough I wouldn't mind avoiding the journey to the great cattle tryst at Crieff come the spring, and I'd be even less eager to travel so far south as Falkirk if the beasts at Crieff proved lacking. But cattle kept hale through the winter? And by fairy magic?"

Jamie shifted on the trestle bench. "Begging pardon, sir, but I said my father uses an ancient Highland remedy to safeguard our cattle in the lean months. 'Tis no witchy magic, nay."

"And what might that be?" Sir Lachlan put in, his voice level and reassuring.

Even so, Jamie found himself at a loss for words and dug his fingers deeper into Cuillin's ratty coat, holding tight to his boyhood companion, his sole connection to home.

"Well, laddie?" Another clansman peered across the table, mirth wreathing his bearded face. "What sort of charm keeps your da's shaggy black beasts the envy of every other cattle-rich laird this side o' the Highland Line?"

"Naught that has to do with witchery," Jamie blurted, feeling conspicuous with so many stares turned his way. "'Tis only a remedy—but an ages-old one. The original was given to my father's father's father by Devorgilla of Doon, Clan MacLean's *cailleach*."

At once, all babble ceased and as Jamie looked round, his spirits lifted to see that the inimitable crone's name had taken the smirk off the other men's faces.

He pulled in a breath, couldn't quite help the slight puffing of his chest. "A Macpherson once gave Devorgilla refuge back when she was young and folk didn't yet appreciate her healing art. In gratitude, she gave my forebear a small clutch of rowan branches tied with red thread. It's still affixed above the byre door, though the clan women hang a fresh cluster beside it each autumn, before the cattle are brought down from the summer pasturings."

Someone harrumphed.

Others exchanged sidelong glances.

"O-ho! And no witchy magic, you say?" A barrel-chested clansman leaned forward, his meaty hands clamped on the table edge. "Och, laddie, I ken some fine braw men who wouldn't cross paths with Devorgilla even if you promised them a roll in the heather with three bonnie, big-breasted lassies. *Naked lassies!*"

Jamie swallowed, some of the swell leaving his chest.

Naked, big-breasted lassies, indeed.

And uttered in the same breath as the venerable Devorgilla.

"Jest as you will," he said, "but so long as we follow the practice, Clan Macpherson enjoys fat cows the whole winter through."

"Havers!" The meaty-handed clansman snorted. "Nigh all cattle beasts are slaughtered and salted on Michaelmas—save a few kept to replenish the next year's stock. Even on Macpherson lands, I'll wager."

"I do not lie," Jamie said, coloring. "And neither does my father, though he surely enjoys . . . bargaining. And, of that I would warn you."

"Aye," someone called from another table, "Munro Macpherson is crafty. But he'll no see you wrong so far as the quality of his beasts."

The man pushed to his feet, glancing round. "Indeed, if you pour enough coin into his coffers and smile through his jabber, he'll look after your cattle till spring and then hand deliver you the finest creatures a Highland heart could desire!"

And mayhap look with more favor on his youngest son.

A fine lad who deserved better and ought not suffer for having been sired by an indifferent father, chiefly or otherwise.

As well Kenneth knew.

He looked over at him, his mind set. "Jamie—is it true your father will care for the beasts through the winter? Deliver them hale and hearty after the first thaws?"

"That is so," Jamie confirmed. "But he'd demand payment now, like as not claiming he'll require the coin to lay in winter fodder or perhaps build an extra byre to house the beasts."

"The coin would be well spent," *she* declared, stepping up to the table and looking far too fetching for such an early hour.

Her lush beauty almost hurting his eyes, Kenneth cocked his head at her, feeling a sharp need to touch and taste her.

"And what do you know of Jamie's father's cattle?" he asked, sending up a silent thanks to the saints that his plaid and the table edge hid the sudden rise in his braies.

"What do I know of Munro Macpherson's cattle?" She slid a glance at Jamie. "Bulls," she said, the challenge in her eyes at strange odds with the delicate pink staining her cheeks. "My father swore by the . . . *craft* of Macpherson bulls; he even secured a few as gifts for his allies."

"Then so be it," Kenneth decided, too aware of how

the top swells of her breasts shimmered in the torchlight to wonder overlong why she hadn't mentioned a connection to Jamie's clan before now—and excusing the coming dent in his coffers with the smile on young Jamie's face.

Much pleased himself, Kenneth stood. "The matter is settled," he declared, lifting his voice. "Macpherson cattle it shall be. This very afternoon, I shall secure sufficient coin to please Munro Macpherson, no matter his demands."

And, he promised himself as the hall broke into a great stir, he'd use the opportunity of retrieving the siller to seek a much needed *remedy* of his own!

One that wouldn't endanger his heart.

And hopefully skilled enough to cure the itch plaguing him!

He turned to frown at that *itch,* but found her gone, vanished as swiftly as she'd appeared.

Only her scent remained, its faint echo teasing and beguiling him, making him want more.

Enough to lose and drown himself in—and propel him from the hall before his men noted his discomfiture and guessed the reason.

A *reason* that slipped from the shadows so soon as he rounded the screens passage and stepped into the curving passage beyond.

He stopped short. One brow arched and his entire body tightened. So much so he risked giving her a slow, deliberate smile.

But she disregarded the warning signs and came right at him, stepping so close that her breasts brushed his chest. So near that her scent swirled around him, inflaming his senses and blotting all thought . . . save dark ones!

"Lass—you dare much," he said, so hard he could scarce breathe.

"I know," she admitted, surprising him. "That is why I waited for you—to tell you the truth away from your men. Especially Jamie."

Kenneth blinked.

This wasn't what he'd expected.

His heart thundering, he gripped the back of her neck, tipping her head so she couldn't look away. "What does Jamie have to do with . . . *this*?"

This time she blinked. "W-with what?"

In answer, he dropped his gaze to where her breasts pressed against his plaid.

"Oh!" She blinked again, moistened her lips. "I lied about Jamie's father's cattle," she said in a rush. "He looked so . . . *besieged* when the others were baiting him and I . . . I wanted to help him."

"And you did—most cleverly," Kenneth owned, snaking an arm around her when she made to pull away. "But I wonder if the lie was worth the risk?"

"The risk?"

"Oh, aye—a great risk." Kenneth nodded. "The one you took in coming so close to me," he said, tightening his hold on her, drawing her closer still. "See you, lass, I am going to kiss you now," he added, already lowering his head.

"Kiss me?" she murmured, even as his mouth slanted over hers. "Knowing you mean to marry me off to someone else?"

"Even then," Kenneth asserted—just before his tongue glided hotly against hers.

Later that day, in the soft light of the gloaming, Kenneth drew rein at the thick, circular base of Dun Telve, one of several hollow-walled brochs nestled deep in the woods of his beloved Glenelg.

Russet-colored bracken and great clusters of wet, late-blooming heather pressed against the broch's ruined walls, the wild tangle of undergrowth nearly blocking the low, stone-linteled entry passage, a sight that reassured him.

Dun Telve looked . . . undisturbed.

Relief sliding through him, he released the breath he'd been holding.

Truth tell, save the differences wrought by the turning seasons, little had changed since he'd last visited this silent remnant of Scotland's distant past. A night he'd sought shelter, a place to secure his coin.

A fortune earned during his toil as a merchant seaman, his years spent as a successful if reluctant gatherer of seabird oil, one of the most highly prized commodities in all Christendom.

His chest tightening, he touched the three vertical scars seaming his left cheek, a forever reminder of days he didn't care to speak of, but would never forget.

Dark days that endcd on a cold, rainy night last spring when he'd slept in Dun Telve's inner courtyard, his heart aching at the unexpected loss of his mother, his good Scots siller stashed within the broch's walls, guilt flooding him for having trespassed on such a sacred place.

Then, as now, the strange stone tower loomed dark against the lowering sky, its strength, even in ruin, filling him with awe.

Knowing better than to rush his movements, he dismounted with care, swinging down onto the black, peat-rich earth as respectfully as he could.

He turned toward the broch, the soft patter of rain on stone and the whispered murmurings of a thousand ancient voices greeting him . . . even if their acceptance came tinged with caution.

Kenneth didn't blame them.

He, too, practiced prudence.

But he could feel them all around him, those broch-dwellers of old, their time here long past, their faces and names as shadowy and distant as the dark of the moon.

Once, they'd danced, sung, and told tales here, yet now they simply watched and guarded, mere shadows of the past, keeping vigil, he sensed, in the deep, ferny woods surrounding the broch.

Ever-present, but quick to melt into the mist if one looked their way too long.

Sure of it, he dipped his head to enter the low-ceilinged entry passage and, as always, his skin prickled when he stepped into the dank, circular interior. The dim enclosure held all the wet chill of autumn, and he welcomed the thin, gray light yet sifting into the roofless ruin, filtering in through tiny gaps in the walls.

He looked round, breathing in the earth-rich scent of leaf mold and cold ash, faint traces of ancient fires, long extinguished and never to burn again.

With luck, nothing more ominous than the echoing

drip of rain would join him and he'd be able to retrieve the coin he needed and be gone before his fancies got the better of him.

Worldly-wise as he considered himself, only those totally lacking caution would forget that some believed such brochs were older than man.

Sithean, the superstitious called them.

Fairy knowes, or forts.

Thin places, where the veil between the worlds might prove a bit translucent. Mysterious portals into the realm of the *Sidhe,* and the point of no return for those unfortunate souls carried off by fairies after darkness falls.

Even so, his susceptibility to such hazards was well tempered—especially with a lusty, willing-armed widow awaiting him.

Leastways, his uncle had assured him she'd welcome his attentions, urging him to visit the buxom, well-made Gunna of the Glen if ever certain manly needs became overpowering.

By all accounts well bitten by the letch herself, the widow was reputed capable of slaking a man's most lascivious thirsts.

A cure Kenneth meant to sample—so soon as possible!

To that end, he made straight for the broch's guard chamber, a tiny cell built into the thickness of the wall near the entrance passage.

Here, too, shadows greeted him, and air thick with the smell of damp, lichened stone. Meager light revealed his hiding place secure, each stone intact—just as he'd left them.

Again, relief washed through him and he squared his

shoulders, flexing his fingers before laying his work-scarred hands on sacred stones.

A grave error for the instant he did, an unearthly light streamed out from the cavity he'd opened—a glow not only illuminating his undisturbed coin pouches, but also his much younger–looking and scar-free hands!

Kenneth froze, his heart slamming against his ribs.

The light pulsed and eddied, no longer coming from the wall, but now slanting down from a summer sun shining through the trees, its golden rays warming the stones beneath his youthful fingers.

Frantic fingers digging ever faster into the fake stone burial cairn he'd built behind *her* cottage.

A wee thatched cottage he could see as clear as yesterday for it stood with a scatter of other such humble, fisherfolk dwellings, the whitewashed line of them crouching together on the slope of a familiar but distant shore, the dank walls of Dun Telve nowhere to be seen!

Only the strangely glowing light and the long ago hiding place he'd erected with such care, believing the mock cairn would keep his savings secure during his absences at sea. And, too, that keeping his coin pouches outside her home might keep her safe as well.

Her, and her aging father.

Should e'er thieving scoundrels ride through their village and suspect they guarded such treasure.

Ne'er would he have believed her father would hand over the greatest treasure of all.

Sell his beautiful, green-eyed daughter to a shipowner more than twice the girl's age.

Or that she'd consent to go with the man.

The betrayal made all the more bitter when her father

offered to help Kenneth gather his savings, claiming neither his daughter nor his own bent-backed self had need of a bastard's savings—the girl's new husband had more gold than they needed, and an untarnished name!

Kenneth blinked, old anger flashing through him. Hot bile rose in his throat, the eerie glow mocking him, increasing in intensity until it shimmered all around him, so brilliant he could see every detail of that long ago day.

Most of all, the observant eyes watching him from behind cracked doors—doors that now swung wide—the fisherfolk stepping out to greet him, their hooded cloaks oddly luminous, the intricately worked silver brooches at their shoulders marking them as anything but simple men of the sea.

A tall, splendidly built youth broke rank with them and strode closer, his magnificent stature and beauty at stark contrast to his humble attire.

A cowherd's rags, naught more.

Recognizing him, Kenneth opened his mouth, but no words came—not that it mattered, for the glowing-robed ancients crowded around Cormac then, one even resting a protective hand on the lad's shoulder as others closed in, shielding him from view.

But the cowherd's words reached Kenneth all the same.

Think hard, my friend, and act wisely.

No peace is so sweet as forgiveness.

Kenneth's jaw dropped, his pulse leaping to a dangerous, heart-drumming speed, but before he could catch himself, Cormac vanished, the ancients and the fishing village disappearing with him.

The brilliant light faded as well, growing dim as it seeped back into the cold, wet stones.

"By the Rood!" Kenneth stared. He ran his hands along the wall and pressed his forehead to the stones, amazement crashing through him.

Had he truly seen such a wonder? Heard Cormac's words?

Seen the faces of the ancients?

If so, only the rush of the wind remained. The same *drip drip* of the rain, and the two coin pouches he'd somehow wrested from his hiding place in the wall.

A gap he'd refilled with great speed, his hands trembling as he replaced the missing stones. Work-worn hands, he noted with relief, for once glad to see the crisscrossing of scars marring hands *she'd* once claimed so beautiful.

So skilled.

And not just at robbing seabird nests!

Remembering, Kenneth's blood chilled anew and the wonder of moments before receded as other, darker emotions surged up to replace them.

Long-seething anger. His determination to never suffer heartache again. And . . . lust.

The insatiable kind that knew but one quenching.

Scowling, he snatched up the coin pouches and took his leave of the broch, his need to sink himself into the sweet, silken heat betwixt Mariota of Dunach's thighs so fierce his hunger for her near blinded him.

Pure need sated . . . no other concerns, her friend had commented.

And he fully agreed.

His needs raging, he swung up onto his saddle and spurred off into the fast fading light.

But not in the direction of Cuidrach.

"Mother o' all the saints! There is naught of substance along Loch Hourn's shore but Cuidrach Castle . . . and that pile o' stanes stands in ruin!"

His opinion aired, Ewan the Witty paced back and forth in the dripping woods at the edge of Kintail, his every step hindered by the clinging, soaking bracken slapping at his thighs, his glowering face darker than the descending night, his entire wrath aimed at Wee Finlay.

"You are mad," he seethed, "crazed as a loon if you think the Lady Mariota would hie herself to such a place!"

"That'll be yourself—what's mad," Finlay shot back. "If you can't recognize the truth when it's laid at your feet!"

Ewan's face turned red. *"The truth?"*

Finlay glared, said nothing.

"I will tell you the truth!" Ewan roared. "For days we've been stumbling through these empty, forsaken hills and you have yet to find your magic-eyed fox!"

He raised bushy brows at the smaller man, ignoring the others and their corner-of-the-mouth mumblings. "How many false foxes have we followed, I ask you? Four? Six?"

"Three," Wee Finlay admitted, his gnarled fists thrust against his hips.

"And now you'd have us follow yet another such sorry

creature into the wilds of Glenelg . . . right to the black shores of Loch Hourn?"

Finlay shrugged.

"Have you stuffed your ears to all our talk about the *urisgean* known to guard these parts?" Ewan the Witty jabbed a finger at the towering black outline of Kintail's peaks. "Ravening beasts, they are, I tell you. And a thousand times more fearsome than the Each Uisge that had done with our own poor alewife back in Assynt!"

"Even so, the Lady Mariota can be nowhere else," Finlay insisted, puffing his chest. "This fox was the right one—I swear it."

"Then why wasn't he carrying the lute on his red-furred back?" one of the others wanted to know.

"Och, well . . . such matters are beyond my ken," Finlay returned. "But some might say he's too clever to make such a mistake."

"The mistake will be yours if we continue into such benighted territory and do not find what we seek," Ewan charged, his stare unyielding.

"Did you not hear what *they* said?" Finlay demanded, equally undaunted.

Turning a deaf ear to the hoots of the others, he jerked a glance at the small farmery they'd happened upon earlier.

Far below them now, and only a cluster of thatched cot houses and a few scraggly byres, the humble spread was still in view at the head of the glen.

Leastways for those whose vision wasn't dimmed by spleen and fury.

Or ignorance.

The fox had led them there.

Finlay knew it.

Their friendly blether with the farmer proved it!

"Well," he prodded, letting his own stare grow bold. "You heard the farm folk."

"Och, now, to be sure and I did," Ewan confirmed with a conspiratorial wink at the others. "A fox has been harrying the farmer's best broody hens and two lassies passed this way a while ago—strangers to these parts. One flame-haired, the other dark."

Finlay nodded. "And they were heading toward Loch Hourn . . . to the ruins of Clan MacKenzies' Cuidrach Castle."

Ewan the Witty snorted. "Do you ken how many flame-haired lassies walk these hills?" he snapped, kicking free of a clump of bracken that had somehow wrapped itself around his leg. "As for the herring widow, dark-haired wenches are even more common—there's as many of them as sand on the shore!"

"But how many travel only of an e'en?" Finlay sent another glance at the now-sleeping farm. "And not only refuse to give their names but head off unescorted into lands known to be . . . dangerous?"

Ewan looked up at the night sky, blew out a breath.

"I say you, Finlay," he growled, "if the Lady Mariota and the golden lute are not at Cuidrach Castle, you *will* be the Each Uisge's next meal. And if I must dredge the whole of the River Inver to find the beastie!"

Wee Finlay gave a curt nod and said nothing.

He wasn't the muddle-headed one. And 'twas well he knew the disadvantages of being a somewhat short-of-stature, leathery old man.

But he had his wits about him, even if others didn't.

And, he decided, as he helped himself to a swill of heather ale from his belt flask, he was beginning to wish they ne'er did find the Lady Mariota and her friend.

Or the wretched lute!

There were some who simply deserved to be plagued by ill fortune and mishap.

And Ewan the Witty was one of them.

Chapter Seven

❧

A good many sea miles away, in the deep of a misty evening, Devorgilla's heart skittered, the flash of familiar red fur and the sparkle of gold catching her by surprise as she knelt before the Clach na Gruagach, the Isle of Doon's revered Stone of the Fairy Woman.

She gave a little cackle of pleasure, a cozy warmth spreading through her ancient bones. But she hadn't expected to see her little friend again so soon.

Or the golden lute . . .

Not that she'd doubted the wee fox's ability.

A rather new but trusted companion, he'd already proved himself a worthy helpmate—and certainly more adventurous than her own dear Mab who preferred dozing before Devorgilla's hearth fire, it being beneath the dignity of her feline years to go traipsing through bog-filled moors and wild mountain fastnesses.

Unlike Somerled, who thrived on such magical missions.

"Ach, laddie—here is a surprise!" the crone enthused, tipping the last of her offering of goat's milk onto the base of the sacred stone.

Quiet as the night, the fox watched with steady eyes as she set aside the now empty ewer and pushed to her feet with a discreet clucking of her tongue, an affectation she allowed herself to disguise the creaking of her knees.

The only bane of age that truly annoyed her.

But one she couldn't help, so she beamed delight at the little fox and looked on as he nosed the lute toward her.

"You are a welcome sight," she fussed over him, reaching down to smooth his silky red fur. "O-o-oh, to be sure, and you are!"

But Somerled only angled his head, tapped the lute with his paw.

"Aye, a fine braw laddie," Devorgilla praised, squinting against the lute's brilliance.

Wrought of fairy gold and studded with jewels, it glowed as if lit by an inner fire, its light shining even brighter when she gathered it into her hands and ran loving fingers over its warm, slightly vibrating surface.

"By all the fates," she crooned, "I vow he is as pleased to be returned to us as we are to have him again, eh?"

The fox blinked in answer, his gaze solemn.

Earnest enough to make Devorgilla lift a grizzled brow.

Something about the evening's stillness, or perhaps the way the moon hung so low above the hills, let her know her own powers were yet needed.

And in more ways than she'd planned to use them!

Tightening her fingers around the lute, she nudged at a

clump of deer grass, struggled to capture the message humming just beneath the surface of the night.

That two deserving souls needed to learn to trust again, she knew. Caught in a place betwixt and between, they were—and aching! So much had been apparent some long nights ago when the innocent peats smoldering on her hearthstone suddenly turned into burning crisps of parchment!

Love sonnets, the scribblings were, and penned by the hand of greed and ambition rather than honest passion. A great stirk of a cross-grained lout who'd only pretended to care for his adoring, deep-pursed lady.

"Fiend seize and keep him," the crone huffed, her ire rising.

As for the *other* one, the good lad, earlier this very e'en, she'd glimpsed him in the steam rising from her cook pot—a fierce scowl on his handsome face, his heart still shuttered.

And now, somewhere across the night sea, the stubborn fool rode . . . elsewhere.

"Tush!" she sniffed, glancing at the moonlit waters. "Lusty widows, indeed!"

Aye, the Keeper of Cuidrach had a few lessons yet to learn.

But mayhap she did as well if Somerled's piercing stare meant anything.

"You'd best tell me," she urged him. "Say on—be the talebearer I know you are."

But the little fox only looked away across the Sea of the Hebrides toward the distant mainland coast, the taut set of his shoulders and his perked ears revealing all the crone needed to hear.

"Humph!" She sent a disdainful glance in the same direction, scorning not the land or the sea, dear as both were to her, but the dastards lurking there, creeping through the darkness, ill winds swirling in their wake.

"Dire, indeed," she assured Somerled, then drew a quivering breath, hoping her skills were up to a challenge.

"How close are they?" she queried, misliking the great number of them.

But before Somerled could respond, she hobbled over to the basket that held her dinner—a small portion of roasted gannet, the seabird meat tender and succulent. Two cooked eggs and a honey-smeared bannock, a flagon of heather ale.

Sustenance to give her strength for the trek back to her cottage. Simple but filling fare for one of her years—but a veritable feast for her little friend.

Victuals she surrendered gladly, arranging them on a cloth spread at the base of the Clach na Gruagach. And only when the fox had sated himself, did the she cock her head and listen with her heart to Somerled's tale.

His adventures.

And warnings.

Devorgilla sighed, looking out to sea again, then back at her little friend.

"Ach, you have the rights of it," she agreed. "We must keep a wary eye. If only I kent what. . . ."

But Somerled was no longer paying her heed, his attention now on the clump of deer grass she'd poked with her toe.

The high-growing grass was moving, swaying to and fro as if stirred by an unseen hand.

And that on a queer windless night, the chill air stiller than still.

Devorgilla's breath caught, especially when her little friend threw her a knowing, *watch-this,* kind of glance. Sitting back on his haunches, he lifted a paw again, this time in a well-recognized gesture of caution—even as a tiny field mouse scurried out from the grass and hurried past them, making for a tumble of boulders.

"A mouse?" Devorgilla blinked after the scampering beastie, watching him flit between two hulking stones, his little body disappearing into a crack no wider than a wink.

For long, she peered at the crevice and then she understood, and clapped her hands in glee.

"O-o-oh, but that will serve," she crowed, comprehension tingling through her.

"If a certain lassie is as observant as she is willful."

'Twas a sweet bit glen, opening just off Kenneth's own Glenelg.

A place that ought to hold the very essence of peace. Even on such a gray and drizzly night. But this night, the gray struck him as darker than usual, the shadows of the wood, a deeper black than comfortable.

Worse, he imagined distant eyes watching him. He was barely restraining himself from turning in his saddle and peering deeper than was wise into the birches that seemed to close round him, stifling rather than pleasing him as such Highland woods usually did.

Instead, he shivered and fixed his gaze on the path before him, frowning.

Sakes, even the rain annoyed him more than any true-blooded Highlander ought admit!

In no good humor, he considered reining round then and there. Digging in his heels and tearing down the narrow little glen the same way he'd come.

But a strange wind blew through the darkness, its hollow whistle carrying . . . hushed laments.

Nay, scoldings.

A truth he'd swear on the morrow, for the whispers dogged him no matter how fast he rode, disapproval ringing in his ears, persistent like the clanging of a bell clapper.

A fool and his folly.

Fate will soon be manifest—no matter whose skirts he lifted.

The admonishment hit him like an upended bucket of iced water, the taunt slicing through him, making his cheeks burn.

And unfairly.

He was not riding into ruin.

And if he'd ne'er partaken of the solace awaiting him at the end of this particular side glen, he'd surely slaked his ease with enough fair widows to justify visiting this one.

Whether the wind approved or nay.

The hot pulsing in his loins gave him scarce choice.

But when, a short while later, a flicker of lights pricked the chill dusk, letting him know he'd found the widow's cottage, the throbbing at his groin diminished, dwindling as quickly as a snuffed out candle flame.

And with the dwindling came a cackle on the wind.

A triumphant sounding cackle.

Reining in, he swiveled round, glaring into the shadows, but saw . . . nothing.

Nor did he feel anything *there,* where he'd had such an itch just moments ago.

Unsettled, and determined to air whoever's skirts he desired, he jerked back round and glowered at the widow's tidy turf-and-wattle cottage.

Glowered, because his need, so insistent since thundering away from Dun Telve, now proved as stubbornly aloof as the silent hills surrounding him.

He drew a hand over his brow, wishing himself back at Cuidrach. But before he could be away, the door of the cottage opened and a woman appeared. A well-made one—and wearing only a scanty undergown.

If that!

Kenneth swallowed and weighed the chances that she couldn't see him, sitting his horse as he was, half hidden by the trees at the edge of the clearing.

But her direct eye said otherwise—a hungry stare he felt all over him.

And whether he desired a tumble with her or no, honor forbade him from cantering away. So he dismounted and strode forward, his mind whirling for a chivalrous . . . excuse.

"Keeper of Cuidrach—I welcome you!" Gunna of the Glen called, her voice low pitched. Rich and smooth.

Just as he would have expected, considering the lushness of her curves.

Indeed, any other time, she would have fired his most heated dreams.

But not now, not on this ill-fated night.

"Lady, I greet you," he said, keenly aware of the absence of heat that should have been pulsing into his loins. "I am come to—"

"I ken why you are here," she supplied, fingering the long plait of her hair. "Your uncle sent word that I might expect you."

"I am sure he did," Kenneth acknowledged, the neck opening of his tunic growing tighter by the moment—especially when she began *really* toying with her braid.

A thick coil of glossiness, raven as his own, he glimpsed its sooty darkness repeated in the prominent, *V*-shaped triangle at the top of her thighs—a luxuriant thatch, clearly visible through the thin cloth of her low-cut shift.

As were her generous breasts, the large, well-defined nipples.

"Lady, you . . . take my breath," he said honestly, watching as she curled her fingers around her braid's thickness and moved her hand slowly up and down its black-gleaming length. "Even so, my reason for being here is not what you think. I—"

"Och, I ken what you seek," she purred, the glide of her fingers turning even more sensuous. "You will be well served, do not doubt it."

She stepped closer, her musky scent rising between them. "Come away in then, and—partake!"

Kenneth shifted, glancing at his horse, but before he could take a step backward, she circled strong fingers around his arm, pulled him inside.

And her cottage *did* welcome.

A wee bittie place, it glowed with warmth. Wafting

peat smoke thickened the air and blackened the walls, but a swift look-around showed a swept earthen floor and a rough-hewn table that looked less than sturdy but was notably well-scrubbed.

But she was turning to face him then, the candlelight showing her not quite so young as he'd first thought, but undeniably alluring.

"You require sustenance," she said, gesturing to a platter of oatcakes and cheese on the table. Even the cold, sliced breast of a fat capon. A well-filled jug of ale.

But the cottage's sole chair, a simple three-legged stool by the shape of it, proved hidden beneath the damp expanse of a homespun kirtle.

A gown she snatched up so soon as his gaze lit upon its freshly-laundered folds.

"Aye, you have caught me at my washing," she admitted, indicating a steaming washtub Kenneth hadn't yet noticed.

"This is my best kirtle," she said, hanging the gown on a wall peg. "My other one is yet in yon wash kettle—so dinna think I greet every man who darkens my door quite so . . . invitingly!"

Coming close again, she smoothed a hand over his groin. "But you, sir . . . ahhh, let us just say, I am pleased you caught me thusly—even if you do not seem quite so *eager* as those who usually come to call!"

Kenneth froze at her touch, trying not to grimace.

She lifted a brow . . . and squeezed.

"O-o-oh, but you are a fine-made man," she purred. "Mayhap if you see what a well-made woman I am, you will grow even finer!"

The words spoken, she rid herself of her undershift

and stood before him naked and glorious, her creamy skin luminescent in the candle glow, her bountiful curves and the dark triangle of her womanhood, dangerously apparent.

But before he could look too closely, a sudden blast of wind shook the cottage, sweeping in through the smoke hole in the ceiling. Eddies of peat ash swirled into the air—right into Kenneth's face!

"By the Rood!" he spluttered, spitting out ash and rubbing his eyes.

"Och, mercy me!" Gunna of the Glen grabbed her undergown, dabbed at his face.

A calculated move, to be sure, for with every circular rub of the cloth, her full breasts brushed his chest and the lush thicket of her female curls teased across his thigh.

"Here, hold tight lest you overbalance afore you can see again," she urged, seizing his hand and pressing his fingers to an unmistakable damp and silken heat. "A firm grip just *there* and—"

"Nay, I see fine already," Kenneth blurted, extricating himself.

Quick as winking, he nabbed the undershift and whirled it around her shoulders, covering her breasts if not the vee of curls so evident between her shapely thighs.

"Och, I see as well." She looked at him, her face coloring. "So you did not come here for the reason I'd expected?"

Kenneth winced at the hurt in her eyes. But it couldn't be helped. He couldn't salve her feelings at the cost of another's.

"Och, lass, 'tis true enough I came here desiring your . . . attentions," he admitted. "But, see you, somewhere along the way, it came to me that I'd best seek such comforts elsewhere."

Gunna of the Glen eyed him, comprehension replacing the hurt on her face.

A wistful softness that made her appear younger than her years, and surprisingly . . . vulnerable.

"You are a very beautiful woman," Kenneth spoke true and reached to smooth his knuckles down her cheek. "So desirable that, were I made otherwise, I would wish to lie with you for days and days, but—"

"Your heart belongs to another," she finished for him, catching his hand and kissing his fingers before he could lift them from her cheek.

"Dinna fash yourself," she said quickly. "I once knew that kind of love myself—with my late husband, the saints rest his soul. 'Tis missing him and what we shared, that keeps my door opened to those who might bring me a night's forgetful solace!"

Kenneth looked at her, her admission touching him deeply, making him ache for something he'd long ago stopped believing in.

Something he wanted to trust in again.

If only he could.

"Your needs are well met?" he asked, pushing thoughts of *her* from his mind—especially thoughts of the might and status of her father.

What such a man might think of him.

But the widow was smiling at him, *now* a welcome distraction. "I live in amity with everyone in these parts, ne'er you worry," she said, donning her undergown. "See you, bitter feuds and reprisals are always forgotten when men turn their minds to . . . other things!"

"I am glad to hear it," Kenneth said, moving ever so tactfully toward the door. "Nevertheless, I would leave some coin with you—for whate'er your heart fancies."

She blinked, looking almost hesitant, but not quite.

"You are kind." She watched as he fumbled in the money purse at his belt and slapped a handful of coins on a wall shelf. "I would not mind cloth for a new gown. My usual visitors are not overconcerned with such needs."

"Well, then, it is settled," Kenneth rushed on, already half out the door. "You have my siller, and, come spring, I will have my men bring you a fat milch cow—and a few goats as well."

Her eyes glimmered at that, and she touched a hand to her cheek.

"You are a fine man, Kenneth of Cuidrach," she said, giving him a tremulous smile. "Your lady is more than fortunate."

"She is not my lady," Kenneth amended, unable to lie.

"So-o-o." The widow raised arching brows. "Then you must see that she is. If she is a wise woman, she will not need much convincing."

But a short while later, as Kenneth spurred his steed ever faster toward Cuidrach, the only thing he knew was that it wasn't Cuidrach urging him to such speed, but *her.*

The flame-haired minx he had no intention of letting slip from his grasp.

If ever he could hope to have her.

A possibility that seemed more than unlikely, now that he knew her true identity.

Indeed, as he finally neared Cuidrach, the numerous gaps in the curtain walls and, in particular, the decrepit state of the gatehouse, only underscored the vast differences in their worlds.

Her status as daughter of a much-respected warrior laird, whether the man was wroth with her or no.

And his taint as bastard son of scoundrel so dark-hearted many in Kintail still refused to utter his name.

Kenneth frowned. Such was a stain even his new style as Keeper of Cuidrach couldn't erase.

Nor did he wish to see his half-ruinous holding judged against Archibald Macnicol's Dunach Castle, a strength he was sure would prove magnificent.

And impregnable.

As unconquerable as he suspected the old laird would be if e'er one such as he were to desire his daughter's hand.

The man's approval and consent.

A blessing Kenneth's honor sorely wanted.

Nay, *needed*.

And knowing it, he kneed his horse forward, his narrow-eyed stare not missing Cuidrach's bent and rusted portcullis. How the spike-tipped ironwork hung at such a crazy angle.

Vowing to have a new one made so soon as he could, he clattered through the gatehouse pend, determined to do what he hadn't done in years . . . pray.

And to any saint that might listen.

But before he could reach Cuidrach's bare-walled little chapel, a movement in the shadows near the castle well caught his eye and all thought of piousness fled. Indeed, the urges that had so plagued him earlier, then vanished, returned with a vengeance at the sight of *her*.

She came toward him across the moonlit bailey, her hair loose and tumbling around her shoulders. A rippling, gleaming skein of liquid bronze that spilled clear to her hips.

Glistening waves that took his breath and . . . enchanted him.

"You return late," she said, reaching him at last, handing him a wineskin. "I have been . . . waiting. Watching for you."

"In the cold dark, my lady? At this hour?" He accepted the proffered wine, drank gladly—and tried not to drink in her scent as well.

A perfume made all the more disturbing for the bright wash of moonlight gilding her curves, the glimpse of her flimsy night robe beneath the woolen cloak she hadn't bothered to fasten.

"It is because of the cold dark, and the hour, that I am here." She cut a glance toward the keep, pushed her hair back over her shoulders.

The movement caused the front of her mantle to gape a bit wider and Kenneth swallowed a groan. His entire body tightened and heat sluiced through him, pooling in his vitals. Never in his life had he been more . . . *aware* of a woman.

Saints, but that wee slip of a gown clung to her! *Made him burn.* He inhaled sharply, his heart thumping so fiercely he wondered she didn't hear its thudding beat, the hot rush of his blood.

Feel his need, the want consuming him.

But she only blinked and moistened her lips. "I feared something might've happened to you."

"Enough to leave the warmth of your bed?"

She flushed, looked down, clearly seeing her unbound hair, the transparency of her nightshift. Yet she made no move to cover herself. "It *is* obvious I was abed, isn't it?"

Kenneth nodded, met her gaze and held it. The saints knew he was too hard to risk looking lower!

"What isn't obvious is why you came out here." He stood rigid, not seeing her curves, but *sensing* them, feeling them rubbing all over him, wrapping around him.

Addling his wits to the point he wondered he could even string words together.

So he frowned.

A dark scowl that helped immensely.

"You could have easily caught me inside," he said, feeling better already. "On my way through the hall."

"I did not want your men to hear us." She cast another glance at the keep. "There is something else, see you. Something I must know. When you kiss—"

"*Kissed* you?" His brows shot upward. "You came out here to be kissed?"

"Nay," she denied—and so quickly he felt a sharp stab of disappointment. "Though I am woman enough to admit I . . . enjoyed your kiss!"

The disappointment vanished.

"Yet?" he prodded, tempted to flash her his most winning smile. But her eyes held shadows, he could see them now, and knew something troubled her.

"What is it, lass? I say you—you can ask me anything."

"Then . . ." She hesitated. "You said you wished to find a husband for me. I would know if you returned so late because you were busy initiating such . . . *arrangements*? I thought you might have been."

"You thought wrong." Kenneth rammed a hand through his hair and looked up at the starry night sky.

What a clumsy-tongued fool he'd been—setting himself up for her to ask the one thing he couldn't answer.

Didn't want to answer.

He strode to his horse instead, bought thinking time by patting the two bulging coin pouches still tied to his saddle. "I did as I said I would—I was gathering coin to purchase cattle from young Jamie's da."

He did not mention his visit to the widow.

Or how he'd been on the way to Cuidrach's chapel when she'd stopped him to seek an answer to just the question she'd posed.

An answer he'd hoped would allow him to make her his.

And as if the saints had heard him after all, that answer came to him now.

The name of a man he could claim as a possible husband for her.

"I would know the names of any men you may wish to speak to about me," she said, making him wonder if she were privy to his soul.

Indeed, she was peering at him through the moonlight, a frown crinkling her brow. "I am sure I will not be willing to consider a single one of them."

"O-o-oh, there is one we shouldn't discount." Kenneth scratched his chin, tried not to smile. "A man of strength, integrity and honor—though he can be a bit difficult to locate."

The little pucker in her forehead deepened. "Who is he?"

"A very great man. Indeed, the finest I know."

"And his name?"

"Duncan Strongbow," Kenneth told her, and hoped the saints would forgive him.

The saints, his uncle, and certain overly soft-hearted Sassunach.

Chapter Eight

✦

A roll in the heather with three bonnie, big-breasted lassies.

Naked lassies!

The words circled in Jamie's head, plaguing him as they'd done for some nights now, giving him no peace, and doing disastrous things to his man-parts.

An annoyance he meant to address this very e'en, before he suffered another sleepless night thinking about fulsome, unclothed womenfolk.

A dip in the ancient burnt mound would soothe him.

And if such a luxury didn't slake the twitching at his groin, a long soak in the heated waters of the stone-slabbed bathing tank would surely ease his other muscles, send him into a dreamless sleep.

One not filled with round, bouncing breasts and sweet succulent thighs.

Lush, well-curved bottoms—totally bare!

Closing his mind to such images, he eyed the stones he'd set to heating on a well-doing birch fire. Already they glowed and popped with increasing heat, the sight and sound of them making him feel connected to the ancient ones who'd created such a unique communal bathing facility.

Leastways, that was what he and others believed the stone-lined water tank must be, set into the earth as the pit was, near a well-running burn, and with charred, burnt stones at its bottom.

Immediately upon discovering the pit, Sir Lachlan and a few others declared it may have been used by hunters, for cooking large sides of meat, but Jamie and the younger knights decided it'd been a communal bathing tank—and with heated water, once white-hot stones had been plunged into its depths.

They'd conjured images of scantily-clad or naked wenches. Brazen, bold-eyed maids who took pleasure in bathing war-weary valiants.

In especial, the careful tending and washing of certain manly accoutrements!

Jamie groaned.

His manly accoutrement needed more than careful tending!

Scowling, for it'd been more than a season since he'd last fumbled beneath the skirts of a bonnie kitchen lass at Eilean Creag Castle, he snatched two lengths of wood and began rolling the white-hot stones from the fire to the water tank, tipping them into the pit until the water hissed and sizzled, steam rising up all around him.

But the steam only reminded him of the warmth of soft, pliant female bodies, so he threw off his plaid and made short work of other hindering *constrictions,* then leapt into the water.

"Ahhh . . ." he sighed as blessed heat swirled around his shoulders. "I've died and awakened in the land o' angels . . ."

At once, his brows snapped together.

He should not have thought of . . . angels.

And he should have known better than to bathe in heated water—in his present, agitated state.

"Och, aye, I must've thrown off my wits with my plaid!" he muttered, and took an indignant swat at the rising clouds of steam.

He tried to ignore how the water's warmth made his already embarrassingly long man-piece grow even longer!

Longer and . . . harder.

And twitching so ferociously there remained but one way out of his current pain.

Would that he'd sank into *cold* water.

But he hadn't, so he gritted his teeth, heaved himself to his feet, and, turning his face to the heavens, closed his eyes and took the aching *matter* to hand.

"Tchach, my lady, you err if you think there is aught wrong with me finding pleasure as I can." Nessa slid a glance at Mariota as they made their way to the burnt mound recently discovered during the clearing of under-brush from near Cuidrach's curtain walls.

"Aye," she added, brushing aside a low-hanging pine bough, "mayhap a good long soak in blissfully heated water will banish the cold from your bones and—"

"My bones are just fine," Mariota snapped, irritation swirling in her breast.

What troubled her was being so . . . confused.

Puzzled by the immensity of her attraction to the Keeper. Why his voice melted her, its deep smoothness pure seduction to her senses. Or why even the most fleeting glance at him made her feel all soft and warm inside, rousing feelings in her that didn't bear examination.

Not when he persisted in wanting to rid himself of her—see her whisked away to wed some paragon named Sir Duncan Strongbow!

Her pulse jerking at the notion, she blew out an aggravated breath. "Och, nay, Nessa, you err, not me. I am most assuredly not . . . cold."

Nessa sniffed. "Then a bit stiff-necked, mayhap? For truth, Lachlan says—"

"So now he is Lachlan?" Mariota stepped around a patch of nettles, swishing her skirts to avoid a clump of bracken. "Since when did you stop calling him *sir*?"

"O-o-oh, perhaps since he brought me out here the other night." Nessa sighed, beamed a knowing smile. "He bathed me by moonlight, my lady—made me feel more a woman than I've e'er done!"

Mariota stared straight ahead at the track through the black pinewood, setting her jaw against the softness in her friend's voice, a *tenderness* that sent sharp little pangs ripping through her.

Faith, but she missed feeling like a woman.

Knowing the joys of a man.

Total, absorbing intimacy and . . . love.

Not that a man had ever truly loved her—as she now knew.

Intimacy, she'd experienced. The kind that made a woman's heart pound and stole her breath, made her ache all over and fear she'd never ever be sated. And, saints help her, but that sweetness, too, she missed.

Especially since *his* arrival at Cuidrach.

She bit her lip, her heart swelling just thinking about him.

Already she knew the potency of his kisses. Slow, deep kisses she'd come to crave. Kisses, and other . . . intimacies. Deep, dark longings that stunned her. Desires he'd wakened in her that burned to be slaked—as the prickling rush of tingles across her most tender parts proved.

Ignoring those tingles as best she could, she hastened to catch up with Nessa, touching a hand to the other woman's sleeve. "Are you certain no one will be using the burnt mound?"

"Hah!" Nessa hooted. "Are you hoping *he* might be there? Bathing, perhaps?"

"I didn't mean him," Mariota denied. "I wouldn't want to surprise . . . anyone."

"We won't." Nessa grabbed her arm and pulled her through the thick-growing pines. "Lachlan says the men are working on the gaps in the curtain wall today, and on the other side of the castle. We'll have the burnt mound to ourselves. Lachlan—"

"Oh!" Mariota stumbled over a root, snatched her arm from Nessa's grasp. "Have done dragging me along! And if you say 'Lachlan says' one more time, you can sink yourself into the heated water without my company."

"Och, my goodness me!" Nessa froze, her face running scarlet. "We already have company, and he's—I believe he's . . ."

"Nay, he can't be!" Mariota stared through the trees at the naked man standing in the middle of the burnt mound.

Young James Macpherson it was, for, in that moment only a fool would call him Jamie *the Small*.

"Oh-dear-saints," Mariota gasped. "He truly is!"

Unable to look away, she gaped as he lightly stroked his incredible length, fingered and squeezed the swollen, plum-sized head.

Her heart thundering, she glanced at Nessa. "Mayhap he is about to . . . take care of *necessities*?"

"O-o-oh, aye, to be sure and he is, my lady, but not the kind you mean."

And another look at him proved it.

Standing in profile, his auburn-maned head thrown back like some ancient Gaelic war-god, his magnificent body glistening with water droplets, young Jamie was just sliding his fingers around the thickness of his engorged shaft.

Tight, tight, he curled those fingers . . . and stroked.

Furiously.

Until Nessa sneezed.

At once, Jamie's hand stilled and he whirled toward them, his fingers still wrapped around his jutting man-hood, his eyes wide with horror as he scanned the trees.

"That will be yourself and too many hours spent frolicking beneath the moon!" Mariota charged Nessa as they backed away. "And that on cold Highland nights."

"He did not see us," Nessa insisted as they slipped deeper into the trees. "Anyone could have sneezed. A garrison man. One of the glen folk, out gathering nuts for winter. Mayhap searching for containers of bog butter, forgotten in the peat hereabouts?"

Nut-gathering glen folk searching for bog butter!
Mariota bit her tongue, sorely doubting it.

Young Jamie had seen them, and there'd be consequences to pay.

Hours later and still convinced of it, embarrassment sent her on another march around the little anteroom off Cuidrach's great hall—the one room that seemed too tiny and dark to attract the attention of knights used to castles of much greater pomp and grandeur.

Nor those who would seek nuts or, worse, centuries-old wooden containers of rancid yellow butter left buried in peat bogs by a folk that was no more.

Here she felt safe.

No one would come looking for her, asking why she'd been peeking at a self-pleasuring young lad tending his own personal needs deep in Cuidrach's most remote pinewood.

Truth tell, she'd never seen anyone set foot in the little room—save Cuillin and he'd followed her here now.

Not that his somewhat smelly presence bothered her.

And judging by his snores, he slept much too soundly to fret about her cares.

Or where she'd been that e'en.

What she'd seen.

As well, what she'd . . . learned.

The revelation that the tingling heat that had swept her upon seeing the young knight *tend* himself, were tingles caused by *him*.

Not strapping young Jamie with his shock of bronze-colored hair and oh-so-impressive man-goods.

Nor even intimate memories of the late Bastard of

Drumodyn, the great stirk of a Highland lout whose once-cherished face grew more dim by the day.

Nay, she'd thought of *him.*

The Keeper of Cuidrach in all his deep, dark sensuality. His smoldering, soul-searing gaze and the languid yearning he roused in her. Unexpected feelings that burned with such bright-edged intensity, she'd almost swear she wouldn't be able to breathe much longer unless he soon touched her again.

Really touched her.

And everywhere.

Let her feel the hardness of his body, so hot and masculine, pressing against hers. Gave her deep-slaking kisses, one for every hour she'd hungered. Long, slow kisses, full of soft, warm breath and sensuously sliding tongues.

The kind of kisses that would set off a firestorm inside her and send rivers of molten, throbbing heat spinning to her core.

Kisses that would make him forget a man named Sir Duncan Strongbow.

And any others that might cross his mind!

Frowning, she bit back a frustrated little cry and fussed at her skirts, dug her hands into its folds to still her trembling fingers.

Truth tell, all of her trembled—not just her fingers!

Even her breath hitched, came shallow and unsteady.

Night after night, she'd seen every garrison man beneath Cuidrach's roof in some state of nakedness, many fully unclothed. They paraded about the hall, unashamed of their well-trained physiques, as they saw to their evening ablutions or dressed of a morn. Some, perhaps, even took a mite of pleasure in having two sets of feminine eyes assess and appreciate their . . . grandeur.

Aye, she'd glimpsed the lot of them.

All save one.

And of those she *had* seen, nary a man had been roused.

Until tonight.

Her palms damping, she closed her eyes, but the image of Jamie's jutting manhood remained. The sight stood branded on her memory in vivid detail, would likely invade her dreams. Unsettling and tormenting her—but not for reasons a lady ought admit!

Even now, in this dank little anteroom and with the cold night air streaming through the arrow slit, a floodtide of hot and shivery excitement spilled through her at the thought of *him*.

How the Keeper would have looked standing there full naked and aroused, raw hunger pouring off him, desire racing through her as his engorged length filled and stretched even more beneath her heated gaze.

He was the one she ached to see.

Faith, more than that, she could already feel him inside her!

So much so, her entire body tensed and her heart knocked wildly against her ribs. She bit her lip at the liquid heat pooling low by her thighs, stifling a gasp at the exquisite pulsing.

But the gasp escaped anyway, and with its release, she frowned, frustration damping the pleasurable sensations whirling inside her.

Truth was, she ought not be *whirling* at all.

Not for a man determined to see her gone.

And lest she wished to melt into a puddle of quivering female heat when he next turned his piercing gaze on her, she'd best learn to subdue more than gasps!

Imagining such deliciousness was as close to the sensually attractive Keeper of Cuidrach as she ought to allow herself.

True and intimate closeness would prove far too heady.

Exceedingly dangerous.

Hot and achy all the same, she resumed her pacing, shot a glance at Cuillin, not surprised to find the old dog watching her with his milky, all-seeing eyes.

As if he knew exactly how torn she was . . . how deeply she yearned, yet how much she feared.

"Ach, laddie." She went over to him and scratched behind his scruffy, tattered ears. "Did you e'er burn with such impossible need? Such unquenched desires?"

But he only looked at her, one scraggly brow raised.

Indeed, he soon lost interest in her, his rheumy gaze latching on to a tiny shadow flitting about near the wine casks stored in one corner of the anteroom.

A mouse.

And a most industrious one, for he darted hither and thither, even scrambling onto one of the wine barrels only to leap down again—almost as if he sought to attract attention.

"'Tis only a bittie mouse," Mariota assured Cuillin, thinking he couldn't see aught but the wee beastie's fast-moving shadow.

To her surprise, Cuillin proved her wrong.

His cloudy eyes narrowing with stealthy purpose, he stretched to his feet, only to hunker down and slink forward, his now-sharp gaze fixed on his tiny, gray-coated prey.

But the mouse had other ideas, shooting with great speed to the far wall where he spun around to stare with tiny, black-beaded eyes at the stiff-legged dog, almost taunting him to catch him.

A feat the aged beast attempted with vigor, even if his awkward gait didn't match the strength of his hunting-dog heart.

He still moved faster than Mariota could bear, for, away from the pile of wine casks, the mouse had nowhere to go.

Indeed, the little creature streaked along the base of the wall, his panic giving Cuillin fresh heart. His eyes lighting, the dog made a great lunge, slip-sliding to a halt mere inches from the mouse.

Or, from the looks of it, right on top of him.

Mariota rushed forward. "Cuillin! Dinna touch that mouse!"

But rather than devouring his hoped-for treat, the old dog nosed the base of the wall, snuffling the damp stones and whining, his prize nowhere in sight.

The mouse was gone.

"Mercy—you didn't eat him, did you?" She eyed the dog, but he only slid her a perplexed look and sank back on his bony haunches.

Flummoxed as well, Mariota spun round to stare at the wine casks. But there, too, nothing moved.

Instead, a thick silence descended, broken only by Cuillin's whines and the sound of his paw scrabbling at the stone wall.

Comprehension—and relief—flooded her.

Cuillin might be aged, but his mind wasn't dimmed. Ne'er would he scratch at a wall—without reason.

She wheeled back around, expecting to see the dog fussing at a mouse hole, but the only irregularity in the wall proved a barely-there crack.

And far too narrow for even a mouse to wriggle through.

Or was it?

Dropping to her knees, she peered at the vertical line seaming the stone masonry. An ordinary-looking crack, though Cuillin's pawings seemed to have loosened the mortar and a smallish black gap peeked at her from between the stones, perhaps just wide enough for a thin mouse.

Or a very determined one.

Intrigued, she ran a finger along the crack. Her probing loosened a few pebble-sized bits of walling that tumbled to the floor in a puff of stone dust. At once, Cuillin squeezed close, his large body pressing her against the wall.

A wall she would've sworn moved beneath her weight!

"Have a care, laddie!" She righted herself, slanting a narrowed glance at the dog.

But he ignored her and thrust his head forward to sniff the fallen masonry and nudge at the crevice.

Nay, not a crevice, but a gap—and one that grew ever wider, screeching and shuddering as only stone can.

Especially when Cuillin gave the wall a great shove and the heavy door swung inward, revealing a secret passage beyond.

A musty void filled with shadow and damp, its crudely

cut steps circling down into darkness, the only sign of life being a pair of tiny, black-glowing eyes that stared at them from the third step before the mouse gave a startled *squeak* and sped away into the gloom.

Mariota's heart skittered, her breath catching as she looked down the spiral of ancient stone steps.

Cuillin barked.

And from somewhere uncomfortably near, steadily approaching footfalls heralded someone's imminent arrival.

Familiar footsteps.

Smooth, and confident . . . knee-wateringly masculine.

"Mercy!" she swore as she scraped her hands and broke fingernails tugging the door-of-stone into place.

And not before time, a faint shifting in the air minded her.

The selfsame crackling disturbance that always alerted her to his approach—and proved the futileness of any attempts to resist him.

"Lady," came his deep voice behind her, just moments after the secret door fell into place with a quiet *clump*. "One of my younger knights tells me you might be suffering from the ague?"

"I want you, Nessa."

Deep in the blackness of the autumn night, the garrison captain's words hung in the cold air, vibrating off the snug walls of the tiny cap house, a remote hideaway at the far end of Cuidrach's least frequented wall-walk.

Sir Lachlan and Nessa's sweetest haven.

Swept clean, and freed of cobwebs, the guardroom now boasted a fine-burning brazier, a plump, heather-stuffed pallet wide enough for two, and a good supply of fine and warm woolen plaids.

A retreat the lovers sought so often as chance and duty allowed. Here, away from the ruckus of the hall, they indulged their need to touch, taste, and enjoy.

Their privacy assured because the Keeper of Cuidrach would ne'er disrupt his most loyal man's pleasure.

And the others wouldn't dare.

Erstwhile first squire to Duncan MacKenzie, the Black Stag of Kintail, and later household knight to the Black Stag's friend, Sir Marmaduke Strongbow, Lachlan Macrae commanded respect.

As he also attracted feminine . . . esteem.

Even if now, his heart belonged to only one.

Full naked and straddling his hips, his chosen heartmate stroked his bare back, easing her hands across his broad, well-muscled shoulders, then caressing down his arms to his hands, lacing her fingers with his. Squeezing tight.

She gave a throaty sigh, quite certain she'd soon not be able to contain the joy he gave her. Just breathing in his scent, all clean, musky male, filled her with hot, languorous ecstasy.

Heat sluicing through her, she released his hands to glide her palms over his back again, absorbing the feel and texture of his skin, drenching herself in his essence.

Desperate craving tingling at her core, she shivered, anticipation clenching inside her. "'Tis good that you want me," she breathed, aching for release. "I could not bear it if you did not!"

"Ach, Nessa-lass, I do more than want you. I burn for you. And have done from the first moment I saw you—as well you know!" he vowed, his voice husky with need. "And dinna think to stop what you are doing, for if you do, I swear the sun shall not rise on the morrow."

"The sun always rises, my lord . . . as do you!" She looked down, admiring how the brazier's glow sent bands of light and shadow across his gleaming, naked flesh. "But ne'er you worry—I shall not stop."

As if she could!

But she did pause long enough to lower her sleek, female heat directly onto the sensitive small of his back and rub his smooth, warm skin with slow, sinuous circles.

Just enough to let him feel the hot, fluid moistness of her arousal and know beyond all doubt that she desired and wanted him with equal fervor.

"You are a man like no other," she purred, keenly aware of the moisture damping her inner thighs. "I have ne'er—"

"Ahhh, but you spent moments this day gazing on a man who truly is . . . *other* than the most of us." Flipping over, he seized her hips, guiding her slick female heat right down against the thick, hot length of his hardness. "Did the sight not stir you, my lady?"

He stirred her, his own male-parts so beautiful at full-stretch, and well enough made to send sheets of fire racing through any female appreciative of the delicious burning a masterful lover could ignite in a woman.

"I await your answer," he said, shifting his hips just enough so that his tarse brushed even more intimately against her tingling heat. "The lad told us what happened—all of it."

Nessa wet her lips, the feel of him throbbing so hotly against her, stealing her breath. " 'Tis true we saw more than his . . . great size," she admitted, a new kind of heat searing her cheeks. "But, nay, he did not rouse me—save to make me thank the saints I must not take my pleasure likewise!"

"Jamie needn't trouble himself again, either—for a while, leastways," he told her, sliding a hand down between them to thread his fingers into her damp nether curls.

He toyed lightly with them as he spoke. "There is a lusty widow just o'er a few hills from here—Gunna of the Glen. Kenneth has ordered Jamie to pay her a visit!"

Nessa lifted a brow. "And yourself?"

"Myself?" Astonishment flooded Lachlan's face. "Do you not ken how well pleased I am . . . *here*?" he asked, slipping his hand deeper between her thighs, stroking and caressing.

"As I hope are you!" he added, with a knowing touch to a certain especially sensitive place. "A thousand beckoning joy wives could not lure me away."

"From me?"

"Aye, from you . . . the sweetest, most lush bit of womanhood I have e'er had the pleasure to claim," he vowed, his middle finger circling.

Nessa sighed, parted her legs another few inches.

Ripples of intense pleasure streamed out from where he rubbed with such focused concentration and her sighs became moans, her body tightening and trembling with bliss. But even through the haze of arousal one word haunted her, hovering on the edge of her pleasure until it burst to the front of her mind.

Joy wives.

The word took hold of her, and not because of her own

darkly handsome knight, but because of another, equally beautiful man—mayhap even a bit more so.

A knight she hoped would soon take his *joy* with her lady!

"Lachlan," she said, her voice sounding distant as she struggled to speak through the pleasure clouding her senses, "this joy wife, Gunna of the Glen, does Sir Kenneth pay her visits?"

She flushed furiously, but she had to know.

For her lady's sake.

In especial, because she suspected Hugh Alesone's betrayal with Elizabeth Paterson was still a lancing pain in Mariota's heart, the memory tainting her judgment, not letting her trust a *good* man.

Leastways, a man Nessa believed was good!

And apparently he was, for Lachlan snorted, his dark eyes lighting with amusement. "Kenneth take his ease with a joy woman?"

He looked up at her from between her legs, his chin hovering just a hot breath above her pulsing heat. "Sweet lass, Gunna of the Glen is widowed—not a joy woman," he explained, drawing a slow finger up and down the very seam of her as he spoke.

"She is lonely, aye, and welcomes a tumble. But Kenneth has no desire to sample her charms." He dropped a light kiss there, where his finger stroked her. "He wouldn't visit her if she were cut of such cloth. He'd sooner slice off his best piece before he'd lay a hand on a . . . fallen woman."

Nessa blinked, an unpleasant iciness slanting though her. *"A fallen woman?"*

Lachlan nodded, his dark gaze on the exposed vee of

her womanhood, his questing finger busy again. "Ach, pay him no heed, sweeting," he said, passion thrumming in his voice. "I'd fight beside him till I was felled, but he has queer notions about women—only beds widows."

"But not this Gunna of the Glen? She is widowed."

Lachlan looked up at her, blew a hot breath across her trembling flesh. "He wants *your* widow," he said, his dark gaze locking with hers.

"Lady Mariota?"

He nodded. "The very one. She has ruined him for all others—not that he will yet admit it," he observed, and licked her. "Sakes, just the other night I heard him tell her he means to find her a husband. If so, he's said naught of it to me."

Nessa's eyes widened at that, but she had other, more grave concerns.

Ones she wasn't privileged to share.

"But why does he bed only widows? Why does he keep himself from other women?"

"Not other women, but the specter of one. 'Tis a long tale," Lachlan told her true, and took another taste of her. "I'll share it with you after I've sated myself on you—and not a moment before."

"But—"

"No buts, my lady, only your pleasure."

And with that, he looked back down at the lush feast spread so lavishly before him and resumed his . . . attentions.

Chapter Nine

❖

"*T*he ague?"

Mariota spun around, pulled in a sharp breath, her heart slamming into her throat. She stared at *him*, guilt rendering her incapable of more than those two words.

"So I said, my lady." The Keeper of Cuidrach folded his arms across his chest and gave her a dark look, the intensity of him swirling into the anteroom, filling the tiny space, making her go soft all over.

"Aye, the . . . ague," he repeated, looking right at her, his gaze burning her. "You did not mishear me, nay."

"But I do not understand."

She looked back at him, genuine confusion warring with the way his deeply rich voice slid all over her, how the sensual heat of him wrapped round her, filling her until she almost couldn't breathe.

And he hadn't even stepped into the room.

He simply stood in the doorway, bold as night and darkly magnificent, his provocative presence claiming possession.

Unsettling and . . . exciting her.

"Och, come, lass, what is there not to understand?" He tilted his head, his eyes narrowing ever so slightly. "Dinna tell me you've ne'er heard of the ague?"

He stepped from the shadows then, a strange light in his eyes, an almost-smile playing at his lips. "It makes people . . . sneeze."

"Oh!" Mariota's eyes flew wide, comprehension flooding her.

"Aye, my lady, you were seen." He came closer, flashed her an amused-looking smile. "Seen, and heard."

Mariota's mouth went dry. Her heart squeezed with embarrassment.

"We did not go to the burnt mound with ill intent—I swear it," she choked, seeing no point in lying.

Or telling him it'd been Nessa who'd sneezed.

Though she did consider hiding stinging nettles in a certain guardroom pallet if that one e'er again sneezed so inopportunely.

Her heart thundering, she lifted her chin. "We only wished to bathe," she added, trying not to see how his eyes glittered, pay heed to the nervous flutter in her stomach. "We will both apologize to the lad if you think we ought?"

"O-o-oh, nay, that would not be wise." He shook his head, the amused-looking smile now turning disarming. "Some things are best left as they are. I dinna think young Jamie would appreciate being reminded of his . . . folly."

And her folly?

His words minded her of it—how often she'd imagined coming across *him* in such a state and what then might've happened.

"As you wish then," she said, well aware her face was flaming. "I have brothers as I've told you. I know young men suffer such . . . discomforts."

"Only young men?" He arched a brow, traced a finger along the curve of her jaw, the fullness of her lower lip. "As a widow, you ought ken that all men have such needs?"

She swallowed, his mention of her supposed widowhood making it impossible to speak, his nearness and the way he kept sliding his finger back and forth across her lips, making *her* needs dampen and pulse.

And with the urgent pulsing came sanity.

Enough to step away from him and draw a shaky breath. "Did you seek me just to tell me you knew I witnessed Jamie's *discomfort* or was there another reason?" she asked, her voice sounding more clipped than she would have liked. "Perhaps that you've sent a word to this Strongbow paladin?"

To her surprise, something flickered in his eyes—a look almost like pain.

Or regret.

"Aye, we must indeed speak of him, but never you mind. He can wait." His eyes darkened, his gaze slipping to her mouth, her breasts, the last traces of his amusement fading.

"You look feverish," he said, studying her. "Perhaps we should see to your discomforts before we speak of my . . . friend."

"*My* discomforts?" Mariota's eyes flew wide, all else forgotten as a lightning streak of sensual thrills shot through her.

But he only lifted his hands, showing her a leather-wrapped flagon and a small silver-edged drinking cup.

"Uisge-beatha," he told her, his smile returning. "Fine Highland spirits, and a sure cure for whate'er ills are troubling you. Ague, or . . . otherwise!"

"I know what *uisge-beatha* is," she said, guilt making her defensive. "And naught troubles me. Not this night."

That last, at least, wasn't a falsehood.

Truth was, she'd been troubled—nay, consumed— every night since he'd walked into her life.

"Indeed, I am feeling well," she emphasized, willing it so.

"Truth tell?" One raven-black brow shot upward, almost as if he'd peered inside her . . . knew her thoughts.

Or perhaps could tell she'd been snooping about the antechamber, peering down secret passages that, by rights, were his.

Shamed at the possibility, she edged away from the crack in the wall. The seam that now seemed to jump out at her. Or, equally damning, the faint haze of stone dust she was sure still hung in the air.

He'd be certain to speed her to Sir Duncan Strongbow if he knew she'd been putting her nose where it didn't belong, ferreting out the secrets of his keep.

So she held her silence and hoped he wouldn't notice.

Likewise, her scraped hands and broken fingernails, evidence of her discovery.

She took a deep breath and released it, not even sure why she didn't want him to know. But even just the notion of telling him made her tongue feel weighted down. Worse, she imagined gnarled but strong fingers pressing against her lips, sealing them.

Warning her.

A chill tore down her spine at that foolhardiness, and she shuddered, taking a few slow, deep breaths until the strange sensations lessened.

If even they would with him closing the space between them again, coming toward her with smooth, fluid grace, his movements almost like a predator's—with her the prey.

"Feeling well or no," he said, stopping less than a hand's breadth in front of her, "I'd urge you to drink a bit of the *uisge-beatha*. Indeed, I insist."

"I don't often drink water of life," she resisted, only too aware of the potent drink's power, its almost instantaneous ability to loosen inhibitions.

Her already weakened defenses.

"Nay, I do not think so," she declined again, shaking her head.

"Ah, but this night you shall make an exception—for me," he said, undaunted.

And giving her another of those dark smiles that made her stomach flutter. Looking as if he knew it, he plucked the stopper from the flagon and poured an all-too-generous portion into the little silver-gilt cup.

"Och, aye, a few sips will do you good—only one pleasure burns a sweeter heat than such fine Highland spirits!"

"And what might that be?" some devil made her ask.

To her surprise, he laughed. A rich, deeply pleasing laughter that curled round her heart, softening and warming her in ways that a whole tun of Highland spirits couldn't hope to achieve.

She looked at him, her heart splitting open, eager to welcome his warmth, but the moment had passed and his expression was serious again, his dark eyes guarded.

"If you must ask what pleasure I mean, lass, then your late husband was not overly . . . *good* to you."

"My late—" Mariota blinked, caught herself just in time.

Guilt pinching her, she eyed the gleaming swirl of innocent-looking liquid, her pulse leaping. Her heart skittered, anticipation of the drink's seductive warmth spooling through her, urging her to . . . enjoy.

Forget nonexistent husbands, family she missed, and suitors she didn't wish to hear about, and, for one sweet evening, pretend that all was right in her world.

But, faith, the fumes alone stung her eyes, searing the back of her throat and making her breath catch!

"Here, lass." Kenneth eased the cup into her hand. "Drink."

"I should not—"

"The *uisge-beatha* will help your . . . ague," he said, closing his fingers over hers, guiding the cup to her lips.

She blinked again, and scrunched her nose as the drink slid down her throat, its burning smoothness a welcoming bliss.

A sweet liquid fire that spread through her, slowly warming her cheeks and every other place in and outside her body. And, just as she'd known would happen, tilting the earth beneath her feet just enough to soften the edges of her resistance.

Blurring the reasons she knew he ought not touch her.

Minding her of why she so wanted to touch *him.*

Fearing that *want* might be written all over her, she wiped the backs of her fingers across her lips.

And forgot completely to hide her broken nails.

He noticed at once, tossing aside the cup of *uisge-beatha* he'd just poured himself to seize her hand, thrust it into the light of a wall torch.

A muscle jerked in his jaw as he examined her scraped palm, the torn and ragged nails. "Merciful saints, what have you done?" he demanded, his brow furrowing.

Darkening with anger for not having noticed before.

Anger that coursed through him now for letting his own misgivings and doubts send him to her side with a flagon of spirits clutched in his hand rather than the smooth words and confidence that might have served him so much better!

"Sakes, lass—you've shredded the palms of both your hands, ripped your nails . . ." He shook his head, wished he knew healing craft, had a salve to soothe her pain.

But there, too, Cuidrach was lacking—he hadn't yet taken time to sort the healing goods his uncle's wife had given him, knew scarce little about such things, having always ignored his own aches and pains.

"I-I was trying to open one of the wine casks," she was saying, her voice tremulous as she spoke the lie. "The scrapes are not so bad. I can see to them later—I have balm and a basket of sphagnum moss abovestairs."

Kenneth said nothing.

He knew she was lying.

The pile of wine casks looked as undisturbed as the day he and his men had carted them into the anteroom. And did he have any doubts, a fine layer of dust, wholly unmarred by female finger marks, bespoke his assessment of her falsehood.

But however she'd injured her hands, the truth could wait.

This night he needed all his skill to address a matter of much more urgency.

And not his incredible need to touch and taste her, to sweep her into his arms and carry her to his bed and just sink his hard, aching self deep inside her. Lose his cares in the sweet, womanly wonder of her.

Make her his own.

But such folly would not be wise . . . yet.

Though a wee bit of . . . *sampling* would no doubt be satisfying for them both!

If the saints had any mercy, she'd agree.

Willing it so, he held fast to her hand—but gently—his entire body so taut with need, he could scarce think much less remember the words he'd been rehearsing for days, ever since riding away from Gunna of the Glen's cottage.

The night destiny clamped its iron-hard grip on him, ruining him for all but one woman, leaving him no choice but to make her his own.

Even if he had to break his honor to do so.

Put his faith in a *pretend* marital candidate to hold her here until he could convince her—and her father—that *he* was the only man for her.

A worthy husband.

So samplings would have to do . . . for now.

He'd savor them to the fullest, tucking each golden moment deep into his heart, to warm and comfort him if he failed.

Shoving that thought from his mind, he brought her hand to his lips and pressed a kiss to her abraded palm. "Lady," he began, his voice huskier, more raw-sounding than he would have wished. "I shall assure a fresh ewer of wine is brought to your bedside every night so soon as darkness falls. Even more if you so desire. But ne'er again do such damage to your hands."

He kissed the soft skin of her inner wrist, looked deep into her eyes. "That, you must promise me."

She met his gaze, flushed a little. "I vow, sir, that I have needs greater than wine can quench," she said, the words so soft they could have been the rustling of the wind.

"But the wine would be welcome, aye," she added, her eyes luminous, shimmering green pools in the torchlight. "I thank you," she said, the three words balm to his soul, her low-pitched, smoky voice sending waves of heat pulsing through his loins.

"For the wine," she added, "and for thinking of my comfort."

Kenneth near choked.

Her comfort.

She'd think otherwise if she knew how many sleepless hours he'd spent trying to think of ways to please a certain northern chieftain she purportedly no longer wanted to see.

Ways to make the man smile on his daughter again— if indeed a void loomed between them.

And, too, ways to breach the pain of losing her if she discovered his plan before time and fled Cuidrach—or, worse, if she stayed and eventually shunned him.

Not as a pass-the-nights-hotly lover, but as a forever mate.

A husband.

"You needn't thank me," he said at last, his voice gruff, the words nowise soft and dreamy as hers had been.

His words fell between them like pebbles dropped into a still pool.

He pulled in a deep breath, exhaled slowly, and still ill ease snatched at him, his gut clenching with the unpleasantness of his task.

"See you," he began, picking his words carefully, "you declined my offer to see you safely returned to your father, and now I—"

"Och, I see," she said, the softness out of her voice. "You still want to be rid of me. Wish to see me sent elsewhere?"

"Nay . . . I mean, aye," Kenneth blurted, making a grand muddle of it, the back of his neck burning so fiercely he wondered he didn't burst into flame. "What I want is to know you safe. And, aye, for life!"

As my wife—if you'd have me, his heart roared at her.

"Cuidrach is not yet a safe place," he tried again, amazed he could speak so casually. "Its curtain walls are riddled with gaps, the gatehouse almost beyond repair. But there are—"

"But there are what? Safer places?" Her eyes flew wide. "Dinna think to send me to a nunnery," she said, backing away from him. "I would sooner walk naked to Glasgow and take up Nessa's trade as herring wife!"

"Sweet lass, you mistake," Kenneth said, that, at least, being the truth of it.

Plunging himself into the only way he saw to possibly hold on to her was what he was about to do, not doom her to a life of bread-and-water penances and piety.

"Sweet, you call me?" She stared at him as if he were about to steal the breath from her. "If you find me so . . .

delectable, you'd ken I'd wither and perish in such confinement."

Kenneth bit back a curse, rammed a hand through his hair.

To be sure, he found her delectable.

So tempting, in fact, his whole body thrummed with wanting her!

She raised her hands as if to ward him away. "For truth, I cannot think of a worse fate. A woman was meant for . . . other things. I—"

"You are surely no lass to be buried under a veil, locked behind cloister walls." Kenneth took her by the shoulders, looked into her eyes. "And such a thought ne'er entered my mind, was not what I was about to say."

She shook free of his grasp, puffed a wisp of hair off her face. "Then what *did* you mean to say?"

He winced—but deep inside, where she couldn't see, wouldn't know he was about to lie . . . or at least bend the truth to suit his purposes.

But *he* knew and the knowledge pained him.

Even with well-meaning intentions.

He inhaled deeply, rushing the words, "I meant to say that although Cuidrach is not yet restored to its fullest strength—some might even call it half-ruined—there are greater dangers outside these walls and," he paused, drew another breath, "with winter coming, I'd urge you to simply stay here and enjoy the protection I can offer you until spring."

She jammed her hands on her hips, tilting her head. "And in the spring?"

"By then I will have made arrangements for a worthy

husband for you," he said. *And hopefully found a way to assure you and your father that I am he,* his heart added.

"And if I do not wish to wed?"

If I have even an ounce of MacKenzie blood in me, you will wish it long before the first thaw touches the hills, his determination answered.

"All women wish to wed. 'Tis the way of things," he *said.* "You ought know—as a widow. I did not think the thought of another husband would distress you so greatly."

"Then you erred," she countered, something flaring in her eyes.

A flash of torment or anger, quickly replaced by a shimmering brightness he hoped wasn't tears.

"Not all women who wish are fortunate enough to see their hopes and dreams fulfilled," she said, swiping a hand across her cheek. "Did you not know that? Or that some women believe they've won their dreams—only to be betrayed? Or left branded as a fallen woman, when all they'd desired was a man's undying love? His heart . . . and given solely to her?"

Kenneth stiffened, something dark and cold shifting in the deepest, most private corner of his heart, something that pinched and prodded, relentless in its efforts to mind him of its existence . . . the dangers.

The past.

He cleared his throat, wished the passion pouring off her could flow into him, banish the chill and hurt inside him.

His doubts and fears of ne'er being good enough.

Not measuring up to the name he carried, the new title he bore with such pride.

But she only peered at him, her eyes large and stormy.

He frowned. "Ach, lass, I know the pain of loving unwisely," he admitted, his mood darkening. "Dinna think I know naught of such things. I do, and my hope for you is that, in time, you will be pleased with the . . . arrangements I can make for you, maybe even find love again."

"Love?" She looked at him, the cynicism on her face surprising him.

Turning away, she went to the pile of wine casks and poured herself a generous helping of his *uisge-beatha,* downing the spirits more swiftly than he could blink.

She coughed, her back to him, and a great tremor shook her, the fire of the potent Highland drink rippling the length of her.

But when she faced him again, she was every inch the warrior laird's daughter.

In truth, the beautiful and proud daughter of *hundreds* of warrior lairds, the bold legacy of each one inscribed on every golden inch of her.

So much so, he could almost see the steel gleaming in her backbone.

He *knew* he could taste her, feel the subtle welling of her iron will, the unbending pride of generations of pure, unadulterated Highland blood.

Finest Highland blood, borne of chieftains who wore their tartans and feathers with arrogance and pride, men extravagantly brave who feared nothing, but whose hearts could weep at the beauty of a Highland sunset.

The poignancy of deep blue shadows edging across a Highland loch on a winter afternoon.

Such great men had molded her and he should have admitted himself lost the first moment he glimpsed her silhouetted so boldly in the tower window.

The saints knew he'd felt it.

As he felt something now.

An unmistakable stirring, a crackling tension that pulsed with such intensity he could feel its currents swirling around them, stealing the chill from the air and even drawing the shadows from the corners, filling each one with shivery, trembling light.

And hope.

Clarity.

His heart began to pound.

She shook out her skirts and dusted her hands.

"The man I loved is dead," she said, the words crisp, and filled with finality. "He was my life, see you? The air I needed to breathe, the sun's warmth of my every day. And, aye, the sated bliss of all my nights. Hugh Alesone was his name, his style, the Bastard of Drumodyn."

She paused, a glimmer of vulnerability in her eyes, its gleam giving lie to her calm. Her straight back and lifted chin. "I have no wish to risk loving and losing another."

"And accepting the comforts of another?" Kenneth stepped closer, drawn by her seductive warmth, almost propelled toward her by the strange quivering in the air.

His desire to banish the tinge of sorrow hovering just beneath her words.

She met his eye, drew a trembling breath. "Are *you* offering these comforts, Kenneth of Cuidrach?"

"I am."

"And might these . . . *comforts* be something other than ewers of wine and a richly-dressed bedchamber? Fine viands and a well-doing fire every e'en?"

Kenneth blew out a slow breath. "They are different, aye," he admitted.

The words, the first step toward his goal.

She stepped closer, touched a hand to his chest, curled her fingers into his plaid. "And for how long are you offering such . . . succor?"

Kenneth swallowed, drawing strength from the hope beginning to blaze in his heart. "Only for the nonce, my lady," he made himself say. "So long as you remain beneath my roof."

His gut clenched on the words.

But the flame in his heart brightened and warmed him. So long as he had her near he'd be winning.

Almost as if she agreed, she gave him a tremulous smile . . . and lifted her hands to the Nordic silver brooch at her shoulder.

"Then so be it." She undid the clasp, let her cloak slip to the floor. "Give me this *comfort* you offer, for I have been empty and hollow for too long."

"Lass, you will not regret this," Kenneth heard himself say, his own words this time, and wrenched from the deep of his soul. "That, I swear to you."

He reached for her, pulling her to him until her body melted against his and all flickers of resistance vanished as if they'd never been.

She threw her arms around him, sliding her hands around his neck and threading her fingers in his hair, urging him closer, their lips crashing together. Melding in a rough, devouring kiss that ripped away the walls of the little anteroom and left them alone in their own world of pure, streaming bliss.

Exhilaration and triumph pounding through him, he seized her face in his hands, angling his head to deepen the kiss, slanting his mouth over hers and thrusting his tongue deep into the warmth of her mouth. He drowned himself in the taste and feel of her, claiming her, even as her lush, female softness rocked against him with equal fervor, each urgent press of her hips, consuming him.

From somewhere beyond the roaring inside him, he heard her moan low in her throat as she opened her lips wider, welcomed the sensuous in-and-out glides of his tongue. A lascivious plundering, an erotic mating she matched slide for sinuous slide as he made good his promise, giving her the solace she needed, and slaking his own in a tantalizing whirl of tangled tongues, hot breath, and aching, sated sighs.

A bliss he'd been wanting too long to let unfold on the cold stone floor of a dank-smelling anteroom, and with a sly-eyed ancient mongrel as witness.

That one's presence alone, and the dog's rapt, unblinking stare, gave him the strength to break the kiss.

His heart thundering, he rested his forehead against hers, his breath ragged. "Lady," he said, his deep voice intense, urgent, "would you enjoy further such comforts, I vow your bedchamber would better suit our needs."

In answer, she delighted him by taking his hand in hers, lacing their fingers. "Sir, I have heard you have ne'er yet spent even one night in your magnificent bed," she said, pulling him with her to the door. "Mayhap it is time?"

And it was, Kenneth knew, the inevitability of it, the *portent,* watering his knees.

But just before he made to step over the unmoving old hound sprawled across the threshold, he shot a last glance at the little antechamber, wondered how such a humble room could have borne such glory.

Determined to hold on to his happiness, he felt himself smiling as he led his lady toward the stairs leading up to her bedchamber.

Life at Cuidrach was good indeed.

And by the spring it would only be better.

But life was not so blessed in all of Scotland.

Indeed, there were places where the hills wept.

In one such place, many leagues away from Cuidrach and at an hour when most old and ailing Highland chieftains would be tucked comfortably in their beds, a plump and young bed-warmer pressed to their sides, Archibald Macnicol stood on the parapet-walk of Dunach Castle, glaring out across miles of jagged coastline and islets, his hands clenched in angry fists, the fierce throbbing at his temples fouling an already black mood.

Still a formidable name in Scotland's far north, if no longer quite so puissant a man, the Macnicol laird's failing health had yet to rob him of his impressive stature, even if he now stood with a bit of a stoop and needed longer to cross his castle's vast great hall than a hump-backed and withered *cailleach* twice his years.

A great stirk of a man in his prime, his plaid-hung shoulders still carried an enviable width and, although his shaggy, once-red mane of hair was now generously tinged with gray, he took some small satisfaction in its continued thickness, just as he appreciated the fullness of his well-curled beard.

What he did not appreciate was the badgering of his middle son, Donald.

One of the few he had left.

Regrettably, Donald was also the most annoying.

"Och, guidsakes—what *is* this?" Archibald grumbled, not meeting his son's eye, his gaze fixed instead on the stretch of moon-washed sand far below his castle walls.

"Have you forgotten I am an old done man?" he snapped, not taking his stare off the long North Sea combers breaking on the shore.

A shore that, just now, shimmered a fine molten silver, but that, come the morn, would glow like burnished gold set alight by the rising sun.

Nigh the selfsame color as *her* flaming hair.

And the sole reason he only made the difficult trek up to his wall-walk at such ungodly hours as this.

As if Donald didn't know!

"Since time was, we have looked after our own," the persistent whelp kept at him. "Defended our honor. We could still—"

"Aye, and so we could!" Archibald roared, wheeling round to scowl at his son.

A scowl that immediately deepened because, of all his seed, *this one* so resembled Archibald himself.

In years so long past, it hurt his aging, aching head to think of them.

He jabbed a finger in Donald's chest, poking hard. "Hah, laddie, to be sure, and we could chase down the black-hearted cravens who'd dare come chapping at our door, accusing a Macnicol of murder," he groused. "Or rather, *you* and your brothers could, with a party of men. Without me. You ken I am failing mightily these days," he added, and clutched a hand to his broad, barrel-chest and wheezed.

But only long enough to catch a flicker of concern on his son's handsome face.

When it didn't come, Archibald spat over the parapet's crenellated wall and jammed his fists against his hips.

"Saints of mercy!" he bellowed. "*Since time was,* you say. Bah, I say!" Seething, he didn't trouble to lower his voice. Indeed, he hoped the wind carried his fury the whole heathery length and breadth of Scotland.

Hoped the very hills shook with his wrath.

"Aye, we could do all that," he said again, his voice somewhat less than a shout now. "But you forget one thing. *That lassie* is no longer a Macnicol! She washed her hands of our fine blood the day she turned her back on me in favor of a self-serving poltroon every man, woman, and bairn beneath this roof warned her against!"

"But—"

"Dinna you but me, laddie. You were there—saw it all." Hot gall rising in his throat, Archibald coughed, thumped a balled fist against his chest until the spasm subsided. "Her shame now rides on the backs of everyone in this clan, and if she *did* plunge a dagger into that up-jumped bastard's heart, good riddance, I say. Him, and all his empty-winded claims to lofty ancestry! As for her— she's only reaped what she sowed."

But rather than share his anger, Donald's face clouded with sympathy.

"She is your only daughter," he said, fumbling beneath his plaid as if he had an itch. "And she remains my sister. I still love her even if you do not. Nor would I see her honor tarnished, or know her trussed and tossed to the Each Uisge of Assynt if those dastards catch her."

"Hah! The water horse would spit her out if he kent—" Archibald broke off, stared at the great war ax Donald was pulling out from beneath his plaid.

Archibald's war ax.

A wicked piece of weaponry that *should* be hanging on the wall of the great hall, over Archibald's laird's chair, where it'd remained, untouched, since the last time he'd wielded it in battle—over a decade ago.

And only Donald would dare lay a finger to it.

"God's blood—I dinna believe what I am seeing!" Archibald's eyes bugged. Sakes, he could feel his face turning purple. "No one touches that war ax but me, as well you know!"

"On my soul, I did not fetch the thing up here to vex you," Donald gave back, clutching the ax without even a hint of relinquishing it. "Truth tell, I thought you might wish to test its grip again? Perhaps even its swing."

"And why would I be a-wishing to do that?" Archibald glowered at him. "Me, with all my frailness? My coughs and wheezing."

But his son only arched a brow, ran his hand down the long shaft of the ax, his fingers trailing over the countless indentations cut into the age-worn wood.

"One notch for each of your battle victories," Donald

minded him, holding out the ax. "Will you not reconsider adding a new one? A notch for rescuing your daughter?"

But Archibald clamped his jaw and turned away, his fixed stare on the horizon again, his hands fisted tighter than ever.

He would not add to his misery by letting his son see him cry.

Chapter Ten

❦

The years had not been kind to Cuidrach, perched on its cliff above Scotland's western coast. And not few were those who whispered that sheer will alone kept the half-ruinous keep from disappearing stone by stone onto the rocks below.

Sheer will, and mayhap an indomitable spirit.

One that dwelt within the living rock of the castle walls and waited, aching to be whole again, to exchange the loneliness of its shores for laughter and warmth. Nights filled with revel, storytelling, and cheer.

Perhaps, too, the soft moans and cries of lovers, intimately entwined.

But sorrow leaves a memory like no other, and decades spent silent and deserted always take their toll.

A burden only lifted by the bright-burning joy of exultation, a truth that now swept Mariota with such blinding brilliance she feared her heart would burst.

Her own tragedies forgotten, she clung to Kenneth's hand as they hastened up the turnpike stair, taking the curving stone steps two at a time. And even that wasn't fast enough, for ne'er had she burned so deliciously, craving until the whole of her body quivered, her *want* so deep and desperate.

A madness consuming her.

Even the night around her pulsed with sensual promise, as if Cuidrach echoed her need, her happiness.

Joyed with her, and shared her anticipation.

An impression that intensified the closer they came to her bedchamber, for the door stood ajar and the soft glow of the hearth fire spilled from within, welcoming them.

As did the deer- and sheepskin rugs spread before the fire, gentle, fragrant flames filling the room with the smoky-sweet scent of peat and strewn aromatic herbs.

The addition of the latter made Mariota's nape prickle and her stomach flutter with suspicion. Ne'er before had anyone bothered to toss dried herbs onto the fire.

Every wall sconce blazed as well, thick wax candles flickering on iron prickets throughout the chamber, the soft golden light illuminating the drawn bed curtains and a simple repast of cold meats and ale laid out on a table near one of the window embrasures.

An ewer of ale accompanied by not one, but *two* drinking cups!

Preparations to seduction.

And she knew exactly whose hand had readied such a cozy nest.

A well-meaning meddler who'd also unlatched the shutters to allow the night breeze to flow in through the high arched windows. Fresh, brisk air holding only the faintest trace of rain, but perfect for cooling hot, sweat-drenched bodies.

Refreshing and restorative—so deepest need could be slaked anew.

Her need escaped her in a soft sigh, ripples of desire sliding through her as Kenneth shut and bolted the door. And when he turned around to face her, his own need simmered in his midnight eyes.

"Oh, lass, tell me I am not dreaming," he said, dragging her against him, his hands sweeping down her back to splay across her buttocks, his fingers cupping and kneading her plump, rounded flesh. "Saints, but I have longed for you. So long, so many nights . . ."

"And I for you," Mariota owned, dizzy with need, an unquenchable burning. "I did not think we—"

"Sweet lass, do not speak of what we *cannot* do—but what we shall," he pledged, tightening his arms around her, then drawing back to look into her eyes.

A look that stopped her heart with its intensity.

She shivered again, feeling drawn inside him, as if she were falling into his soul. An endless tumble, a spiraling glide into inevitability, thrumming and powerful.

Impossible to deny.

"Sweet precious lass," he said again, the wonder in his voice hinting that he felt it, too.

The pull toward each other . . . the deep belonging and rightness.

His eyes darkened then, his gaze heating, turning so intimate that long, liquid pulls of astonishing pleasure swirled through the lowest part of her belly. Staggering whirls of sensation that left her breathless and made her heart pound harder with each pulsing moment.

"Do you know you make my breasts swell?" she whispered, the admission shocking her so soon as it slipped from her lips, but her breasts *were* swelling, and so acutely they hurt.

An aching, piercing need winding so tight inside her she'd swear she was about to splinter.

"Do I now?" he purred, a teasing light in his eye. "And do you know you make *me* swell?" He leaned close, dragging his mouth over hers in a quick, searing kiss. "So you see—we are well suited!"

Mariota flushed, reveling in the pleasure of him.

The way he was looking at her.

His gaze smoldering, he inhaled deeply, exhaling only after a long moment. "Mayhap you would also like to know that your scent makes me burn to devour you," he purred, his dark eyes narrowing with lust.

A need that echoed her own exquisite aching.

He kissed her again, an open-mouthed kiss with just enough sweep of tongue to melt her. "Be warned, sweetness—you do not know what you do to me."

"I know I want you. Do not think my urges are any less powerful." She flushed at the words, but she couldn't have held them back had someone thrust a blade against her throat—too overwhelming was her need for him.

Her ache.

And seeing it, his eyes blazed even hotter.

He gave a husky growl, peered so deeply into her eyes that he brushed her soul, almost penetrating her darkest secrets.

Secrets well-cloaked by the urgency of their need—a burning, living desperation twisting between and all around them. A mutual blaze manifested in the pleasure crashing through her, the hot wetness pulsing across her womanhood, and the thick bulge at his groin. A breathstealingly intimate pressure against the softness of her belly, the throbbing heat of him scorching her through their clothes.

Tingly heat that shimmered across her most tender flesh as warm, slick moisture damped her thighs, the musky scent of her arousal drifting up between them like a sex-drenched fog.

Leaning closer, he traced the tip of his tongue up the side of her neck, nipped at her earlobe. "There can be no going back, Mariota-lass. Lest you naysay me now," he warned, some still coherent glimmer of honor forcing the words.

He slanted his mouth over hers, kissed her yet again. Hard and swift this time, almost desperate. "One chance, lady. Speak now, or we slake our needs. Thoroughly, and without regrets."

"Regrets?" She reached between them, caressed down his length, pressing her palm against him, squeezing, before she withdrew her hand. "For truth, I have none and shall not—unless you can look me in the eye and tell me you would still wish me wed . . . after this?"

Kenneth stood rigid, unable to breathe. Her touch, though brief, had near caused him to explode.

Her words shook him. "I *would* see you wed," he compromised, "but only to a man you love and desire. Can you accept that?"

"Oh, aye." She nodded, and her smile warmed him so much he almost feared he'd waken any moment.

Find himself sprawled across his pallet in the hall, surrounded by sleeping men and the nightly chorus of snores and other unmentionable deep-slumbering-male noises that accompanied him into his dreams each night.

But *she* looked a dream to him, her kiss-swollen lips, begging eyes, and quickened breath undoing him.

In especial, her begging eyes.

Hot, needy eyes, full of hunger and longing.

He swallowed, his throat tightening with emotion. Ne'er had a woman gazed at him with such wide-open yearning.

She glowed with her pleasure in him, in *them,* and seeing her desire ripped away more barriers he'd ne'er thought to lose.

He closed his eyes, braced himself for his capitulation. "'Tis too late now, sweetness," he said, his heart racing, his senses saturated with wanting her. "I couldna cease if—"

"Cease?" She clutched at him, her startled tone flooding him with such triumph he imagined the room spun.

"O-o-oh, nay, I told you—no stopping," she protested, the full softness of her breasts crushing against him, the rubbing of her firm, shapely thighs on his, near causing him to spill. "I need, want, and hunger for this closeness with you . . . every intimacy a man and woman can share."

Kenneth stilled on the words, not quite sure he'd heard them, so loudly did his ears buzz with the hot rush of his blood, the whirring of his senses.

Every intimacy a man and woman can share.

He groaned, the very thought making him even harder.

"O-o-oh, we will share intimacies," he promised her, caressing her cheek. "Soon you shall be sprawled naked across yon bed, your breasts straining for my attention and your legs spread wide, fully opened for me, lass, and hiding nothing but the damp slickness of your arousal."

He touched his fingers to her lips when she tried to speak, hushed her. "Nay, do not say anything . . . yet, my lady. Just listen and hear how much I desire you. Truth tell, I can even taste you."

"Taste me?"

"Aye, taste you—and for the longest time," he vowed, holding her gaze. "And after I've sated myself on you, I will slide deep inside you, glide smoothly in and out of your silken heat, reveling in the tight, sleek wetness of you until I can take no more and throw back my head to call out your name."

Raptures they would both soon enjoy—a bliss he knew would change his life forever.

"See you, Mariota, I want you as I have ne'er wanted another," he told her, lighting soft, slow kisses across her brow, down the smooth curve of her cheek, her neck, and lower.

"And those are the *intimacies* I would give you," he vowed, claiming her mouth in a voracious kiss that probed and plundered.

An intimate melding made even more tantalizing by the sweep of her tongue against his. Again and again, until, gasping, they broke apart, the wild pounding of their hearts a loud drumming in the silent room.

"I want those intimacies," she said, her voice soft, yet powerful enough to bring him to his knees. "And I would return them . . . gladly."

That did it.

Forgetting every caution he'd practiced since a certain long ago day, Kenneth reached for the lacings of her gown, undoing them with surprising ease.

His entire body clenched when the bodice fell away

without resistance, leaving her lovely, full-rounded breasts to spill free.

The surprising absence of an undergown fully exposed her, and the chill night air did its part to bedevil him by making her nipples pucker right before his eyes.

Kenneth groaned, lust squeezing him beyond endurance. "You are glorious, my lady. So beautiful in your nakedness. Come, move into the candlelight so I can see you better, look on your sweetness."

"O-o-oh, aye," she sighed, the sultry, low pitch of her voice so soft he scarce heard her.

But she did as he asked and stepped up to a brace of candles, turning so the light spilled across her naked breasts. "This is good . . . so good," she breathed, her nipples tightening even more.

And this time he was sure he heard her.

The surge of heat pouring into his groin confirmed it—as did the way she arched her body for him, the movement lifting her breasts, offering their ripeness, the roused flush spreading across their swells, stealing his breath.

He stared at her ruched nipples. The beautifully swollen teats and the tiny tightened folds of her aureoles fascinated him. "Nay, lass, 'tis more than good," he breathed, licking his fingers, then lighting them on her nipples, caressing and *feeling* them.

"Such intensity as this is rare, and we shall spend each other much satisfaction and . . . comfort," he heard himself saying, some still-wary part of himself grateful he hadn't blurted how much he loved her.

Needed her.

And for more than the intoxication of playing with her nipples or sinking into her sleek female heat!

"Total contentment," she agreed, giving a quick, downward tug to her gown, a swift jerk that sent the garment sliding down her legs to pool in a rumpled mass at her feet.

Ravishingly naked, she gave a proud toss of her head, flicked her braid over her shoulder. "Bliss, aye," she said then, a spark of fire in her eye. "For so long as you allow me to stay beneath your roof."

Kenneth frowned. "For so long as the fates give us," he amended, wincing at the notion he might have just called undue attention to their . . . arrangement.

A possibility given credence when a sudden gusting wind rattled the shutters, causing one to crack loudly against the tower wall. The resounding *bang* jarred the night's quiet, but proved nowise near so unsettling as the cackle he would have sworn he heard just before the gale-like blast died away.

Suspicion nipping, he crossed the room and refastened the loose shutter, fully expecting her to comment on the gleeful hoot when he turned back around, but she only locked gazes with him and stepped out of her tangled gown.

Torturing him even more, she lifted and plumped her breasts, then walked quite unashamedly to the cloth-lined tub of bathing water someone had placed near a well-doing little brazier in the corner.

Thin wisps of herb-scented steam rose off the water to curl up toward the ceiling rafters, the bath's purpose and his lady's intent sending a jolt of objection streaking to his core.

"Och, nay, lassie." He seized her arm, pulled her back just as she lifted her leg to step into the tub. "That willna do—not this night."

"No bath?" She lowered her foot to the padded toweling spread around the bathing tub, the movement making her breasts sway. "But I thought—"

"You thought wrong." His blood on fire, he tightened his grip on her, needing the balance, so heady had been the flash he'd caught of deep red curls and tender female flesh. "To be sure, you can bathe if you wish. We shall both bathe. But later, not now, this moment."

"You prefer to wash . . . later?"

He nodded, his throat too tight to speak.

She looked at him, and he looked *there,* his lust so fierce he could hardly breathe.

But, blessedly he could, because the musky-dark scent of her arousal rose up even more strongly now, its intoxication making him dizzy with desire.

She slipped free of his grasp and dipped a hand in the water, swirling her fingers across its rippling surface. "I do not understand—the water is still warm." Her brow puckered. "I would know myself . . . well ready for you."

"O-o-ooh, that you are, lass. More than you know!" He inhaled deeply, his need almost splitting him. "But, see you, I would have you as you are."

"As I am?"

" 'Tis your scent and *your* taste I want all o'er me, not whate'er scent might come out of yon little clay pot of soap!"

She blinked at that, the widening of her eyes and her bright flush revealing better than words that she'd comprehended.

A flush that deepened alarmingly, even if she kept her chin raised and made no attempt to shield her nakedness. "You know I am not without experience. That I desire you as only a woman who has loved, and loved well, can want a man," she said, an emotion that could have been embarrassment flitting across her face. "Nor am I ashamed of my body—or my ache to know passion again."

She paused, glanced at the steaming tub, her face now flaming in earnest. "But I ne'er went to Hugh's bed without first—"

"You bathed but several hours ago if I heard aright— as did I, if only at the castle well," Kenneth minded her, understanding her concern.

Even if he found it sorely misplaced.

He took her chin, forcing her to meet his eye. "I am not your late Hugh Alesone, lady, and more the pity for him, if he did not appreciate certain *enticements*," he said, determining to wipe the man's memory off her, however long he needed.

"Hear me well, sweeting. 'Tis you, and you alone, I want." He released her, unbuckled his sword belt. "No other lass, no false scents designed to rob a man of the true beauty and pleasure of a woman!"

"But—"

"Lady, I have told you, I am no courtly knight, overfond of fineries and airs." His gaze not leaving her, he tossed aside his belt and blade. "I am bastard-born and was raised in a thatched cot-house so small the whole of it would fit three times into this bedchamber. 'Twas a good life despite its roughness, and to this day I still count my pleasures in the riches of this earth. The great blue hills, the mist on the braes, and other . . . *natural delights*."

He reached out a quick hand then, dragged his fingers across the dampness of her center, then brought his hand to his lips, inhaling deep before he licked the glistening moisture clinging to his skin.

" 'Tis the goodness of you I savor. Naught else," he said, stripping off his plaid and tunic. "And you are good, lass. So blessedly tempting I could ne'er tire of tasting you—as I've already told you."

Mariota's nipples tightened and a delicious weightiness spread through her belly. "I would enjoy you . . . tasting me."

"I just have, minx, and your taste pleases me so much I find myself craving more." He looked at her, hot desire glittering in his eyes. "I will devour you—there, where you burn the hottest and your essence gathers so sweetly."

Mariota's heart gave a great leap of excitement, her body shuddering with thrilling need.

Hugh had licked her down there, and often. But the throbbing hunger now beating between her thighs felt far sweeter than that one's most ardent endeavors—and *he* hadn't even touched his tongue to her yet!

"Would you like that, Mariota?" He brought his fingers to his nose again, then, holding her gaze, inhaled. "Do you know how much I burn to scent you? Feast on your sweetness? Lap up every delicious drop of your woman's dew?"

Woman's dew.

The term knifed Mariota's heart. One of Hugh the Bastard's most favored phrases—mentioned at least once in over half the love sonnets he'd penned for her.

Now she understood the man's attachment to . . . woman's dew.

Like as not, as much as he could get of it and from as many sources!

Bile rising in her throat, she pressed a hand to her breast, blinking against the darkness rushing at her, the way the floor suddenly dipped beneath her feet, unbalancing her.

"Aye! 'Tis well I ken how much men crave such base pleasures," she blurted, the words bursting from a dark place in her heart, a cold place forever branded with the Bastard of Drumodyn's dead-glazed stare, the taunting eyes of Elizabeth Paterson.

But then *he* dropped to his knees before her, his hands gripping her hips as he pressed his face to the soft curve of her belly. At once, a great tremor tore through her, its power sweeping away the hurtful images and replacing them with such golden melting bliss she wondered she could contain it inside her and not burst.

A stinging heat jabbed into the backs of her eyes, near blinding her. Tears. Hot, burning ones that made her blink and swallow until they went away.

Archibald Macnicol's daughter didn't cry.

But she did allow her heart to thunder and her hands to curl into fists, as if the clenching of her fingers could hold fast to the warmth inside her, the joy her Keeper was giving her.

"Not base, lass. Ne'er that," he murmured, rubbing his mouth on her soft skin, his warm breath a tantalizing sweetness teasing her nether curls. He looked up her, his eyes almost black with passion. "'Tis heaven on earth to taste your need and breathe in your desire. Dinna e'er think otherwise."

As if to prove it, he swept his hands down the backs of her thighs, easing her legs apart just enough to allow him to touch his tongue to her. Only a light flick across her

throbbing flesh, but a light flick he ended with a decidedly wicked curl—one that circled and swirled over the
tiny bud of swollen urgency at the top of her womanhood.

Circled, swirled, and . . . suckled.

"Oh-dear-saints," Mariota cried, Hugh Alesone and his
whore fading into oblivion.

Gasping, she clutched her Keeper's shoulders, her fingers digging into him lest her knees buckled. "O-o-oh, I
can't bear it. . . ."

"Ahhh, but you can," he disagreed, and licked her.

Long, broad-tongued strokes, each one dragging
across her wetness, probing her softness as if he truly relished the taste, scent, and feel of her.

"You are so lovely," he breathed, his voice thick with
raw need. "And far too delicious not to be savored to the
fullest."

A sigh escaped her, her body both trembling and
tightening as she twined her fingers into the thick silk of
his hair, pulled him more firmly against her, needing
him closer to the hot, needy, ache pulsing where he
licked her.

She held fast to him, moaning her pleasure, rocking
her hips against him. "I thought I'd known this pleasure,"
she gasped, breathless. "But I have ne'er . . . *ooooh!*"

"O-o-oh, aye, that's my good lass," Kenneth agreed,
and plunged his tongue even deeper inside her this time,
touched a questing finger to the little nub pulsing so hotly
at the heart of her sleek female heat. "Take your pleasure,
minx . . . shatter for me."

A fast approaching triumph, its certainty racing ever
closer as he circled his finger. Licked and tasted her, his
swirling tongue pushing her to greater heights, the des-

peration of her arousal firing his own blood until he burned with equal ferocity.

Mayhap even more, for the instant she cried out with her release, his control spiraled away, his own groan of pleasure blending with hers, a damp, telltale stain suddenly marring the front of his braies.

A disaster he hoped to hide by pushing to his feet so smoothly as his *depleted condition* would allow, then yanking off his boots and shoving down his stained hose with a swiftness a lesser man would ne'er have been able to achieve.

His quickly snatched up plaid spared him further shame—as did the wits to hold it in front of him until her lush nakedness and pungent arousal worked their magic again.

She turned wide eyes on him, still visibly trembling, her breath gradually slowing. "You have made me whole again," she vowed, her voice soft with the after-ripples of her release, her flushed skin and the wonder on her face already reviving the familiar, throbbing hunger.

He shoved a hand through his hair, released a breath he hoped did not sound too shaky. "Dinna think I did not find my own pleasure," he managed, hoping she'd never guess the truth of his words.

"Even so, I would ease your need as well." She tilted her head and began unplaiting her hair, loosening the strands until they streamed to her hips, a red-gold curtain of silk gleaming with the reflection of the hearth fire. "And if I might use your own words—do not think I will not enjoy myself!"

"You have already undone me." He stroked her glistening hair, brushed a kiss across her temple. "But I would ne'er weary of pleasing you, or enjoying the pleasure you bring me. Having you the way I want you—fully."

"Aye, completely." She slid her arms around his waist, splaying her hands across his chest, her fingers lightly plucking at his chest hair. "You have unleashed a deep hunger in me, my braw Keeper, and I find myself wanting . . . more."

"And you shall have more. All that I can give," he promised, hot desire pulsing into his loins, letting him swell and lengthen again.

Harden so fiercely he dropped the plaid and swept her up in his arms, cradling her high against his chest to kiss her roughly on the lips before he carried her across the room and lowered her to the bed.

"Nay, not yet." She stopped him when he made to stretch out beside her. "You have seen my nakedness—and you know I joyed in having you see it. But now I would look at you. Step back and let me see the man who has made me a woman again."

"Made you a woman again?" Kenneth swallowed his astonishment.

He stared at her, saw every lush, golden inch of her sprawled so invitingly across the bed, and wondered not for the first time at the mysteries of the female mind.

The misconceptions they could spin.

Sakes, he could scarce breathe for wanting her, needing her. Already, he craved the taste of her again! Burned to drink in her scent, saturate his senses with its dark, feminine musk.

Bathe in it if he could!

Instead, he did as she'd asked, stepping back so she

could regard him. "For truth," he said as her gaze flitted over him, "a more *womanly* female than you ne'er walked this earth."

"I am pleased if you think so."

"Think so?" He lifted a brow, his own gaze moving over her, marveling at her proud breasts and slightly rounded belly, the red-gold triangle topping her thighs, her beautifully curved hips. *Her ripeness.* "I do not think so, I *know* so," he vowed, his loins heavy with desire.

"You are walking glory, my lady," he added, craving her beyond any lust he'd ever before experienced.

Not a wee dainty bit of a female, one who'd blow away at the first blast of a black north wind, Mariota of Dunach was well-made. A full woman, her bold curves and height made her a true Highlander's most rousing dream.

And Kenneth was a true Heilander if e'er one lived and breathed.

"Ooooh, aye," he purred, feasting on her beauty, "I have wished you mine from the beginning—the moment I first glimpsed you."

But she only took her lip between her teeth and tilted her head, continuing her perusal of him.

Not that he minded.

Though nowise of young Jamie's extraordinary endowment, he could stand beside the best of men and be proud, even cast many in shadow. A sentiment his lady apparently agreed with, for her eyes were widening with flattering awe—and there could be no mistaking where she'd fixed her gaze!

Indeed, she couldn't look away.

Taller than most men, his shoulders spanned a great width as well. Silky dark hair, raven black and glistening, brushed those shoulders, a shimmering skein, riffled by the night breeze pouring in through the windows.

Her gaze drifted lower, to the slabbed muscles of his chest, beautiful masculine skin agleam in the glow of the hearth fire, the light dusting of crisp black hairs arrowing downward, exciting her. Heating her blood until deep, trickling desire stirred between her legs again.

Aye, there could be no question. Full naked and magnificent, the Keeper of Cuidrach took her breath away.

Her whole body quivered just looking at him. Ne'er had she seen a more beautiful man.

"Will I suit?" His voice came low, husky. Almost amused. "To spend you *solace* and comfort? Of course, only for the—"

"Time we have," she finished for him, a sharp pang lancing her at the thought of parting.

The strictures of their borrowed bliss.

And they hadn't even yet *comforted* each other.

Not truly.

Her breath quickening with something that felt too much like annoyance, Mariota tore her gaze from the part of him she was certain might be difficult to fit inside her, and looked instead at his handsome face.

A scarred but wonderful face. One she knew she could gaze upon forever and ne'er see enough.

Especially when he looked at her with such a shamelessly seductive smile.

A smile she wanted for keeps—as she wanted the man!

Biting her lip, she pushed up on her elbows, fast-beating little bits of resentment pricking the haze of her arousal.

"Before we begin our true *solacing,* tell me again that

you will not press me to marry against my will," she said softly, watching him.

His brows arched. "You would speak of this . . . now? When I am standing naked before you?"

"Especially when you are naked in front of me," she returned, her gaze sweeping him. "See you, this Strongbow or whoe'er you might have in mind, might not appreciate the *comfort* we are about to share. Mutually pleasing to us, or nay."

"Och, no one will mind," Kenneth said, perhaps a mite too quickly. "Truth tell, I suspect Duncan Strongbow, at least, would be pleased to know I saw to your . . . *needs.*"

Needs he meant to address now, before risking another disaster.

A distinct possibility considering how long it'd been since he'd taken his ease with a woman, and how very much he burned for this one.

His loins heavy and aching, he stretched out beside her and drew her close, savoring her warm, rounded loveliness. "Nay, lass, dinna even think of any other man this night," he urged her, smoothing his hand over the soft fullness of her breasts, letting his thumb circle and rub her tightened nipples.

"Think only of us—our need for each other," he added, gliding his hand lower, slipping his fingers between her thighs to toy with her damp curls and gently stroke the tender flesh of her cleft.

She opened her mouth as if to protest, but closed it as quickly. Trembling instead, she spread her legs wider, giving him greater access as she lifted her hips, rocked against his circling fingers, sweet little breathless gasps assuring him of her pleasure, sealing his own.

Saints, she was his undoing.

Sleek and slippery as liquid silk, hot as molten honey, lithe, warm, and pliant in his arms. She welcomed his stroking, writhing against him when he slid first one finger, then a second inside her, slowly easing them in and out of her.

And driving himself ever closer to the edge, each dip of his fingers into her soft, wet heat turning him to granite.

"Have done," she cried, arching against his hand, her movements urgent, insistent. *"Please,"* she begged, and opened her legs wider, spreading them. "I have waited so long."

It was all Kenneth needed to hear.

And see.

Thrusting all else from his mind, he rolled on top of her, nearly losing control again at the feel of her warm body beneath his. "Look at me, lass," he murmured, pausing at her entrance, "see my pleasure in you—now, as I join us."

"O-o-oh," she gasped, lifting her hips, her body urging him inside her.

"Can you see my need—my joy in you? Can you feel me coming in you now?" he breathed, easing into her, filling her one sweet, slow inch at time, sliding deep.

"Aye, I feel you, all of you . . . oh, sweet bliss . . ." She shuddered beneath him then, clamping her legs around him, clutching him to her, forcing him deeper. "Dinna stop . . . so good, so good," she cried, digging her fingers into his hair as he glided in and out of her in a beautiful joining, a coupling more exquisite than anything Kenneth had ever known.

Long, slow strokes at first; smooth, deep, and rhythmic. So wondrous, he wanted to make it last forever, her sweet whimpers of pleasure helping him to hold back even as his own blood flamed. His need spiraling, he claimed her lips in a hot, savage kiss, plunged deeper.

His restraint broke and he rode her faster, thrusting hard and deep, their mutual craving hurtling them to a crashing, cataclysmic release.

And afterward, as they both drifted, the world itself seeming distant and a wondrous peace buoying him, somewhere in the darkness of his mind, he remembered a long ago night in Eilean Creag's great hall and how he'd scoffed at the suggestion he needed a wife.

Turned a deaf ear to insistent urgings that only a woman could bring light and warmth to Cuidrach's empty walls, make his own life . . . complete.

Now, at last, he understood his kinsmen.

And vowed to tell them they were right.

Chapter Eleven

❧

"Can you not forget Duncan Strongbow, my lady?"

Wishing she would, Kenneth folded his arms across his chest and kept his gaze on the towering cloud masses drifting across Loch Hourn's night-blackened waters.

"I've promised not to press an unwanted suitor on you and I can swear to you that Sir Duncan, of all men, would ne'er consider a lady who didn't want him," he said, wondering how he could spin such a yarn at this ungodly hour, and with the lassitude of their lovemaking still deep in his bones.

He drew a breath and hoped she hadn't detected the tinge of desperation he was sure he'd heard in his voice. "If you will return to bed, lass, I shall answer whate'er else you would know on the morrow."

But Mariota Macnicol had other plans.

That much he could tell . . . even without directly looking at her.

Wrapped in an exquisite furred bed-robe no one save

his long-nosed garrison captain could have slipped into her hands, she ignored his every hint to return to sleep and only settled deeper into the cushioned comforts of her most favored window seat.

Without doubt, she was well prepared to remain in the cozy bench-lined embrasure until he revealed more about a puissant Highland paragon he wasn't about to admit didn't exist!

Leastways not in the form of one single man.

He frowned, stepping deeper into the window embrasure so the chill night air could cool his heated flesh if not banish the impending sense of doom closing in on him with ever stealthier leaps and bounds.

Already, he regretted his fool idea to use the combined names of his far-famed uncle and that one's chivalrous Sassunach friend, Sir Marmaduke Strongbow, to purchase much-needed thinking time.

Wife-and-aging-warrior-laird-winning time.

A respite he sorely needed.

Especially now that his demons rode him again, the whole ring-tailed lot of them returning with a vengeance to banish the bliss that lulled him into such a sound slumber after tasting his lady's sweetness.

His lady.

He stiffened, the muscle beneath his left eye twitching again. Like it or no, his sudden inability to think of her as anything but his, proved one of the most pressing reasons he needed time.

Not just to think, but to marshal his wits and fight his demons.

His demons, and the emotions *she'd* wakened inside him. Stirrings that went deeper than the physical pleasure he'd found in slaking his burning need for her. Things he hadn't felt or experienced in so very long.

Truth be told, mayhap never.

Wonders he hadn't even believed in.

Leastways, no longer.

Struggling to conceal how deeply she'd affected him, he swallowed hard, the ramifications of allowing himself to care, to *love* her, pounding through his head.

And, wise or no, he was certain he loved her.

Why else would just the thought of losing her strike him as more loathsome than spending the rest of his days in the dank confines of a dungeon?

A rat-infested dungeon with naught but moldy bread and soured water to live on.

His mouth setting in a taut line, he stepped closer to the embrasure's high, arched-topped window. At once, the silence of the night closed down about him and he drew a hand over his brow, knew himself lost.

Defeated, and on a warring field of his own choosing.

Scowling now, he gripped the window ledge and looked out at the dim shining water, the great thrusting mass of the Bastard Stone.

Etched black against the gray and silver of the moonlit night, the massive rock formation seemed to glower back at him. In especial, the tall door-like opening gouged through the blackness of the cliff face.

Kenneth shuddered, drawing his plaid more closely around his naked body. Saints, a more fanciful man might even imagine he saw someone struggling to balance atop the precarious natural-made arch.

Someone Kenneth now recognized, and knew would soon plunge headlong into the yawning darkness below, the starry-eyed young man's hopes and dreams forever dashed on the jagged, waiting rocks.

Not wanting to see the fall, Kenneth closed his eyes and dragged a hand back through his hair. Drew a deep breath of the damp night air.

Aye, he needed all his wits, and time.

And like it or no, Duncan Strongbow would help him gain both.

If need be, with assistance from a similarly named friend or two.

Magnus MacLean came to mind.

A suitor he could claim proved to be a great flat-footed oaf—so long as Magnus MacKinnon and Donall MacLean, two of the finest younger chieftains in the Western Isles, ne'er got wind of the deception.

The possibilities were as endless as his need to keep his lady by his side.

There, where she stood just now if the prickling awareness spreading through him was any indication.

And it was.

A light touch to his arm proved it. "Did a woman do that to you?"

"A woman?" Kenneth turned to her, his mind still half-bound to the Bastard Stone, young Cormac's tragic fate.

She flushed, the stain clearly visible in the moon glow—as was just the hint of a certain vee of lush red curls, peeping at him through the slight gap in her bed-robe.

Kenneth lifted his gaze. "Did a woman do what?"

"The scars." Her own gaze pierced him, probed deep. "If you will not speak of Duncan Strongbow, perhaps you will tell me who marked your handsome face?"

His handsome face?

Kenneth blinked, his heart dipping. It'd been a long while since a woman had called him handsome.

But she was staring at him, her green eyes all soft and aglow as she lifted a hand, traced the three vertical scars seaming his left cheek, her questing fingers brushing against his own. "They look—"

"I ken how they look, my lady." He lowered his hand at once, clutched the cold stone of the window ledge.

Saints, he hadn't realized he'd been fingering the scars. Pale slashes, needle-thin, and often mistaken for scratches left on his face by a furious woman's raking talons.

In truth, the marks of a past he could ne'er outrun.

A legacy tied to a woman, aye.

But caused by his own clumsiness.

No one else's.

And just the sliver of the memory sent chills down his spine, filled him with the horrors of that day. Wincing, his fingers tightened on the window ledge, the smell of the cold northern sea, streaming wet rock, and his own blood suddenly heavy on the damp night air.

Thick and cloying. And so real-seeming, he could almost taste the bitterness on his tongue. Clenching his jaw, he glanced at his lady, hoped she wouldn't notice his discomfiture, the chills sliding up and down his spine.

The inherited torments he doubted he could e'er cast off his shoulders.

He kept his gaze on her, his longing, his hopes to win her, almost causing the room to spin. Blessedly, the lingering musk of their joining still clung to the bedsheets. And powerfully enough to waft across the room, even drift into the closeness of the embrasure.

A glorious scent, his redemption and strength.

Living proof that St. Girta's Isle, bird oil, and even the Orcades, were finally behind him.

And especially . . . *her.*

The fisherman's daughter whose green eyes, however lovely, had ne'er stared at him so unwaveringly as Mariota's—or so filled with compassion.

Mayhap even sympathy.

The last thing he wanted from *this* green-eyed vixen.

His shoulders tensing, he let go of the window ledge, rubbed a hand over his face.

"A woman did not make the scars," he said, turning to face her. "I fell, see you? Lost my footing on a narrow ledge while being lowered on a rope down one of Hirta, St. Girta's Isle's, most treacherous sea cliffs—I plunged into the sea, my lady."

He angled his head so the flame of a nearby wall torch could illuminate the scars. " 'Twas the jagged rock face of the cliff that sliced open my cheek—not the slashing nails of a woman scorned."

Och, nay.

He'd been the betrayed one.

But now, so many cold and empty years later, he thanked the saints for that long-ago perfidy. Even the anger and hurt that'd distracted him, tainting his usual concentration and balance until he'd placed a foot exactly where he shouldn't have.

And the fall had done more than scar his face—it'd jarred him into remembering those he loved best.

His mother, may the Almighty bless her soul and keep her, and his half-sister, Juliana, now well-wed, and happily, to his uncle's son and heir, Robbie MacKenzie.

He smoothed the folds of his plaid, a lump rising in his throat. Hot and burning, a thickness he doubted could e'er be swallowed. But his mother and sister had needed him direly at the time, sustained themselves on the help he sent them, so often as he could.

Hard-earned monies he'd hoard and then see delivered into their hands—even during the rough times when he'd not known where he'd next lay his head or when he might enjoy more than salt herring and ale for his next meal.

On their own in one of Glenelg's darkest, most remote corners, his mother and Juliana had needed the help more.

The plunge down Hirta's razor-sharp sea cliffs made him realize how much he'd needed them.

A blow from fate that was also the beginning of the end of his days as one of most sought-after bird-oil gatherers in all the Western and Northern Isles.

His heart gave a lurch, his mind filling with the image of seabirds, wheeling and screaming all around him. Crying their rage, swooping in to attack. Hearing them now, he shuddered, wiped his palms on his plaid.

He had no cause to complain. The good God knows, had his life been . . . otherwise, he would not be standing here today, his losses far greater than three pale lines marring his cheek.

Greater than he would have e'er dreamed.

One look at his lady, so desirous and desirable, proved it.

And thinking of her, he closed his eyes and inhaled deeply, drawing in the scent of her.

His mind filled with her image, the joys they'd so recently shared. The ecstasy and wonder. *The closeness.*

Saints, the immensity of his pleasure in her, the depth of his need, near overwhelmed him.

And not just because of her lush, warm curves; the promise of hours spent in heated, carnal delight. Truth be told, simply gathering her in his arms and holding her proved an irresistible bliss.

The sweetest intoxication.

And in ways no one else had e'er stirred him.

Swallowing against the tightness in his throat, he slid another glance at the dark silhouette of the Bastard Stone, wishing poor Cormac's plunge to the sea had been as fortuitous as his own.

Good fortune that regarded him quietly, her remarkable eyes looking deep, seeing . . . everything. "God be thanked you were not killed," she said, her voice soft, minding him of what he'd revealed.

And what he hadn't.

"A fall. I would ne'er have guessed." She stood with one hand pressed to her breast, something too close to sympathy flitting across her face. "Yet, still—"

"But you knew I earned my coin at sea?"

She nodded, her eyes luminous in the moonlight. "I have heard talk, aye."

"I imagine you have," he said, touching her cheek with a work-roughened hand. " 'Tis no secret. All ken that I hired out on any galley that would take me on, toiled for years as a gatherer of bird oil. A plunderer of cliff-side nests, for the chicks gave the most and richest oil. In especial, the young fulmar petrels."

He paused, reached to toy with the ends of her hair. " 'Tis a foul trade and one I wish I'd ne'er practiced, but bird oil is prized all over Christendom. The sea traders of

the Hansa League will pay nigh any price for the oil—
they reap fine profits from churchmen everywhere, all
eager for a goodly supply. The holy men consider the oil
sacred and use it for lamps, anointing, even preserving
corpses. Physicians vie for it as well. The market is endless, and greedy."

Mariota lifted a brow. "But you are not greed-driven,"
she said, hearing his words, but listening deeper. "That
much I know—just from having seen you with your
men."

Faith, all at Cuidrach knew he'd paid more than triple
a fair price for the cattle he'd ordered from young Jamie's
father.

And everyone knew why.

Her heart swelled and began to thump. Even now,
weeks later, his men still wagged proud tongues about
how the new Keeper had put such shine in the young
Macpherson's eyes.

Good of heart, they'd called him. The best yet of
Cuidrach's long line of bastard Keepers.

A man like no other.

Sure of it, her gaze slipped past him, out the high,
arched windows to the moonlit glint of Loch Hourn far
below. She welcomed the freshening wind blowing in
from the sea, enjoyed its rain-washed purity.

She drew a deep breath of the chill air, letting the wind
clear her mind. To be sure, the Keeper of Cuidrach was a
man different than most—a man possessed of the sleek
grace of a night-stalking predator, his every move and
thought, carefully executed, mayhap even fluid.

Ever at ease.

And sure.

That, too, anyone could see.

Mariota's brow knitted and she slid a glance at him. Such men did not easily stumble. Save perhaps over the slumbering bulk of a certain ancient beastie, e'er determined to plop his great, shaggy self in the path of his hapless two-legged friends.

Nay, Kenneth MacKenzie was not a man given to careless missteps.

But he could have been . . . pushed.

Driven to clumsiness by . . . circumstance.

At the realization, a powerful emotion surged into Mariota's breast. Hot, tight bands sliding round her ribcage, pinpricks of unexpected jealousy jabbing at her heart.

"So it was a woman," she said, running with her instinct, taking a risk. "She may not have scratched your face, but she scarred you all the same—enough for you to not have your mind where it ought to have been when you were on that cliff."

His sharp intake of breath answered her.

The sudden shuttering of his handsome face.

"It makes gloomy telling," he said, and bit back a curse when her eyes clouded upon the words.

But there'd been no point in keeping silent; the truth already thrummed all through her.

Leastways, what she believed must be the truth.

"Aye, there was a woman on my mind that day." He paced back to the window, looked out at the night, the stars gleaming in cold beauty above the loch. "Her name was Maili, a maid in full blossom of youth when I met her. Her eyes sparkled and her cheeks dimpled when she'd smile and her hair rippled like golden silk. She was a fisherman's daughter and lived with her father in a cottage in a wee bit coastal village in the far north, not far from Durness. She mended nets and wove rush baskets for the fisherfolk—"

"Until you came along and she set her heart—"

"Not her heart," Kenneth corrected, rubbing the back of his neck. "That she ne'er gave me—as I learned to my cost." He glanced at her, wanting her to understand. "'Twas my own heart that was shredded. All I'd e'er believed in, knocked out from under me so swiftly I thought the world would ne'er stop spinning."

His *true* lady looked down, plucked at the embroidered edge of her bed-robe. "You loved her that deeply?"

"At the time, aye. She was young, exceedingly fair, and . . . flatteringly attentive." Kenneth let out a long breath, forcing the tension from his shoulders. "Seeing her the first time was like having the sun burst through a gray fog—I was bedazzled and smitten . . . blinded."

Mariota's head snapped up. "And she was not equally . . . moved?"

He glanced at the hearth fire, his expression unreadable.

Not that it mattered.

His silence said everything.

A stony-eyed mole could see that his experience with the fisherman's dimple-cheeked daughter had torn his soul, defeated him.

Mariota shivered, despite the warm thickness of her bed-robe. Faith, she could *smell* the other woman's deceit, even over such a distance and so many years.

A living, waking nightmare, much like her own.

Only she'd been warned.

Squaring her shoulders, she kept her chin raised, marveling at how little her own hurts pained her. Faith, she couldn't even conjure Hugh the Bastard's face.

Or his whore's.

She only saw *his* face, and ached to soothe him.

"I thought that was the way of it," she said, her stomach clenching in fury at any woman who could have such a good man on his knees, then betray and gut him. "Did you ne'er have reason to—"

"Doubt her? Suspect she'd forget me, cast me aside the instant someone better came along?"

He looked at her, the words hanging between them. Each one dredged from his soul, offered to her to do with what she would.

"Nay, I had no idea."

Mariota stared at him, the outrage in her belly tightening to a small, hard knot.

"Nor had I considered that her father might not hold me . . . suitable."

He paused to look intently at her. "See you, I was well-paid for my skill at sea and although I sent help to my mother and sister, I was also saving for a future with Maili. I'd planned to wed her, wanted a family—so soon as I'd amassed enough to quit the sea. But she—"

"Left you for another?"

"Nay, her father *sold* her to another," Kenneth said, absently stroking the scars on his cheek. "An aging fisherman he was, and friendly with sea merchants and shipowners. Friendly enough to notice the eye one of them cast on Maili. That man was nearly twice her age, and my employer on more than one occasion."

He looked aside, ran a hand down over his chin. "He

was also much deeper-pursed than I could e'er have hoped to be at the time, and . . . he wasn't a bastard. All reasons, I was later told, that Maili agreed to marry him. And happily, though I cannot vouch for that, as I ne'er saw her again. It was her father who told me."

"I think the greater loss was hers," Mariota said, not missing the rigid set of his jaw, or how the muscles around his eyes were tightening. "I am sorry . . . do not know what to say."

"There is naught to be said. Not o'er things long past and no longer of importance. Though the saints know, I should have been wary . . . bastard-born as I am."

"Och, aye, that is so." Mariota nodded, well aware her eyes must be flashing. "'Twas an unsanctioned mating that spawned you, to be sure, Kenneth of Cuidrach."

She stepped closer, tapped his chest with a finger. "You, and many more like you throughout these fair hills. And beyond. Even the good King Robert Bruce had his bastards—and loved them well! Two of my own father's by-blows grew to manhood within Dunach's walls, joining our household after their lady mothers' succumbed to fevers."

"I am not shamed by my heritage." He eased her finger from his chest. "But other things should have warned me."

"Indeed?" Mariota tilted her head, her heart thumping. "I already ken how much your lady mother loved you—all speak of your devotion to her. Was it your father? Did he treat you ill?"

But rather than answer her, he only set his mouth in a hard, tight line.

Her own blood heating, she grabbed his arm, squeezing tight when he made to turn back to the window. "O-o-oh, nay, Sir Keeper, do not hide your hurt from me. Think you I could come to age in a keep full of men and not learn to read their every mood?"

"Ah, but I no longer hurt, lass," Kenneth returned, wondering at the truth of it.

Not about his roaming-eyed scoundrel of a father and that one's legendary infamy. Truth tell, he had it on best authority from his uncle's own lady wife, that, in death, his father had finally found the peace he'd ne'er enjoyed in life.

Even forgiveness from those he'd caused immeasurable hurt.

Including Kenneth.

And now, since coming to Cuidrach, he no longer hurt over Maili, either.

He only had difficulty accepting *why* he no longer hurt!

The possibilities made his head ache and his mouth go dry. He crossed his arms and peered out at the Bastard Stone again, his heart recognizing the parallels even when his wits told him to ignore them.

Unlike Cormac, Kenneth had given his youthful heart to a common-bred lass who'd let greed and ambition taint their love. Or what he'd thought had been love. The cowherd, the first true Keeper of Cuidrach, if only in spirit, had won the heart of a noble's daughter.

A maid who, by all accounting, had loved him in return.

And now Kenneth wore similar shoes—and found himself afraid to walk in them.

The reason stood staring at him now, her green eyes narrowed, demanding an answer.

Melting his heart.

"Dinna tell me you do not ache. I think every inch of you hurts," she fired at him, her expression daring him to deny it. "Save perhaps . . . *certain* inches," she added, her gaze slipping low. " 'Tis well I know you suffer no lackings . . . there."

Kenneth blew out a breath, glanced at the ceiling.

"Ach, lass, I ne'er spoke more true words." He gentled his knuckles along her jaw. "But I will speak more plain ones now. See you, if seeing Maili for the first time was like the sun breaking through mist, meeting *you* was like having the light of a thousand sunbursts illuminate the darkest winter night."

He peeled her fingers from his arm, and lifted her hand to his lips. "Indeed, the whole of a dark winter!" he added, kissing her fingertips.

"Yet you would see me wedded and bedded by this . . . Duncan Strongbow?"

"He is a . . . possible option to consider, aye," Kenneth hedged, the words stale ash on his tongue. "For the now."

Until he could banish the concerns sitting so heavily on his shoulders.

"And later?" She tipped her head, peered at him. "Come spring, will you hasten me into another man's safekeeping? His arms?"

Kenneth flushed, heat snaking up his neck.

Now he knew why he so hated lies.

Deceptions.

He stiffened, looking round for inspiration, his gaze lighting on the row of aumbries set into the far wall.

Not one, but four well-secured wall cupboards, two on either side of the hearth. Each one masoned into the thickness of the walling, their placement in the bedchamber proving Ranald the Redoubtable's faith in Cuidrach's strength, the braw men patrolling the bastard keep's formidable ramparts.

Formidable in that one's day, he silently corrected, his blood chilling at the thought of the holding's present gap-fraught walls.

Unthinkable, should they face an attack before Cuidrach could be fully refurbished

In especial, with women in the keep.

And him, knightly title or no, more adept at robbing seabird nests than fending off sword-swinging assailants.

Frowning, he heaved a sigh.

Galling or no, she would be better off wedded and bedded by one Duncan Strongbow.

Better yet, a real man of such ilk.

But he'd be damned if he'd relinquish her.

Not now.

He'd simply have to face his demons, prove himself worthy once and for all time.

Something his gut told him he'd soon have the chance to do.

"You long devil," Gunna of the Glen purred some nights later as she smoothed her hand over Jamie the Small's groin. She looked at him through lowered lashes, her breath quickening, her dark eyes heated. "I was not told to expect such . . . *pleasure.*"

Jamie flushed.

Words failed him. And even if he could think of something bold to say, with the whole length of him trembling and his tongue tied in knots, anything he could get past his lips would've been an unintelligible mumble.

A gruff *hurrumph* at best.

So he blurted the first thing that came to mind. "Someone shoulda warned you—there are times I doona fit."

But the widow only smiled. "Ahhh, Jamie, I have yet to see a sword I cannot sheathe." She pressed her palm against him and stepped closer so the hardened peaks of her breasts rubbed against his equally naked chest.

"Nor have I ever run from the push of a . . . pike staff," she added, and brushed the honeyed warmth of her lips across his mouth. "You will glide in just fine. And to the hilt, I promise you."

But Jamie had his doubts.

Even if Gunna of the Glen showed no signs of concern.

He could scarce breathe. Ne'er had he been so hard and tight.

In especial when she seized his hands and brought them to her breasts, clamping his fingers on her nipples—hard-swollen teats he soon found himself squeezing and pulling on, even as his chest constricted to a painful degree and, saints help him, his toes began to curl!

She busied herself nuzzling her silky, dark head against his chest hair and squeezing him *down there,* her deft fingers making him crazy, the heady scent of attar of roses rising up from the black skeins of her hair to intoxicate him and further befuddle his already scattered wits.

"O-o-oh, Saints Maria and Joseph!" he moaned, half-torn by the urge to rip off the rest of his clothes and yank the hot-eyed widow even tighter against him, taking her right against the smoke-blackened wall of her cottage, yet equally compelled to hie himself away before his head split from the things she was doing to him.

There was only so much goodness a man could bear.

But *that part of him* swelled and grew, stretching even longer than he'd known was possible, the urgent pounding at his loins rooting him in place as surely as the neat rows of herrings she'd strung above her hearth fire.

Just the place he ought not have looked for the orange-blue flames lapping at the peats on her hearth only minded him that he'd likely spend a thousand years sitting on the hottest hob in hell for indulging in such naked, carnal abandon with a sinfully alluring woman at least ten summers his elder!

And, he realized with another flood of heat up his neck, he was now well and truly naked.

Somehow, without him even noticing, she'd freed him of his boots, hose, and his braies, and was holding him in her hands, gazing down at his full-jutting tarse as if she'd ne'er seen the like.

"M'mmm, but you *are* a splendidly-built man," she purred again, her eyes growing ever wider. "They ought style you *Destrier.*"

War-horse.

His face flaming even hotter, Jamie looked down.

But he didn't share her astonishment. He'd known he'd fill both her hands, even stacked one atop the other. Her fingers didn't meet, either, the plum-shaped tip well topping the curve by her thumb.

Truth tell, *three* hands would be hard-pressed to contain him.

"I tried to tell you," he got out, his voice little more than a rasp, for she'd dropped to her knees and was . . . *licking* him. "Not many lasses are able—"

"Then more's the pity for those unfortunates," the widow murmured, gently kneading his ballocks as she opened her lips over him.

"Holy saints!" Jamie cried, clenching his hands.

"Shush, you, and just enjoy," she murmured, stroking him. "I was told you need such *comforting*—and so do I."

Looking up at him, she swirled her tongue around the thickness of him, moving her head up and down, again and again, each suctioning pull drawing him deeper into the sweet warmth of her mouth until his nails drew blood from his palms and his toes dug into the cold earth of her hard-packed floor.

A floor that suddenly tilted beneath him as the night went black and all the stars in the heavens rushed into the little cot-house, spinning around him as he threw back his head and roared, his seed spilling hotly into the widow's throat, the great need he'd been carrying so long, thoroughly quenched and sated.

But hours later, when the half-light mists before sunrise crept round the cottage and Jamie lay depleted for the seventh time in the widow's arms and neither the lush curves of her body nor her sultry glances could stir him, she rose from the pallet to stand above him, her nakedness no less glorious for the dimness of the hour, the heat in her eyes now of an entirely different nature.

"You are a man of spirit and hot blood, James of the Heather," she said, straddling his thighs so he had a clear view of the sooty curls of her womanhood. "I wonder if you also might have courage enough to pass on a warning to a mutual friend?"

"Courage?" Jamie swallowed, used all his strength to lift his gaze from *there* to her face. "Lady, I will lean a strong shoulder into any wind that comes at me. In especial, for a friend."

She arched a glossy black brow. "And if a part of my warning might prove displeasing to that friend?"

"Even then. If the learning of it will be of use," Jamie vowed, his heart thundering.

But, saints, she'd moved a bit closer and a band of moonlight bathed her in silver and shadow, the shimmering light slanting across her full, round breasts and emphasizing the mysterious darkness beckoning so irresistibly from betwixt her shapely thighs.

His entire body tightening again, Jamie curled his hands around her ankles, stifling a groan. "And who is this friend? You have not said."

"I did not say because I am only guessing," she said, smoothing her hair back over her shoulder, the gesture improving the view almost more than Jamie could bear. "So tell me, James Macpherson, does the name Mariota Macnicol have any meaning to you? To your *Keeper*?"

Jamie near choked.

His *need* froze.

Unthinkable, if Gunna of the Glen had heard of the embarrassment at the burnt mound.

But she only gave a small sigh and fixed him with her dark, smoldering stare. "I see it is as I thought," she said, her voice low-pitched and smoky, but also cautious. "She is your Keeper's lady?"

Jamie nodded. "So everyone says . . . or hopes," he amended, the smooth warmth of her calves beneath his fingers and the attar of roses, along with her own heady musk, making it hard for him to concentrate. "I think he is well smitten with her."

"Then you must warn him anon," she said, holding his gaze. "Tell him I have had . . . unwelcome visitors. He will know I am not usually wont to turn away companionship. But these were men of no fine grain. Rough-looking devils who—"

"By the Rood! Did they harm you?" Jamie made to leap to his feet, but she dropped swiftly to her knees, began rubbing her slippery, female heat in slow circles across his groin.

His breath catching, Jamie slid a glance at his sword belt, discarded near the door. "You must tell me, lady. I will shred them to ribbons, run them through if—"

"No need," she said, and kissed him, the sweet warmth of her lips sending heat pouring into his loins again.

"See you," she said, breaking the kiss, "I have lived alone long enough to ken how to disperse undesired *guests*. I simply told them I was suffering a woman's malaise the day they came to call."

Jamie flushed. "And these . . . men asked about the Lady Mariota?"

The widow nodded, began lowering herself onto him—as if sheathing him might soften her answer. "You must tell Sir Kenneth these men are looking for his lady," she said, already rising and falling on him. "Her, and her tiring woman."

Some dim memory cut through the haze of Jamie's lust, a comment heard in passing. "The Each Uisge!" he exclaimed, reaching for her, grasping her well-rounded hips. "These will be the men she was running from, the ones who meant to sacrifice her to the water horse of Assynt!"

"That may be," Gunna of the Glen agreed, riding him

hard and fast now. "But they want her for another reason as well," she added, her back arching. "A grave one."

Jamie scarce heard her, raw lust roaring through him, stealing his wits and hurtling him toward his eighth *shattering*.

"Grave?"

"Even worse," the widow confided, her voice a faint echo just as he loosed himself. "I would not heed a word they say, but the men seeking Mariota Macnicol, claim she is a murderess."

Chapter Twelve

❖

Kenneth froze on the turnpike stairs, too stunned and disbelieving to move. He *did* drop one of the bags of coin he'd been clutching, and stared it, watching as it thumped down a few of the curving stone steps before coming to rest with a dull-sounding *plump*.

Not one to greet disaster gladly, he blew out a gusty breath and eyed his men as well—in especial Jamie the Small.

The one who'd brought such astonishing tidings.

Ill tidings.

But Jamie, too, was staring at the loosed bag of siller. And not mere slack-jawed gawping. Och, nay, the young knight stood straight as if he'd swallowed a lance, his whole great body stiff as stone. And ne'er had Kenneth seen the lad's face flushed a brighter red.

Nor had he e'er seen him look so miserable.

So utterly stricken.

But then, at the moment, he wouldn't give two pins to see his own expression, either. Truth tell, with anger burning him like a flame, he could almost feel steam pouring out of his ears.

And he knew the muscle beneath his eye would soon be twitching up a storm.

A MacKenzie plague, annoying and unavoidable.

So he just stared back at Jamie, shock hollowing him.

"A murderess?" Kenneth's breath stopped. His outrage echoed in the tight stairwell. "And of not one, but *two* men?"

Jamie gulped audibly and nodded, his misery palpable.

The other men crowding the steps exchanged glances.

No one spoke.

Each man held one or two coin pouches in a white-knuckled grip and stared owl-eyed.

But not at Kenneth.

Och, nay, to a man, the lack-hearts made a great show of studying their feet, the wall, or the bulging leather bags in their hands—the lot of them peering anywhere but at the dark-scowling Keeper of Cuidrach.

Ignoring them all—save Jamie—Kenneth lowered his own remaining coin pouches to the stone-slabbed landing and folded his arms across his chest.

"So-o-o." He narrowed his eyes at the strapping young man who'd just come pounding up the stairs, flush-faced and breathless. "Make the sun shine again, Macpherson. Tell me I mishrard you."

Do not ruin the day I'd hoped to start rebuilding my life again!

But Jamie only shook his head and rammed a hand through his shaggy, bronze-bright hair.

And seeing his discomfiture, Kenneth cleared his

throat and blessed the cool draught pouring into the stair-well through a nearby arrow slit.

"This is not to be borne," he said, pushing the words past his fury. "A slayer of two men? Hah, I say!"

His temples pounding, he shot a glance at Lachlan, two steps below him. "Be on with the siller," he ordered his grim-faced captain, "see the coins stashed in the four aumbries. Assure the locks are stout—and hang a tapestry o'er the whole of them."

"You still want the coin deposited in *her* chamber?" a deep voice queried from farther down the turnpike stair.

"Now, when such dastards might assault us any hour?" another called, his cry reaping a round of hearty agreement.

"In especial, now!" Kenneth returned, more sure of his path than e'er before.

But the throbbing in his head increased, so he closed his eyes, breathed deep. Just long enough to gather his good sense and . . . his control.

Saints, but he felt an urge to curl his fingers around the necks of whate'er gutter-sweeps would dare taint his lady's good name.

For the now, he cleared his throat and rubbed the back of his own neck.

"Aye, to be sure and I wish the coin stored in her bed-chamber—in the aumbries, as I have said," he confirmed, relieved his voice sounded firm.

Untroubled.

"Naught has changed, my good men—and woe be to any who might deem it otherwise," he added, raking them with the best *Keeper* look he could muster.

A fierce-eyed glare that would have made his uncle proud.

Mayhap even Ranald the Redoubtable.

Even so, a spate of quibbling followed. Not a full-blooded stramash, but a belligerent shuffling of feet and few corner-of-the-mouth mutters. A tightening of lips. But finally the men scowled as only Highlanders know how to do, and one by one inclined their heads.

Satisfied, Kenneth waited until they resumed their trudging, circular climb, then caught Jamie by the arm.

"Come, you," he said, the calm of his voice cloaking a seething anger.

His dark brows drawn dangerously low, he dragged the young knight across the landing to a tiny chamber built into the thickness of the wall, pulling him inside, then slamming the door.

He wheeled to face Jamie, his gaze sharpening. "I swear on God's holy name, I have ne'er heard aught so foul."

"Just that!" Jamie agreed, bobbing his auburn head. "I saw it as my bounden duty to warn you, as did the widow. She didn't believe a word the men said."

He looked down then, brushed a speck of lint off his plaid. "See you, she said they were a meaner sort and—"

"Think you I'd hold them for any other?" Kenneth strode to the little room's chink of a window, stopped and swung around. "Hear me well, lad, I do not believe any of this. And if my lady *did* thrust a dagger in some man's heart, I'll vow she had good reason!"

Jamie's chin jutted. "I dinna believe it, either."

But for all his bluster and indignation, Kenneth's favorite couldn't quite meet his eyes.

Indeed, every time Kenneth narrowed his gaze on him, the lad plucked at his plaid or looked down at his over-large feet.

Opened his mouth as if to say something, only to shut it like a trap before a single word emerged.

Kenneth frowned.

"Tell me again who she is supposed to have dirked? Her husband? This Hugh Alesone?" He began pacing again, slanted a dark look at the young knight. "The Bastard of Drumodyn, I believe he was styled?"

"Aye, that one." Jamie confirmed, a fresh wash of pink staining his cheeks. "He was found with her dagger in his heart—and in the bed they shared, aye. 'Tis said he was . . . naked, sir."

Kenneth winced. "And the other?"

"A guardsman, as I said." Jamie rubbed his chin with the back of his hand. "He was found just outside her dungeon cell—with a gash on his head."

Kenneth swallowed the bile rising in his throat. "So no one saw these . . . supposed murders happen?" he asked, the cold knot in his gut growing tight and hard.

"I dinna think so."

Kenneth wheeled round again, his fists clenching and unclenching. "So what *do* you think? I can see all o'er you that there is something else."

"H'mmm. Och, well." Jamie blinked, and coughed. "I'm a-thinking these dregs will soon be at our walls. They told Gunna of the Glen they'd heard tell of Cuidrach, knew it stood empty. They suspect she'd head here."

"As well she did," Kenneth agreed, with some significance. "And if they follow, they'll regret it in ways they cannot begin to imagine."

He hoped.

"Oh, to be sure, we'll ready a fine welcome for them if they come," he vowed, tension twisting his innards.

Damping his palms.

He was a highly skilled seaman, not a blooded warrior.

Not allowing doubts to darken his already black mood, he wrapped his hands around his sword belt and prayed the saints the finer techniques of swording his cousin Robbie and Lachlan had taught him would serve him well if it came to it.

But it'd been a long while since those early days at his uncle's Eilean Creag Castle, and he'd not yet had a chance to test his skill.

There wasn't, however, anything wrong or lacking in his ability to recognize ill ease.

In especial, in someone with as honest and open a face as young Jamie.

The lad was keeping something from him.

Something he feared would upset him.

Certain of it, Kenneth ignored the cold seeping into his marrow and turned a black-browed stare on his young friend. "So-o-o," he said again, and folded his arms. "There is still something I must hear, aye? Something you think might be better left unsaid?"

Young James was slow in answering. "It will rouse your ire, sir."

"Not so much as silence," Kenneth owned, his heart thudding. "Or what I have already guessed—just from looking at you."

"Aye, well . . ." Jamie let the words tail away.

" 'Aye, well', indeed."

Kenneth stepped closer, clapped a hand across the younger man's shoulder.

"Now speak," he said in a tone brooking no refusal. "And do not play me for a fool. I would hear . . . everything."

"Have a care, my lady, or you'll spill everything."

"As if I could." Mariota's breath caught at her friend's slip of tongue. "Now—after what you've just told me."

But Nessa simply gave her a long, hard stare and reached for the heavy creel of golden-smoked herrings, wresting the brimming basket from Mariota's arms and plunking it onto the sturdy kitchen table.

"You wouldn't know," she added, wiping her hands, "but such creels are just like the back-creels used for carrying peats and sea-wrack. There's a hinged bottom, see you? That allows the load to be dropped where'er it's desired—and not there, where *that one* lies a-waiting such a savory treat!"

On the last word, Cuillin sat up and raised a paw, his rheumy gaze full of hope.

Glad for the distraction, Mariota shook her head. "Ach, nay, laddie, no herring for you," she crooned, reaching down to grasp the proffered paw. "But a fine soup bone, you shall have," she added, handing him a large, well-fleshed bone.

A prize he carried to a far corner of the kitchen, where he flopped down with a contented grunt, the temptation of the smoked herrings promptly forgotten.

Just as she'd surely slipped from Hugh the Bastard's mind the moment he'd closed his hands on the riper, fleshier curves of the alewife of Assynt.

Mariota shuddered, a red-hot bolt of alarm piercing her fortitude, chills spilling down her spine.

But not because of Hugh Alesone.

Och, nay, a far greater concern plagued her, filled her with uncommon dread and . . . doubt.

The gnawing fear of just how swiftly *he* might wash his hands of her if she revealed her last remaining secret—a disclosure she'd hoped to share with him this very e'en, and would have, had not Nessa learned why he favored widows.

Or, better said, why he despised fallen women.

Tainted women, scorned by God and man.

Shadow souls, cast out by their own families, dead in the eyes of those who'd once loved them. Forgotten women, branded as senseless chits for having followed their hearts and trusted, succumbed to the worst glib-tongued, gentle-handed men.

She drew an uneven breath, her lungs filling with the comforting pungency of wood smoke, roasted meats and salt-dried fish. Fresh-baked bannocks and stout, frothy ale. Not that such homey smells made much difference.

Her heart still skittered out of beat, her blood still firing with fury at the past she couldn't undo.

His past that threatened to withdraw every shred of hope she'd been clinging to.

If he discovered that she was just such a woman as he chose to avoid, her racing pulse taunted her. As did the hot lump in her throat, the stinging heat searing the backs of her eyes.

She bit back a strangled oath and looked around the smoke-hazed kitchen, her gaze going anywhere but to old Cuillin and his bone.

Or Nessa with her all-seeing stare.

A rough-hewn oaken bench stood against the far wall and it was there she turned her attention, aching to cross the room and just sit there, close her eyes and then be somewhere else when she opened them.

Better yet, be someone else.

Someone untarnished.

Unblemished and free.

Instead, she blinked away the tears she refused to spill and turned back to the table. Well-laden with joints of beef, roasted capons, and still-warm loaves of crusty brown bread, it proved the creel of herrings that caught her eye.

And so soon as it did, her stomach fluttered and unfair resentment began beating in her breast.

"The widow must have sent him her entire store of smoked fish," she said, chilled despite the warmth of the cozy, fire-lit kitchen.

"Sent *all* of us, my lady," Nessa amended, examining the herrings. "And a fine batch they are, too. Of equal quality if not superior to my own."

But Mariota scarce heard her, save to recognize that her friend meant to lead her away from a hurtful topic.

A thorn *she'd* plunged into Mariota's side, however well-meant or innocently.

"Och, I understand why the woman sent her herrings," Mariota owned, hoping only she heard the tremor in her voice. "Sir Kenneth is a good Keeper, a great-hearted man. He has promised the widow a fine, fat milch cow and other stock come the spring, assured her of his protection. She is appreciative. . . ."

She tailed off, her pulse thundering as her gaze lit on

the sacks of salt and flour piled near the kitchen door. The crates filled with dried venison, wineskins, and jarred honey. Small, cloth-covered baskets of jellied eggs and fried seabird pasties. Three or four good-sized wheels of cheese, rolled lengths of the finest wool and linen, softest leather for shoes and belts.

Provender and gifts for Gunna of the Glen.

Goods awaiting transport, so soon as some lust-plagued garrison man volunteered to make the journey to the little side-glen where untold pleasures surely awaited him in the grateful widow's arms.

The *lusty* widow's arms.

The back of Mariota's neck grew hot and she swallowed, her mind's eyes seeing a woman with well-fleshed curves and a shimmering curtain of glossy hair, like as not dark, long, and rippling.

A sultry-eyed temptress who moved with languorous grace and bespelled all men who glanced her way, forever besotting those beguiled enough to reach for her.

Sample her bountiful charms.

Her brows snapping together at the image, she swiped a hand beneath her eyes, squared her shoulders.

"The Keeper of Cuidrach will help any glen folk in need," she said, armoring herself with that surety and banishing the *other* thoughts.

Nessa snorted and puffed at a lock of hair falling over her forehead.

"You are letting false fears eat at you," she scoffed, her nimble fingers sorting the herring. " 'Tis young James the widow's like to set her *needs* on—all ken the lad paid her a call. You know he will have . . . pleased her."

She slid a glance at Mariota, one dark brow arching.

"You also know I speak as I find, my lady. If you see fat sizzling and smoking in that fire you're stirring, 'tis your own good self what tossed it there. Your Keeper is too in lov—"

"O-o-oh, do you not see?" Mariota flipped her braid over her shoulder, her heart near bursting. "I am not sure of his feelings! Would that I were. But I . . . I love him."

She glanced aside, blinked furiously.

"Aye, Nessa, I do love him," she admitted. "Deeper and more powerfully than I e'er loved Hugh the Bastard—more than I would have believed possible. 'Tis not fear of losing him to the *lusty widow* that freezes my blood, but dread of losing him if he learns that I was ne'er widowed!"

Her head spinning, she lowered her voice. "What he will do when he discovers I've lied?"

"He will do nothing for he loves you true. And he does, I am sure of it, even if you aren't. His feelings are writ all o'er him—ask anyone in these walls!" Nessa thrust a cup of ale into her hand. "Here, drink, my lady. And dinna you fret."

"You say that so easily." Mariota set down the cup untouched. "Yet it was you who told me of his mother— how a *fallen woman* ruined her life and how, watching her pain, left him with an aversion of such women."

Nessa sniffed. "You are nowise such a woman, and well you know it," she snipped, shaking her head. "Lachlan told me Sir Kenneth's father was lured astray by the guile of a conniving, cold-blooded adulteress. Sir Kenneth's uncle's own lady wife. Or rather, his first wife. A woman wicked and fickle to the bone, by all accounts."

Mariota looked away, unconvinced.

"Dinna you see?" Nessa touched her arm. "'Tis no small wonder such a scandal made him wary of devious women . . . whores and true joy women, the sort without a jot of scruple."

But Mariota only shook her own head, hearing little but the word *whore*.

The selfsame word Hugh the Bastard's men had hurled at her the night he'd died and Elizabeth Paterson had plunged Mariota's dagger into his heart.

As well, a slur she could not deny.

Whether she'd thought she'd loved Hugh Alesone more than life itself, or no.

Steeling herself, she looked back at her friend, wishing she had that one's faith, her confidence.

The saints knew she used to—but that now seemed so very long ago.

"He will not understand, see you?" She dashed a hand across her cheek again. "What you have told me means he has been injured twice. The suffering he saw his mother endure . . . at the hands of a light-skirted female. And then the treachery with his Maili, the fisherman's daughter who married someone else, breaking his heart and rubbing salt in the wound by letting it be known she'd shunned him because of his bastardy, the reputation of his father."

Nessa snorted again. "Men talk of a night in Cuidrach's hall. Duncan MacKenzie's first wife was anything but a casual *light-skirt,* and your Keeper's Maili was a brazen piece he should ne'er have winked at in the first place!"

"Even so . . ." Mariota bit her lip.

Finding it ever harder to breathe, she went to the nearest window, needing the air. "For mercy, Nessa, even if he can accept my vulnerability towards Hugh and believes me when I tell him I e'er thought Hugh would take me to wife, if he learns I lied, he will be devastated."

She wheeled on Nessa then, her anguish a hot clamp around her heart. "He will ne'er trust me, see you? Not after I've kept silent so long."

"And you trust him so little to give him the chance?" Nessa angled her head and clucked her tongue.

"I do not trust myself to bear the pain if he turns from me," Mariota admitted, fear of losing him nigh choking her. "I cannot take that chance."

But then a tiny smile began curving Nessa's lips and she moved away from the worktable to stand before the open kitchen door. "And if I tell you he already trusts you more than you would ever guess?" The smile now reached her eyes, lighting them and making them twinkle. "H'mmm, my lady? What say you to that?"

"I say you've run mad," Mariota returned, her heart beginning to thump all the same. "Or that the moon sickness has finally seized you."

"No moon madness, my lady." Nessa placed a finger to her lips then, glancing over her shoulder into the darkness of the vaulted passage leading away from the kitchen. "Tell me, have you not heard the thudding of feet tramping up and down yon turnpike stairs as we've been working away in here?" she asked, turning back to Mariota. "The muffled mumblings of men underfoot? Many men?"

Mariota frowned. "I have heard nothing," she said, puzzled.

Naught save the crackling of the cook fire, the sound of rain from beyond the unshuttered windows, and, of course, the hammering of her heart.

The occasional grinding of Cuillin's stump-like teeth on his soup bone.

"A shame, that." Nessa looked down, made a show of shaking out her skirts. "See, if you'd listened closely, you might have heard the sounds of trust."

"The sounds of trust?"

"Och, aye . . . sweet, burgeoning trust."

Mariota blinked, straining her ears . . . and still heard nothing unusual.

"I do not understand," she said, truly puzzled. "Speak plain—so clearly as you e'er pride yourself on doing."

"So be it," Nessa agreed, beaming now. "When Lachlan first told me why Sir Kenneth feels such distaste for *fallen women,* I, too, feared he might not listen when you tell him the truth about Hugh the Bastard—that he was your lover and not your husband."

Mariota crossed her arms, feeling chilled again. "What has happened to make you think otherwise?"

"His *trust,* my lady," her friend explained, speaking in riddles again.

She came forward then, gripping Mariota by the arms. "See you, if he loves you enough to trust you as he has ne'er trusted another woman in all these long years, he will not disappoint you when he learns the truth."

Mariota shook free. "And how do you know he trusts me? That is what I would hear!"

Nessa threw another glance at the passage beyond the door arch. "Did you not wonder why I pleaded your help today? Do you not ken me well enough to know I do not need another woman's hand in the kitchen? That I prefer going about such tasks on my own?"

"I did wonder," Mariota admitted, her gaze going

again to the mound of goods near the door. "But I knew there was much to be readied for the widow."

"And so there was," Nessa ceded, smiling again. "But the true reason you are here is because I was asked to keep you occupied until Sir Kenneth and his men could carry his bags of coin up to your bedchamber and store them in the aumbries—"

"His bags of coin?" Mariota stared at her friend, her jaw dropping. "I have heard whisperings that he kept his monies stashed outside the castle, in a broch, I believe? But you say he now—"

She broke off, clamping her lips around the words, unable to form them, for the hot lump that had been lodged in her throat suddenly swelled to such a degree she could scarce breathe much less speak.

Her *heart* melted.

"Aye, my lady, just so," Nessa confirmed.

Looking pleased with herself, she seized Mariota's arm and propelled her toward the door arch. "He'd stashed his wealth in the double-walled thickness of nearby Dun Telve—did so long months ago, Lachlan told me. Well before we even neared Cuidrach."

Mariota's eyes widened, her tongue still too thick to form words.

"You needn't look so flummoxed." Nessa prodded her down the passageway, toward the upward-winding stairs. "'Tis all true. He's fetched his coin here, securing every siller he possesses in the wall cupboards in your chamber. Lachlan says he wishes to prove his trust to you, let you see how much he values and loves you."

"But—"

"Hah! I will hear no *buts,* my lady," Nessa chided,

stopping at the base of the stairs. "Go and see for yourself. He'll be waiting for you, Lachlan swore it."

But even as Mariota's feet carried her upward, each echoing footfall drove a spike of fear deeper into her heart.

If he truly had vested so much trust in her, how could she dare risk breaking it?

She couldn't.

Much as her heart begged her.

The sad truth was, the puissant Archibald Macnicol's only daughter was not so braw as she'd thought.

He didn't care.

Or, rather he cared so much that naught that had gone before mattered to him.

A truth that rocked Kenneth to the roots of his soul the moment the bedchamber door opened and *she* paused on the threshold. Even through the shadows, he could see her eyes widen as her gaze went straight to the magnificent Flemish tapestry flapping gently in the night breeze.

A richly woven gem, and newly hung, its brilliant colors glowed in the light of the hearth fire. Yet another gift from Sir Marmaduke Strongbow, and depicting a romantic woodland scene, the tapestry served its purpose well, its great size completely hiding the four aumbries that, until a few hours ago, had loomed in clear view.

Aumbries now filled with every coin he possessed.

And all his dreams—and more.

He only prayed she'd be honest with him.

Tell him her secrets without him having to pry, something he was determined not to do. Much as keeping his silence pained him.

In especial, when he so wished to reassure her.

But she hadn't yet noticed him, concealed as he was in the blackness of a corner. Instead, astonishment lit her face, her surprise seeming to swirl more thickly around her with every step she took into the room.

Carefully placed steps, for her knees had jellied upon seeing the tapestry. And her heart pounded so loudly upon not finding *him* waiting for her, the sound of its thundering vied with the night wind, a cold wind with the dampness of rain on its breath.

A chill clamminess mirrored in the damping of her palms as she crossed the room and reached for the wall hanging, lifting its edge to see four stout new locks guarding whate'er had been placed in the aumbries.

"The keys are hidden inside your mattress," said a deep voice behind her. "All four of them."

Mariota spun around, her breath snagging.

Her eyes flew even wider. "Faith, but you startled me," she gasped, staring at him. "I did not see you when I came in."

"Nay, you would not have," he owned, smoothing his knuckles down the side of her cheek. "I was in yon corner by the window embrasure."

But she noticed him now.

And even with so much on her mind, her heart dipped and she went liquid, wanting him so much she could hardly breathe.

As if he sensed her need, he stepped closer. So close that his nearness wrapped round her, his sensual heat seducing her ever deeper into a whirling maze of giddy sensation.

"*Sir.*" She breathed the word, unable to say more.

Not with her heart pounding and his dark eyes holding hers, his smoldering gaze making her burn. Faith, she ached for him with such urgency she trembled.

"Were you not told I'd be here . . . waiting for you?"

She nodded, melting when he stroked her hair.

"Then you see that your friend spoke true?" He pulled her to him, slid his hands up and down her back. "We have much to speak of, my heart. But first, you must know that the locks on the aumbries are not meant for you."

Mariota stiffened, an edge of ill ease sluicing through her. "You needn't have told me about the keys," she said as he nuzzled the top of her head, kissed her brow. "I have no need or wish for—"

" 'Tis I who have need, my lady." He eased back from her, holding her at arm's length. "Need for you, as you ought well know. And this night, a great need to know you safe."

Mariota swallowed. "Safe?"

"Aye, safe," he said, his dark gaze solemn.

Unsettling.

"That is why I told you where the keys are." He paused, crushed her to him again. "As well, because I trust you. Ne'er doubt that. No matter what comes."

He trusted her.

Mariota's heart stopped. No three words could have pleased or frightened her more.

As it was, they spooled through her, warming her and taking her breath. But the ill ease inside her bloomed as well. No longer a flickering edge, a growing current of fear slid through her, chilling her.

Consuming her.

She opened her mouth to speak, but before she could, he framed her face with his hands and kissed her hard and swift. His tongue swirled into her mouth to slide against and tangle with hers. Their breath mingled as he deepened the kiss, devouring her as if he sought life-giving sustenance from her. But then he gentled the kiss and pulled back to look at her again, his eyes dark with passion.

Passion, and something else.

Something that quickened her pulse, but not in the way his gaze usually stirred her. Nay, there was an almost stony hardness about his expression, a carefully controlled tinge of anger simmering beneath the blaze of his desire.

Indeed, a terrifying sense of underlying fury throbbed in the air around them. A living thing, bold and untamed, come to join them in the chamber.

"See you, I would know that you have access to yon monies should aught happen to me," he said, his words allaying one fear but adding another. "Only if I know you safe, can I do what I must."

"What you must?"

He nodded, shoved a hand back through his hair.

Dread rising in her throat, Mariota looked at him, comprehension crawling up from the shadows, nipping and nibbling at her until she understood.

And with the realization, his words took on their own ominous meaning.

"Oh dear saints," she cried, memories of the early days at Cuidrach flooding her mind.

Days and nights lived in fear of Hugh's men finding her.

There could be no other reason Kenneth would take

the precaution of assuring she had access to his coin—not unless he wished to know her secure if aught happened to him!

And *he* had no sworn enemies.

None that she knew of, anyway.

Only she did.

"God in Heaven." She clapped her hands to her cheeks. "Ne'er would I have wanted it to come to thi—"

"But *I* want, my lady. I burn to resolve this for you," he vowed, the determination in his voice squeezing her heart, lancing her.

"Men are passing through Kintail, see you? Your late . . . husband's men, and they are looking for you." He touched the hair at her temple, caressed her cheek. "I mea.. to ride out and sort them before they can find you—send them back whence they came. Lest they wish an early reckoning with their Maker."

Mariota stared at him, his words laming her.

Her blood froze.

She'd also heard the hesitation in his voice when he'd said her late *husband's* men.

But his expression was now unreadable, could have been sculpted of granite. Its hardness not aimed at her, but at Hugh Alesone's minions.

Broken men with less scruples than adders. Malcontents who did not fight fair and knew no honor.

Her stomach heaving, her soul began to rip.

A thousand horrors spun in her head, the tapestried walls shifting and contracting before crashing inward to bury her beneath her guilt.

Her deep regret at e'er coming here, involving *him* in such madness.

Or with such devil-damned snakes as Hugh the Bastard's men.

"Nay, I cannot believe it," she denied, willing the moment to be a fearing dream.

He fixed her with a long stare.

"But they are here," he said, then went to the window, stared out at the silver-gilt night. "They stopped at Gunna of the Glen's cottage. Not long before Jamie visited her. 'Twas she who sent the warning."

He glanced over his shoulder at her. "She, too, wishes you well, my lady."

Mariota shook her head, still disbelieving.

"My . . . Hugh the Bastard's men would ne'er come this far, nor venture into Glenelg. Even in Assynt one hears of the dread *urisgean* said to haunt these parts." She joined him at the window, touching a hand to his arm. "It is why I fled here. I ken those men, much as I wish I didn't. They fear no man, but tremble at the unseen."

She drew a shaky breath, shuddered. "'Tis why they sought to offer me to the *Each Uisge*—they wished to appease the beast."

"I suspect they had other reasons," her Keeper said, still staring out the window.

He stood rigid, the set of his shoulders speaking his mood, as did his clenched hands.

"I vow, too," he added, "that there is more to their being here than a wish to toss you to some water horse that might or might not exist."

Mariota's face began to burn.

"'Tis true enough," she said, the words tumbling. "I told you before, every ten years the Assynt water horse is delivered a sacrifice. Folk believe the offering keeps him beneath the river's surface."

She looked down, fussed with her skirts. "This year, he killed before a sacrifice could be made." She spoke quickly, before the image of Hugh's naked whore could rise in her mind. "He ravaged the village alewife and left her broken body on the banks of the Abhainn Inbhir, the River Inver, not far from Drumodyn Castle."

Kenneth glanced at her, one brow raised. "She died near your husband's holding?"

"Close to Hugh Alesone's castle, aye." Mariota forced herself to nod. "Her death increased the wish to serve me up to the beast—to hinder further savagings. Leastways, that is how folk in those parts saw it."

"And why did they choose you?" The brow arched a tiny bit higher. "A warrior laird's daughter?"

Mariota moistened her lips, tried to ignore the sudden damping of her palms. "I was told folk believed the water horse would consider a *lady* a rare treat," she said, forcing herself to hold his gaze. "And . . . Hugh's men did not like me. They will be sore vexed I escaped them."

He didn't look convinced. "And you do not think there could be another reason these men followed you here?"

Mariota blinked, fingers of ice clutching her heart.

Something in his tone, the way he was looking at her, screamed that he knew there was another reason.

A horrible reason.

And one he wanted to hear.

"Well, my lady?" He took her chin, holding her face so she couldn't look away. "No other possibilities?"

"No. I—"

"Think hard, lass." He touched his fingers to her lips,

pressing gently. "And do not speak again until you are prepared to tell the truth."

Terror bit into her then, white-hot misery clamping around her ribs, stealing her breath.

"I—" she began, only to break off and swipe a hand over her cheeks, not surprised to find them damp, streaming with tears.

Scalding tears that continued to spill—especially when she tried to glance aside and her gaze fell across a settle half-hidden in shadow, her swimming vision not yet so poor that she missed the gleaming mail hauberk draped across the settle's cushioned bench.

She also caught the silvery glint of a shiny new war ax propped against the wall.

The one, a knightly accoutrement men donned before heading into battle.

The other, a warrior's weapon, large, wicked, and deadly.

An ax she knew would boast a smooth, notch-free haft and a well-honed but untried blade.

She stared at both, their portent breaking her as dread churned and whirled inside her.

"There is another reason." She straightened her back, making herself meet Kenneth's eyes. "Hugh Alesone's men believe I murdered him. He was found with my dagger buried in his chest."

The words came fast and breathless, but that she'd said them at all filled Kenneth with such numbing triumph he was hard-pressed not to throw back his head and shout with joy.

True, she hadn't said all he'd hoped she'd say, but it was enough.

A beginning.

So he pulled her into his arms and held her, stroking her to cushion the one question he couldn't ignore.

Even though the answer did not matter.

He could not face these men without knowing.

He drew a breath, steeling himself. "And did you, my lady?"

She jerked in his arms, the horror of the truth filling her eyes. "Nay, I did not. I swear to you on—"

"You needn't tell me more—I believe you," Kenneth said, surprising himself with the depth of that belief.

His willingness to wait until she trusted him enough to admit the rest.

For the nonce, he took her face in his hands again and kissed her, sweeter and deeper than before. A *soul*-deep kiss he hoped would shield and protect her heart, warm and sustain her always, if aught happened to him.

Not that he had any intention of leaving this world any time soon.

Not now with such a bright future glimmering on his horizon, on *their* horizon.

Even if she didn't yet know it.

Convinced he'd soon be able to tell her, mayhap even long before spring, he unfastened his plaid and let it drop to the floor. His sword belt followed, an incredible sense of rightness and purpose filling him as he pulled her with him across the room.

"Come you," he said, helping her with her own clothes so that when they tumbled onto the bed, naught separated them but the linen of his braies and her scant nothingness of an undershift.

Time stretched, accommodating their need as he

moved on top of her, loosened his braies. She reached for him, arching her hips to ease his entry even before he could shove her camise above her thighs.

"Pray God do not go seeking them," she cried, clamping her legs around him, rocking against him when he thrust deep inside her. *"Please."*

She clung to him, digging her fingers into his shoulders as he began moving in and out of her. "I could not bear to lose you."

"And you shall not—the saints would ne'er be so unkind," Kenneth breathed, hoping he spoke true.

Determined to *make* it so if he wasn't.

But already his body was tensing, the smooth, fast rhythm of their movements milking him. The tight, wet sleekness of her draining his strength as everything suddenly spun around him and the most intense pleasure he'd ever known burst through him, shattering him.

"That—was—too—soon," he gasped, collapsing against her, his heart hammering. "But I shall make it up to you."

As if to start proving it, he slid one hand over her breast, let his fingers toy with her nipple through the fine linen of her camise. "Aye, lass, I shall make . . . *every-thing* better for you," he promised, his breath still uneven. "If you will only let me."

And somewhere through the drenching haze of their just-sated passion, he thought he heard her say she loved him, though it might have only been a sigh.

Or the fitful night wind.

Not that it mattered . . . yet.

For the moment, it was enough to just hold and stroke her. Perhaps later, they could savor a longer, more languorous joining. Mayhap even two. A glance at the still-darkened windows, and the utter stillness beyond them, reassured him of the possibilities.

Aye, this night, at least, he could give her.

He suspected they had till sunrise.

Chapter Thirteen

❧

The night was too still.

The shadows creeping across Kintail, too well-hung with swords and daggers to be ignored. Even by those who slept so deeply as the well-sated Keeper of Cuidrach, his dreams alive with the succulence of moon-silvered thighs—warm, sleek, and silky. Long, deep kisses, endless and slaking.

Tongue kisses.

Soft, slow, and full of breath.

Scorching kisses, each one more intimate than the last. His need to taste and savor, all-consuming; the wetness between her thighs, an irresistible beckoning, urging him to plunge ever deeper, to claim and possess.

Exquisite thrusts, languid and sweeter than any he'd ever known.

Delicious dreams, heady and intoxicating.

Quicksilver swirls of glory, his minx writhing beneath him, her lush curves clad in naught but the silken spill of her hair, the rapture of her sighs.

Even so, an edge of iciness cut through the languorous warmth of his dream, its black chill sliding ever deeper into Kenneth's contentment, shattering his bliss.

Squeezing everything inside him until his eyes snapped open.

Thick silence rushed him at once, its suffocating presence filling the darkened bedchamber and chilling his blood before he could even blink away the dredges of sleep.

He peered about the room, his senses coming alert as he searched the shadows, but found only emptiness. An odd frozen-in-time quality that brought a worse dread than if all his demons had suddenly escaped from the hither side to manifest before his disbelieving gaze.

Swallowing hard, he sat up in the curtained bed and rubbed his eyes. Tense and breathless, the unquiet grew as he tilted his head to listen and heard . . . nothing.

Only the beating of his own heart. The deep hush where night sounds should have flourished.

She lay motionless, lost in the soundness of sleep, her soft warm curves still cushioning him, her sweet feminine heat a temptation against his thigh.

The taste of her yet lingered on his tongue, conjuring images of last night, heated memories that stirred him. But they stunned him, too, because the contentment he'd found just holding her as she'd slept had satisfied him almost as much as when they'd lain together in hottest passion.

Perhaps even more so.

He glanced at her, his gaze skimming over her full, round breasts. They gleamed in the dim light of the moon, teasing and tempting him in their nakedness, the lush swells begging attention. Even now in this strange moment and after a full night of vigorous lovemaking.

Nay, not quite a full night, the darkness minded.

As did the unnatural calm.

Nothing stirred at all—as a quick glance at the open shutters confirmed.

Indeed, it looked a clear and windless night. Not anywhere near the morn, and with a few stars yet winking in the frosty sky. And with each long-stretching moment, Kenneth came more awake.

More sharply aware of the silence—the prickling at his nape.

There could be only one reason for the quiet, the chills slithering up and down his spine.

He'd guessed wrong.

They hadn't till sunrise.

The Bastard of Drumodyn's men were upon them now. This very hour when the Devil looked after his own and the night was at its darkest.

"God's holy knuckles!" he roared, leaping from the bed. He bounded to the nearest window, for one crazy moment wishing he could blow fireballs against the churls.

Such magic, however ludicrous, would serve him better than the knightly sword belt he was struggling to fasten about his hips.

Naked hips, he realized with sudden dismay.

His brow blackening, he tossed aside the impressively tooled belt and its magnificent brand and began yanking on his clothes.

Dressed at last, he relatched his sword belt, glared out the arched windows. But except for the eerie silence, all appeared as it should.

Not that he was wont to stare out windows at such ungodly hours to make sure.

This night he made an exception.

Took a deep breath and stared into the cold dark with an intensity that made his eyes burn. He let his most piercing gaze take in every fold of this remote upland glen he so loved. Scrutinized the great hills rimming the horizon until his vision blurred.

And when nothing menacing caught his eye, he kept looking. Curled his hands to fists, and scanned the darkness, watching for movement.

Anything unusual.

But nothing more sinister than a few wispy bits of mist drifted across the wooded slopes beyond the gatehouse, and only a dim wash of moonlight spilled into the cobbled bailey.

No pack of wild Hielandmen came tearing from behind the trees, wrapped in plaids and tartan, armed to the teeth and bristling with steel.

Kenneth stood still, frowning. Whether he saw them or no, he could feel them.

Ruffianly characters.

Full of stares and anger . . . bitten by greed.

So he turned his attention on the outbuildings clustered along the inner curtain walls. Each wood-built byre or shed seemed to hunch in the shadows. Blessedly, he could not detect anything else crouching there, sharing the murky gloom.

Only the scent of rain, wet shrubbery, and peat smoke hung in the air, familiar as the dark mass of the Bastard Stone looming up from the still waters of Loch Hourn.

An ordinary night.

But one like no other.

Something hovered unseen, watching and waiting.

And not one of Glenelg's much-feared *urisgean*.

"Och, aye, I'd wager my soul on it," he muttered, rolling his shoulders beneath the unaccustomed weight of mail.

A splendidly crafted hauberk he thanked the saints his uncle had pressed upon him.

As for the battle-ax, its silvery blade glinting so wickedly across the room, he'd wield the thing against anyone who'd dare raise a hand against his lady.

And without mercy.

He only wished he'd spent more time practicing its swing in recent weeks than pulling up weeds and lugging endless barrels of wine into dust-filled storerooms!

"Wager your soul on what, my lord?" The words came from just behind him, his lady's voice husky with sleep and yet laced with all the steel of a warrior laird's daughter.

Whirling from the window, Kenneth's heart seized at her loveliness.

"My soul?" He blinked, her tousle-haired beauty and the fullness of her kiss-swollen lips momentarily blinding him.

Sakes, even though she'd pulled on her undergown, the flimsy material clung to her, molding her shapeliness rather than concealing her charms. And her unbound hair still tumbled to her hips, a glistening swirl of sunfire, richly a-gleam even in the room's deep shadow.

A wanton display to weaken and seduce the boldest of men.

"Aye, your soul," she said, the slight emphasis on the

last word making him wonder if she'd somehow read his thoughts as they'd slept.

Knew better than he how much he lusted for her.

Loved and wanted her.

Needed her.

Watching him closely, she pushed her hair over her shoulder and crossed her arms. The gesture lifted her breasts, plumping them, making his breath catch.

She tilted her head, her gaze unblinking. "I would know what is so grave you'd offer up your soul on its surety?"

"You, my lady, would heat a man so fiercely the hottest flames of hell would seem a reprieve." Kenneth looked at her through the shadowy dark, well aware he hadn't answered her, but his manhood was stirring, the scent of her woman's musk playing havoc with his senses.

He shoved a hand through his hair, his fury of earlier making room for an even greater dread should he fail to keep her safe.

Should Cuidrach's gap-ridden walls prove as disastrous a hazard as he feared.

"Wishing to tempt you is not what brought me from bed." She searched his face, her expression calm as she stepped closer. "You have anger all over you—look more tense than a drawn bowstring. I would know why."

"*Why?*"

Kenneth near choked. He'd just told her why, had she had ears to listen!

"Saints, lass." He blew out a hot breath, shoving a hand through his hair. "God be good, lady, I will not lie— I *am* tense," he admitted, pinning her with his gaze. "And angry. I did not spend years at sea and not develop the ability to sense a change in the wind's direction . . . very often before the shift happens."

The warrior laird's daughter lifted a brow. "And I could not reach womanhood beneath my father's roof and with a slew of quick-tempered, sword-swinging brothers and not guess what troubles you."

She turned to the window, looking down at the deserted bailey. "You're expecting Hugh the Bastard's men—and soon."

Fury-bitten brigands who will charge through your tumbly-stoned gatehouse and into Cuidrach's great open courtyard before any within these walls can stop them.

That truth, she left unsaid.

It was enough that the notion chilled her to the marrow, struck such dread into her heart she could almost feel a cloud of cold darkness moving in on her, surrounding her.

But when she turned back to face him, determination to avert disaster already thrummed all through her.

"There is no other reason you'd be wearing this." She touched his chest, easing aside his plaid to rest her fingers against the silvery-smooth mail beneath. "Or carrying around an ax that would have put a gleam in the eyes of our most fearsome Viking ancestors."

"I see you *are* your father's daughter," he said, stepping beside her at the window. "And I respect that blood highly enough to tell you true, lass—our situation here is grim."

He paused to glance down at the bailey, over to the gatehouse. "You won't be under any illusions about the dangers if these men lay siege to Cuidrach," he went on, the words a statement. "Would that I had a horde of wild-eyed Norsemen to join my men on the walls. As is—"

"As is, I am enough Macnicol to ken how to make myself useful." Careful to stay within the shadow of the window arch, Mariota surveyed the hills rolling away beyond the curtain walls, her gaze studying every crack, hollow, and spur of the steep, rock-strewn slopes. "Hugh's men are as crafty as they are fearless. They will not show themselves until they've assessed our vulnerabilities, are certain—"

"Fair lady, *all* of Cuidrach is a susceptibility," he minded her, his gaze, too, on the nearer hill faces.

In particular, a dark line of Caledonian pines near a great outcropping of rock a good distance from the farthest curve of the curtain walls. Something moved there, and Mariota knew he'd seen it, too, for his mail-clad arm tightened beneath her fingers.

"There!" She jerked his arm, gestured at the heap of jagged, broken stones. "At the edge of those rocks, a shadow—"

"A fox," the Keeper of Cuidrach announced, leaning forward. "A fine red fox, naught else."

And on second glance, she had to agree.

The stealthily moving creature slipped along the base of the outcropping, the brilliance of his coat attracting the moonlight just before he vanished into a gap between the stones.

But he reappeared as quickly, his eye-catching fur looking almost aflame as he scrambled about the boulders as lightly as if he had the feet of a goat.

Or some other kind of fey magic.

"Would that I could secret you away as easily," the

Keeper said as the little fox slipped from view. "But the storeroom will have to do. It is the farthest from the keep's outer walls and can be held to the last. I will place Jamie and his old dog on the door. The dog wouldn't be much use to you if it came to it, but I'd not want him to take a stray bow shot—"

"Dinna worry—I will look after Cuillin." Mariota's heart clenched at the thought of anything happening to the aged dog. "Jamie will serve you better if he uses his brawn to carry kettles of boiling water up to the battlements. That, and anything else that can be hurled from the walls. 'Tis fairly clear they'll breach the gatehouse without difficulty."

Eager to make herself useful, she moved away from the window, dressing as she spoke. "We'll want water to drench the main keep door. It seems sturdy enough, but they may try to fire it if they cannot break through. Nessa and I can—"

"Ho—you weren't listening again." He strode after her. "You and Nessa shall wait out whatever comes in the storeroom off the great hall," he informed her, snatching up his battle ax and tucking it beneath his belt.

"I appreciate your will to help and I'm sure you've seen more than your share of sieges. Or heard the tales. But my men and I will do what must be done." He touched her cheek. "Without endangering you or Nessa."

"But—"

" 'Tis settled, lass." He took her arm, guiding her from the bedchamber. "I have enough of my uncle's blood to defend Cuidrach as befits a MacKenzie and enough of my father in me to outwit scourges as these in ways they'd ne'er dreamed."

"They will not be put off like a pack of whipped curs. They—"

"And," he continued as if she hadn't spoken, "I have too much honor of my own to lose a keep I have sworn to hold."

He glanced at her, releasing her just long enough to open the door. "Nor shall I allow any harm to come to you. Above all, I shall keep you safe."

"But these walls cannot withstand a direct assault," Mariota argued, sure of it. "They are still half in ruin. You ken—"

"There will not be an assault," he said, propelling her down the dimly-lit passage. "I expect they will be at our gates by first light—with demands. Conditions they'll wish met by a certain time, or else. I intend to use that time to lay a trap for them."

Mariota dug in her heels, gaping at him. "A trap?"

He nodded. "A lure, if you will. A surefire means to draw them from Cuidrach to Dun Telve where I and what men I can spare will have done with them one black-hearted miscreant at a time."

"Dun Telve?" Mariota's brow arched. "The broch where you'd stashed your coin?"

"Just so." He smiled, his eyes glinting in the darkness. "They will not ken the coin pouches are no longer there and that an ambush awaits them. Greed will compel them to bargain. Your life in exchange for mine and the siller."

"Nay, 'tis madness," Mariota objected, her heart plummeting. "These men are hard-bitten, stiff-necked dastards well accustomed to waylaying and ill-doings. You will ne'er be able to lead them into a trap. They'll smell an ambush two glens away."

He looked at her, saying nothing for a time. "Mayhap you have the rights of it, but such is a risk I must take."

Mariota flinched, but he only shook his head and glanced at a narrow window cut high in the wall. Already the sky was beginning to pale, the night's dark giving way to a soft, luminous pearl.

"See you, the new day is almost upon us." He smoothed back her hair, drew his knuckles down her cheek. "There is not time to send a rider to my uncle for reinforcements. Eilean Creag is too distant, and—as you know—our walls may well be made of butter."

Mariota opened her mouth, but he raised a hand, silencing her.

"Luring them away is our only option. I will not risk letting them gain entry to the keep."

"You will be killed," she pushed the words past the hot burning in her throat. "Because of me, you and your men will be—"

"Do not underestimate me, lass," he said, disentangling himself when she clutched at him. "I may not have my uncle's vaunted skill with a sword, but I have my wits."

Mariota flushed. "I did not mean—"

"I know what you meant," he said, crushing her in his arms, urging her back against the cold stone of the passage wall, his mouth slanting hard over hers in a swift, furious kiss.

She locked her hands behind his neck, giving herself up to the frantic need raging inside her. A desperation as wild as his fierce, demanding kiss.

A possessive claiming, hot and hungry, fiery enough to send molten heat sluicing all through her even as it increased her dread.

A suffocating panic that welled inside her, darkening the edges of the sweet, golden warmth he'd brought her and threatening with a dark and ugly cold capable of extinguishing all light and joy from her life.

Cut her off at the knees . . . just when she was learning to walk again.

She shuddered, chills sweeping the length of her. She could not bear to lose him.

Not now when she loved so desperately, wished to cling greedily to every moment they had, burned for a *lifetime* of moments.

An eternity is what she wanted.

Not a cold-cast marble effigy to kneel at each night, her fingers stroking stone as she marveled at his valor, bathed his likeness with tears that could ne'er revive him.

He stiffened against her, setting her from him as if he sensed her doubt, felt and understood the icy terror digging its claws into her most vulnerable places.

"Ah, my Mariota minx, know well that I am not about to lose you. Not to marauders—not to . . . any man," he vowed, the words spoken so softly she was sure she'd imagined them.

"Wait!" She tugged on his arm. "What did you mean—"

"I was assuring you've no need to worry—about anything," he said, evading her true question as he urged her down the vaulted corridor. "The curtain walls and battlements will be manned, we'll drop the portcullis, such as it is, and even see extra bolts slid across all the outer doors."

"And if they scale the walls? Push through the larger gaps?" She gathered up her skirts to keep pace with him. "If you meant what I think you meant?"

He shot a glance at her, the look in his eyes telling her he did.

But the moment passed when several of his garrison men rushed by, their naked swords gleaming in the torch-light, their fierce-set faces making even the warrior laird's daughter's breath catch.

"See, lass, I told you—I have good men," the Keeper said, glancing after them. "My uncle gave me some of his best. Sir Lachlan was once his most favored squire, and later served as house knight to Sir Marmaduke. He learned much from those valiants, and thanks to his fore-sight, we already have a goodly supply of stones and quicklime stored along the wall-walk."

He stopped to give her another fast kiss. "We'll be ready for them before the first man breaks from the woods—scaling ladders or no."

"Do you not see?" Mariota shook her head. "Nessa and I can do so much—"

"You and Nessa shall be barricaded in the storeroom," he repeated, pulling her behind him down the turnpike stairs. "You will be safe there—and comfortable. There is surely enough time for you to gather enough foodstuffs and plaids for pallets."

Mariota sniffed, scarce hearing him.

Instead, her ears echoed with the shrieking yells of men rushing castle walls, the cries of the wounded and dying. The *zishing* whine of fire arrows, followed by the crackle and roar of burning pitch; the shudder and splin-tering of smashed wood.

Sounds she'd heard often enough at Dunach and other castles where her father had made his name. Nightmarish horrors she did not want to hear at Cuidrach.

Especially not at Cuidrach!

But her Keeper seemed unconcerned. Far from it, he fair thrummed with the surety of victory as he hastened her down the stairs.

"See you, lass, I will even open one of the wine barrels in the storeroom for you," he promised when they reached the foot of the stair tower. "If Providence is kind, everything will be over before you have time to worry."

"I am worried now." She caught at his arm. "I told you—'tis madness."

"Nay, it is the best we can do." He touched her face, smoothed her hair. "And whether you like it or no, it is the only option we have."

Mariota swallowed and said nothing.

The granite set of his jaw warned of the pointlessness of further objections.

And only made her all the more determined to find a better way. She did not have Archibald Macnicol's blood in her veins for naught.

Or so she hoped.

Chapter Fourteen

✦

Mariota fisted her hands against her hips and peered deep into Cuidrach's kitchen larder. "He's run crazy mad," she mumbled, leaning forward to rummage through the available food stores.

"Growing up with the father I had, I've likely seen more sieges than any man beneath this roof." She flashed an indignant look at Nessa. "And Kenneth MacKenzie knows it!"

"He would know you safe—as he told you," Nessa returned, looking annoyingly unperturbed as she stood beside the cook fire, jabbing at the logs with an iron poker. "It is good-hearted of him to want me in the storeroom with you. I will not forget his concern."

Mariota frowned. "His concern is misplaced," she said, digging deeper into the larder. "Womenfolk are always about during sieges. Who else sees to the wounded when they're brought in for tending? Who keeps the water boiling—as you are now doing? Makes a fuss and bother o'er the valiants when they need an uplifting word?"

"That may be so, my lady, but I vow your Keeper's thoughts are more on having us in a secure corner of the keep than any doubts about our usefulness." Nessa set her poker aside and pressed a hand to the small of her back. "We all know Hugh's men could saunter right up to our high table if they've a mind to it! Sir Kenneth wishes you out of harm's way if that happens."

Frustration began beating in Mariota's breast. "And what about *him*?"

She straightened, threw a hot look at her friend. "I am not pleased about his notion to lure them away. You know Ewan the Witty will ne'er fall for such a ploy."

Nessa snorted. "I would pit your Keeper against that one any day, my lady. Whether these walls are less than invincible or no!"

Mariota sighed. "Mayhap I worry because I have more at stake than you—I am in love with him, could not bear to . . . to—"

"And you think I love my Lachlan less?" Nessa eyed her across the kitchen. "Let us be glad they would know us in a safe corner. Truth is, many are the faint-hearts who'd be only too eager to hide away during a siege, spend those fraught-filled hours far from the chaos and bloodletting."

As if to underscore her point, she brushed at her skirts with unnecessary vigor. "Men and women!"

"You are surely right," Mariota conceded, her vexation spiking. "Even so, I would rather make myself . . . useful."

Determined to do just that, she tossed a cloth-wrapped bundle of salt herring into a large wicker creel on the kitchen's sturdy trestle table and looked around for other thirst-inducing delicacies she could add to her growing stash.

A pile of two-day-old bannocks caught her eye and were seized upon at once, soon to join the salt herring and twisted lengths of dried venison already languishing in her basket. It was a motley assortment of goods not lacking in taste on their own, but viands greatly enhanced by the addition of a thickly-smeared layer of butter or honey.

Embellishments she purposely left out of the innocent-looking basket.

Luckily, Nessa did not appear to notice.

That one seemed far too occupied filling endless barrels with scalding water and, much to Mariota's growing annoyance, extolling Sir Lachlan's knightly virtues.

"I say you," she gushed even now, her eyes going all soft again, "Lachlan will have that rabble of savages wishing they'd ne'er left their northern fastnesses! They'll rue the day they even glanced toward Kintail."

Mariota said nothing.

Nessa hooted.

Her dark eyes glittering, she snatched up her long iron poker and began jabbing at the cook fire with renewed gusto. "Ha, lady! We will soon see them running back to Assynt—and with their forked tails clapped between their legs. If our men let them go!"

"Och, to be sure." Mariota smoothed a cloth over the top of her basket. "The flat-footed louts will all follow Sir Kenneth to Dun Telve and allow themselves to be cut down one at time as they slink through the broch's low and narrow entry passage."

Feeling color rise in her face, she paused and strode to

the window and back again. "And those remaining will hie themselves away. They'll bolt straight back here to seize Cuidrach so soon as they realize our best men lay in wait inside the broch—or in the woods surrounding it!"

Nessa snorted.

"Cuidrach's garrison is large enough to man these walls and send a party to the broch," she argued. "Lachlan says the men are readying themselves even now. They'll be in place, well-armed and hidden, long before Hugh the Bastard's men make their first demands. They—"

"Have you forgotten the sheer number of Hugh's men?" Mariota reached for the basket of victuals, hefting it on her hip. "Far greater a garrison than we have here. In especial, if ours is split."

Nessa leaned the poker against the wall and dusted her hands. "Even so, Sir Kenneth's ploy is the surest tactic we have," she said, gathering up a pile of folded plaids. "If you were not so vexed about his wish to know us safely barricaded in the storeroom, you would see the sense of it."

"*Guid*sakes—I do see the sense of it. Would that I did not! And would that none of this was happening." Mariota swallowed at the agony jabbing holes in her heart. "Ach, Nessa, every man within these walls is about to take great hazards—mayhap even to the loss of life—and that, because of me."

She glanced aside. "That, my friend, is the way of it. And such is a sore burden."

Nessa frowned, flicked a speck of lint off the topmost of the plaids clutched against her breast. The hiss of the logs on the fire and the rolling boil of the kettle filled the silence, the sounds overloud in the warm, smoke-hazed room.

"Lachlan says the men are high of heart," she said at last, still worrying the plaid. "There is not a one amongst them who is not eager to take up his blade."

Mariota drew an uneven breath. "Aye, and in my honor."

And *that* was her problem.

She knew only too well what Cuidrach's men were risking and her own honor would not allow her to do any less for them.

Despite the difficulties.

Standing straight as she could with the food basket jammed against her hip, she gulped back the bile in her throat and wished for about the hundredth time that she'd fled Drumodyn in any direction but the route she'd taken.

Truth tell, she'd barter her soul if she had!

The sweetest bliss under the heavens was not worth the darkness she'd brought to Cuidrach's door.

To a man who'd yearned for only peace and quiet living in his beloved Kintail. And now found himself facing the worst pack of snakes to e'er crawl out of the heather.

She saw him now, in her heart, imagined him up on the parapet-walk or in one of the topmost rooms of the gatehouse tower, waiting. Dark, bold-eyed, and daring, so full of life. Her stomach clenched on the image, her blood running cold.

E'er seeing him *otherwise* was a thought so unbearable she could scarce breathe.

Indeed, the horror of it nigh lamed her.

She loved—and needed him—that much.

"Lachlan says there isn't a man within these walls who wouldn't face down the Devil for you," Nessa blurted, making it worse.

Not trusting her voice, Mariota bit her lip, trying not to wince as guilt-laced dread coiled in her belly.

She tightened her grip on the basket—a sop to her conscience. The carefully chosen delicacies her sole chance to make amends.

But Nessa, Fiend take her, was having none of it.

"O-o-oh, aye, my lady. They are stalwarts and valiants, every one," she enthused, eyeing Mariota with a look that made her grip the basket even more fiercely. "Gallant as any boldly-mounted champion thundering down the lists with his lady's favor flying from his lance."

"Aye, to be sure, men of great valor." Mariota could not have agreed more.

She almost wished it were . . . otherwise.

But it wasn't, so she turned toward the kitchen door before her friend could see the brightness beginning to burn and blur her vision.

The little storeroom off the hall awaited her, no cheering banks of gleeful joust spectators.

Just an overly-besotted, well-meaning friend, an auburn-haired youthful giant of a door sentinel, and a stump-toothed, aged dog.

Everyone else was already in position to greet fate.

Or their Maker, saints forbid.

"I see you frowning—even with your back turned." Nessa's voice carried across the kitchen. "You needn't fash yourself. The men—"

"My mind is on men cut of a different cloth than ours." Mariota paused outside the kitchen arch, her palms damping as she waited for Nessa to join her.

Faith, Kenneth had hinted Sir Lachlan might wish to wed Nessa. Yet now, such a possibility balanced on a sword's edge, the whim of a speeding arrow. Unthinkable, if the good-hearted, dark-eyed garrison captain was suddenly ripped forever from her friend's life.

"'Tis pleased I am to hear you call my men *ours*, my lady."

Mariota jumped, whirled round.

Her Keeper was leaning against the passage wall, smiling at her. "Aye, mayhap it wasn't necessary for me to come looking for you if you are already thinking thusly!"

"I-I thought you were on the battlements?" she gasped, her heart lodged so firmly in her throat she could scarce get the words out.

The creel she was clutching near crashed to the floor.

"O-o-ooh, lassie, you mustn't spill your provisions," he purred, whisking the heavy basket from her with lightning speed. "That would not do. And"—he cocked a brow—"I see your ears are filled with wax again?"

"Wax?" Mariota blinked. "In my ears?"

He nodded and set down her basket. "Just that, my lady," he said, resting his hands on her shoulders. "Something seems to keep you from understanding what I say to you. And, in light of an imminent siege, I thought I'd not only escort you to the storeroom, but inquire if you've at last seen through what I said to you earlier?"

Mariota bit her lip, remembering indeed.

He'd spoken words that had made her weak-kneed, breathless with hope. And he was doing it again now.

"Do you mean something you said about . . . marauders?" Her face began to burn . . . nay, her *eyes*. "Something about not losing me to such men?"

"Ahhh, less wax than I thought," he said, his tone and

the way he was looking at her making her heart fill with joy. "But not quite what I meant."

He captured her face in his hands and gave her a swift kiss. "Can you no do better, lass?"

Mariota's eyes began misting in earnest. She had trouble wrapping her tongue around the words. "Y-you said you would not lose me to . . . any man."

"Indeed, that is what I said—and meant." He slid his arms around her, drawing her close. "And why I was pleased to hear you call my men . . . *ours*."

Mariota dashed a hand over her cheek and wet her lips. "Are you telling me there will not be any riders heading out to prospective suitors?"

He nodded. "I am saying there will be but one suitor, lady, and there is no need to send a rider looking for him, for he is already here, standing before you."

"Oh dear saints," Mariota gasped, her composure breaking. "I do not know what to say . . . thought this Sir Dunc—"

"That one will dance at our wedding, lass, I promise you—if you will have me?" He clutched her to him, holding her so tight she could feel the thundering of his heart. "I meant to wait, see you? Until the spring. Thought to woo you properly, but . . ."

He paused, glancing over his shoulder, as sworded garrison men hurried past behind them. "I will still give you time, lass. So long as you need, just say you'll consider me and I'll—"

"*Consider you?* I would have no other!" she cried, her tears spilling freely now. "Dear saints, I ne'er thought—"

"Ach, dinna mind me if I say some of us *did* think," Nessa beamed, coming through the open kitchen arch.

"And not before time! 'Tis long I've waited to see such a smile on my lady's face again."

Kenneth turned to her. "Lady, I would see her wear such a smile on all of her tomorrows, but for the now, I must take you both to the storeroom."

He pressed a quick kiss to Mariota's brow and picked up her basket. "We will speak when this is past," he said, glancing at her as he led them down the passage. "I've been away from my men too long and must get back to them."

Mariota hastened after him, his words minding her of his plan to lead Hugh the Bastard's men into an ambush. She shuddered anew, the very idea jelling her knees so badly she could scarce keep up with him on the stairs.

He was making a grave error to think they'd be easily fooled or maneuvered.

But neither would he.

One reason she thanked the saints he'd chosen the unassuming little storeroom as her refuge.

And especially that he'd ordered young Jamie to stand guard outside the door and not within.

Indeed, the strapping young knight stood there now, his dog sprawled at his feet. Tall and splendid, Jamie's hand rested lightly on his sword-hilt and every inch of him looked a fine, Highland gallant. His auburn hair gleamed in the torchlight, but his handsome face flushed even brighter at their approach.

"Ladies. Sir Kenneth." He jerked a bow and snatched his hand from his blade. "I greet you—and hope all is to your satisfaction within."

Mariota touched a hand to his mailed sleeve, her throat still too tight for words.

"You will be safe within," Jamie said to her. "While I am not the most battle-probed man in the garrison, I can swing a blade with the rest of them."

"You are a fine sworder—one of the best I have seen," she praised him. "We shall ne'er forget your valor."

"Nor I, lad." Kenneth clapped a hand on his shoulder. "Guard them well." Turning to Mariota, he bracketed her face with his hands and leaned close to brush his lips across hers. "Be safe, my sweet. Jamie will look after you until I return for you."

And with that he hastened away, his long strides carrying him across the hall to his gathering men.

Young Jamie waited until he was gone, then flipped back his plaid to reveal two naked dirks thrust beneath his bolt. "I'm armed for whate'er comes at me and I'll be here until this is done. No one will get past me."

He flashed a smile of dimpled charm and opened the storeroom door with a bit of a flourish. "And if I lose my weapons, I've got two strong hands, so dinna either of you worry!"

"And we will not," Mariota said, clutching her basket again.

She had a plan to assuage her worries.

And Nessa, bless her, would soon be rendered oblivious to fretting of *any* nature.

But the simple words seemed to please the young knight and he made a gallant show of ushering them into the chamber. Not to be bested, Cuillin pushed to his feet and padded in after them.

The old dog made himself comfortable at once, plopping down in front of a tiny, red-glowing brazier. The only halfway warm spot in the room.

Two rushlights burned in wall brackets near the door and someone had placed a small, rough-hewn table and two three-legged stools against the wall. And an earthen-ware jug and two wooden mugs on the table signaled that true to her Keeper's word, someone had opened one of the wine casks.

A more thorough glance showed an animal skin and a folded, somewhat tattered plaid on the floor in a corner, clearly meant for Cuillin's comfort. A thoughtful gesture underscored by the large bowl of water and several well-beefed meat bones lying nearby.

Not that the old dog would budge from his chosen place before the coal brazier.

Otherwise, the little room appeared much as it had the last time she'd been here—when she'd discovered the secret stairs and what she hoped would prove to be a warren of subterranean passages cut into the living rock beneath Cuidrach.

A way out—if only she could induce Nessa to eat enough salt herring and dry bannocks.

And if her friend's ensuing thirst caused her to drink as much of the heady Gascon wine as Mariota hoped she would.

She felt a throb of guilt, wished such measures weren't necessary.

Praying that all would go as planned, she waited until young Jamie left, then leaned back against the closed door and let out her breath.

To her delight, Nessa was already seated at the little table, a butter-less bannock in her hand, a cup of wine at her elbow.

Mariota watched her eat and bit back a smile.

Especially when Nessa plucked a particularly long twist of dried venison from the food basket.

Already, the innocent-looking crack down the opposite wall beckoned.

If she could locate the right underground passage and exit the thing anywhere outside Cuidrach's walls, she was sure she'd be able to find Hugh's men before they loosed a single fire arrow.

She was their prize, after all.

Not a half-ruinous pile of stone and men with whom they had no grievances.

She also possessed enough wit to lead them in circles until Kenneth could send for help from his uncle at Eilean Creag. Once those additional men reached Cuidrach, she knew they'd come looking for her.

Or she'd escape on her own.

For the nonce, all that mattered was getting *out* of Cuidrach, not back in.

If all else failed, she'd think of some feint to employ on Jamie and—

"Oh dear saints!" Chills racing through her, she closed her eyes, Jamie's bright red hair filling her mind.

The little red fox also returned to haunt her.

The creature's glossy fur had gleamed in the moonlight, shone with the same brilliance and color as James Macpherson's proud auburn mane.

Even now, she could still see the fox flitting over the rocks, disappearing in and out of a dark and mysterious gap in a certain rough-stoned outcropping.

And with the memory, came surety.

At last, she knew where Cuidrach's secret passage would lead her. She was certain of it, and the location could not have suited her better.

She need only bide her time.

That, and hope Nessa gorged herself on salt herring and wine.

About the same time, but across wind-tossed waves and surf-beaten shores, the Hebridean Isle of Doon lay in silent slumber. Thick mist rolled in from sea, darkening the sky and turning day to deepest, impenetrable night until no place could have appeared more lonely. Or so full of the echo of older, darker times.

Indeed, the lovely isle that usually rose so blue from the sea took on an eerie silver-black hue, and hills that were e'er praised as romantic and picturesque, now bore a creeping, ominous tinge.

A cold chill swept Doon as well, tearing across the bogs and black pools of the moors. Not that all Doon's folk noted the dark wind's passing.

Devorgilla, in particular, remained in blissful ignorance.

Doon's far-famed *cailleach* and wise woman since before time was, the indomitable crone slept peaceably within the thick, white-washed walls of her cottage. Leastways, she rested so comfortably as her somewhat lumpy pallet of dried heather and bracken allowed.

Snoring lightly, for she'd imbibed a bit more heather ale than was good for a woman of her years, she paid no heed to bumps in her pallet. Not that she would have cared if she did notice them. Too pleasing were her dreams of fearless warriors and magical otherworlds, the wondrous feats of Celtic gods and heroes.

And, as always, her small but tidy dwelling place wrapped her in goodness and quiet, the air pleasantly scented with peat and pungent herbs.

Nay, it was the glaring light burning her tightly-squeezed eyelids that vexed her, trodding so rudely over her much-needed sleep.

Deep *morning* sleep, for at her impressive age, a soul was entitled to slumber when they wished.

And after a long night of spelling and working charms straight through to the small hours, Devorgilla wanted naught more than to sleep.

She would, too.

If it weren't for the infernal light.

A persistent, pulsing *glow* that was spreading through the whole of her cottage.

That she knew without even prying open one tired eyelid.

Determined to remain undisturbed, she rolled onto her side, flung a knotty-elbowed arm over her grizzled head.

Not that it made a whit of difference.

One slit-eyed glance at her two deep-set windows proved what she already knew.

The morn was so gray, so damp and mist-hung, she doubted she'd be able to see her hand in front of her face were she to force her age-stiffened legs to carry her outside.

The eerie glow came from within her cottage.

Truth tell, she didn't even need to look to be certain.

She could *feel* the light seeping into every nook and cranny, inching its blaring brilliance up the walls and across her black-raftered ceiling, every bright, throbbing beat of it stealing her sleep and minding her ancient bones of something she ought not be forgetting.

If only she could remember.

But then she did.

"Daughter of a moonless night!" Her breath catching, she pushed up on an elbow and peered across the room at the only object capable of giving off such light.

But the golden lute resting on her table didn't blaze with the bright, sun-white glare she'd expected. Instead, it shimmered with a soft, luminous glow.

A glow that beckoned in its warmth and lulled with the gently swirling mist flowing over and around the lute's sleek, jewel-encrusted lines.

But even as she stared, her heart knocking in excitement, the mist began to spin, whirling into a column of shimmering light that disappeared inside the lute before she could even blink.

Slack-jawed, she nudged the tri-colored cat curled so close to her heart. "Mab—old lass! Did you see that?" she cried, her eyes widening as the mist reappeared on the lute's side.

Even Mab took notice, arching to her feet to fix the lute with a sharp, feline stare.

Heaving herself to her own feet, Devorgilla pressed a hand to her hip and hobbled to the table. Awe filling her, she clutched its edge and looked on as the mist lost all luminosity.

No longer glowing, it thickened and spread, billowing like an eerie, grayish fog until the lute vanished into its hazy depths.

"Goddess have mercy," she breathed, only half aware of old Mab rubbing against her legs, the feline's loud purring.

Mab only ever purred when *good* magic was underfoot.

Too aged and fond of her comfort to tolerate peculiarities of any other kind, Mab would still be snuggled in the warmth of the pallet plaiding if the swirling mist held danger.

So Devorgilla leaned close, poked at the mist with a crooked finger. "Come," she coaxed, "show me your secrets."

But when a gap appeared in the whirling grayness, only the well-worn wood of the naked tabletop came into view.

If she was even looking at her table, for it seemed to have narrowed to a mere *haft*. Long, smooth, and anything but naked, the well-used wood appeared marred by numberless little notches.

Tiny gashes cut into the shaft of the most fearsome battle-ax she'd ever seen.

A *Norseman's* ax—or such as carried by only the most ferocious warrior men.

"Mab!" Realization hit her hard, splitting her heart with joy and relief. "Och, lass, the fates have been kind— our prayers heard," she crooned, reaching down to gather her little friend into her arms.

And as she stroked Mab's silky-warm fur, another gap in the mist appeared and a large, age-spotted hand reached for the ax. An older man's hand, to be sure, but a strong hand, its grip firm and true.

Unerring.

As was the overwhelming sense of love and forgiveness that flooded the cottage as the old warrior's fingers clenched around the notched shaft.

But before Devorgilla could even swipe at the tears damping her furrowed cheeks, the mist cleared, its vanishing tendrils taking the hand and the ax back whence they'd come.

Nothing remained save the lingering emotion of a lonely man who was braw enough to admit when he'd been wrong.

And hoped to reclaim what he'd lost.

"Ach, Mab." Devorgilla sniffed, blinked the moisture from her eyes. "I do think I'm getting too soft for such meddling."

But as she shuffled back to her pallet, she knew such was simply her lot in life.

And ne'er in a thousand tomorrows would she wish it otherwise.

Chapter Fifteen

✦

Kenneth went to the gatehouse window and peered out into the morning gloom. A light rain fell and mists gathered, slow-drifting curtains that cloaked the hills and thickened the soft, damp air. And as always, the Bastard Stone loomed dark and frowning above Loch Hourn, the cliff's black face and door-like arch minding of the ancient tragedy.

Cormac's legacy, a brooding heritage now his own.

He swallowed, a sense of belonging such as he would ne'er have believed possible making his breath catch and his heart swell with purpose.

Especially now.

I would have no other. His lady's words filled his mind, the joy and wonder he'd heard in them, overwhelming him. He curled his hands to fists and closed his eyes, something inside him tightening and warming, a glowing happiness such as he'd never known.

Opening his eyes, he stared long and hard at Cormac's

nemesis. A new calamity would *not* unfold in the Bastard Stone's shadow.

Not now, in the morning of his life.

And with surety, not a disaster with *her* name on it.

He'd see to that, he vowed, his gaze passing from the heights of that dark-tinged promontory to the loch's rocky shore. A stretch of stony silence with nary a sign or stir of life showing, yet menace lurked near.

Of that, he was certain.

The prickly chills at the back of his neck warned him—as did the continued quiet.

The same eerie hush that had robbed his sleep.

A stillness so deep he'd almost believe all of Kintail watched and waited, holding its breath to see how well the new Keeper *kept* Cuidrach's peace.

Determined to do that and more, he scanned the trees, the skirts of the hills. "Nothing," he said, straining his eyes. "Just a rolling sea of mist and mizzling rain."

"Bah! Mist, rain, and scab-headed despoilers of innocents, I'd wager," one of the garrison men tossed back as he passed by on his way to the parapet wall-walk.

Those remaining voiced hearty accord.

Agreeing as well, Kenneth turned from the window, faced the men bustling about the crowded room.

Mailed and armored men who fussed and fidgeted, fingering the hilts of their swords as they, too, peered out the tower room's windows.

A bearded man, older and barrel-chested, snatched up an ale flask and drank deep. "Tchach! A pox on 'em, I say!"

He slammed down the flask and looked around at the others. "They will have to show some movement soon—

if only to cut and gather gorse and brushwood to torch our door."

"Hah!" another shot back. "They'll no bother to smoke us out when they can just stroll through the holes in yon curtain walls!"

Kenneth frowned.

A small party of his own men were out there now, scrounging about in the mist and rain to collect armloads of gorse and whate'er else might catch quick flame.

Their last-ditch defense if all went wrong—the self-burning of the wooden stairs to their own keep!

Something he did not want to see happen.

But he would—if such measures were needed.

He rubbed a hand down over his mouth and chin, hoping his instincts about the day were wrong.

The day simply . . . odd.

Shadowed, as some days were. Especially in dark and lonely reaches like Glenelg.

He looked out the window again. Nothing had changed. "Ne'er in all broad Scotland have I seen a more still morn," he said, turning back to his men. "Perhaps we are letting a shift in the weather confound us?"

But he knew otherwise.

As did his men—he saw it on their faces.

" 'Tis the hush that e'er falls before a battle. Naught else!" The barrel-chested man reached for the flask again, took a swig, and offered it round. "I've been in enough to know."

"Colm has the rights of it. They will come," Sir Lachlan agreed. He stood by the door to the battlements, but now stepped forward. "I feel it in my bones—can smell their putrid breath."

"And I can feel the heat of their stares," Kenneth agreed.

No matter that a thin rain blew off the loch. The chill wind couldn't banish the scorching fury.

"Aye, hot anger brews out there." Sir Lachlan went to a vacant window and looked out. "Whether the dastards mean to take their time showing themselves or no."

But just when he moved to turn away, the sudden winding of a horn shattered the quiet.

Loud and ululant, the sound shrilled as a huge, broad-built man spurred from the shadows.

"By the Rood—here they are!" Kenneth swore, watching the rider's arrogant approach.

Rough-hewn and draped in a wet, ragged-looking plaid, the man cantered to within easy bow-shot of the gatehouse and raised a booming voice. "Ho! MacKenzie! A word—if you would see this day progress so peaceably as it began!"

"And who speaks so bold?" Kenneth threw back. "I already see the style of you. I would hear your name e'er we exchange . . . words."

"As you will." The big man shrugged, rode closer. "I am Ewan the Witty, garrison captain of Drumodyn Castle in Assynt, the holding of the murdered Hugh Alesone, Bastard of Drumodyn."

"And what is your business here? In my territories?" Kenneth leaned out the window, staring down at the man. "Your liege's name is not known in these parts."

"Mayhap not, but I'll wager the name of his murderess is!" The man sneered up at Kenneth. "'Tis she I seek! The Lady Mariota—Mariota Macnicol of Dunach. Wagging tongues claim you've given her refuge."

Kenneth tensed, his fists clenching. "Prattling tongues do not always speak true. But if the lady is here, 'tis no concern of yours."

"Ha—there speaks a man besotted!" Ewan the Witty barked a laugh and slapped his thigh. "I say you, MacKenzie, hand her over. The lass will have done with you in your sleep. Dirk you in your own bed—after you've pleasured her! Forby, she carries the blood of two men on her hands!"

"'Tis your own blood you'll soon be seeing if you do not mind your tongue, good sir." Kenneth pressed his hands on the window ledge, leaning forward again. "Every stone of this keep will have to fall into the sea before I'd hand over *any* lady to the likes of you."

Ewan the Witty harrumphed. "From the looks of it, your holding already *is* falling into the sea!"

A chorus of hoots and guffaws rose from the trees. A brief outburst, but enough to reveal just how many men rimmed the wood's edge, hid themselves on the slopes.

"Did you hear them, sir?" One of his younger knights edged near. "They sound to be thrice our number."

Kenneth grimaced, keeping his attention on the rider below. "Hear me, you," he yelled to the man, "I'm in no mood for such . . belly-aching this early in the day. I have more to do with my time—as you can see! But if you think to test my strength, then be on with it."

He leaned farther out the window, flashed a challenging smile. "But be warned—when you leave here, some of you might find yourselves shortened by a head!"

This time his men laughed, but already scores of would-be besiegers men streamed down the hills or edged their mounts out from beneath the trees.

Brutish-looking, plaid-hung caterans, many with mail glinting beneath their tartans, they formed a great semicircle behind their leader.

All looked armed to the teeth.

"What say you now, MacKenzie?" Ewan the Witty smirked up at the gatehouse tower. "Some might say the lady's fate doesn't fall to you to decide."

"Others might say we shall see," Kenneth called back. "Aye, my friend, you have been warned—the worse for you if you misjudge my strength."

Sir Lachlan joined him at the window. "Have a care—and keep him talking," he cautioned, low-voiced. "The longer he and his men blether before the door of the gatehouse, the better our chances of getting the others safely out the postern gate. With good fortune, they can be at Dun Telve long before you arrive with yon blackguards."

He clapped a hand on Kenneth's shoulder. "*If* they take your bait."

"They will bite." Kenneth placed his hand over his captain's and squeezed. "I spent too many years with sea merchants and traders not to recognize greed when I see it. That one would cut the throat of his own grandmother for less than a handful of siller."

"Saints of mercy—your strength?" Ewan the Witty burst into laughter again. "I'd not wager on such false hope were I you," he roared. "Your holding is ruinous, the curtain walls looking to crumble at the next good wind. I vow your keep will prove even easier to topple! Think hard before you refuse to let us have the woman. Your raised drawbridge is worm-eaten and half-rotted, and a bairn could breach your portcullis."

Kenneth slid a glance at Sir Lachlan. "Braggart loon. We ought to fire a red-hot bolt right through him—now, before he knows what hit him."

"Let me, sir." The younger knight put his shoulders back, swelling his chest. "I'd send a bolt right through his honey hole, I would!"

"Dinna think to launch arrows at us," the lout below yelled then, almost as if he'd heard their exchange. "We have ropes and grappling hooks. And know this—we are as many as sands on the shore. For each of us that you might shoot down, another score will rise to take his place!"

He spurred closer, raised a balled fist. "Yield the lady and we shall leave in peace. Your lives will be spared and your moldering keep left intact—such as it is!"

Sir Lachlan gripped Kenneth's elbow. "*Now,*" he urged. "Make your bid."

Kenneth pressed his lips together, heat flashing all through him. "God's bones, Lachlan," he seethed, "you ken—there's naught I wouldn't give to know my lady safe. I want her secure and happy. Mayhap even more than I care for my own life. Certainly, my pride. But . . ." He paused, blowing out a breath.

What was pride, or even Cuidrach, when she had but to cross a room and all else ceased to exist?

Truth was, he'd fallen irrevocably in love with her. She was his treasure and reason. His life. And any price, no matter how dear or galling, was worth saving her from the men gathered around his walls.

"That ruffian speaks true words, my friend." Lachlan squeezed Kenneth's elbow, manly commiseration in his dark eyes. "We all know Cuidrach won't hold against them. Let that reality sweeten what you must do."

"Damnation," Kenneth swore, his gut tightening all the same. "I say you, I've supped with the Devil before, and more times than I would have liked. But ne'er with such a short spoon!"

But he turned back to the window, raised his voice. "So, Ewan of Drumodyn. You vow to leave us in peace if we surrender the lady. How say you if I offer you something of greater value than her worth?"

He paused, the words hot daggers in his heart, making him feel dirty inside.

Ewan the Witty spat and dragged his arm over his bearded face. "What could be of more worth than that one's murderous neck? Seeing my lord's death avenged at last?"

But a spark of interest flickered across the man's upturned face. Indeed, the rat's eyes glittered like a serpent's.

Bile heavy on his tongue, Kenneth again lifted his voice. "What is of more worth? I say you—a fortune to line your coffers and your men's for the rest of your days?"

Silence followed, but not before the wretch flashed Kenneth a triumphant smile.

"A blood deed requires payment in kind—and the lady is also marked as a sacrifice to Assynt's Each Uisge. Her value is high. Mayhap too high for the likes of you!" He stared up at Kenneth, made a show of scratching his beard. "But your offer is worth . . . considering!"

Before Kenneth could reply, the big man swung round to confer with his men. When he wheeled back again, the unmistakable gleam of greed lit the whole of his coarse features.

"How great a fortune do you have in mind, Keeper of Cuidrach?" he demanded, and Kenneth's pulse leapt at the excitement in the man's eyes.

Smelling victory, Kenneth leaned through the window arch, hoped his own expression wasn't quite so revealing. "For you—enough bags of good Scots siller to purchase ten of your Drumodyn Castle. And for myself—your word that you will leave Kintail and ne'er set foot here again."

"Hech! You cast tall promises, Bastard MacKenzie." Ewan the Witty cocked his head, his eyes narrowing. "See you, I am an honest man, true to my friends and firm to my word. But why should I trust yours?"

"Because . . ." Kenneth drew a long breath, wished he weren't so aware of the dampness of his palms. ". . . My coin is not kept here," he lied, certain the untruth stood emblazoned across his forehead.

"My wealth is . . . otherwise, and I shall lead you there. If you are not satisfied by the number of coin pouches and how well-filled they are, I'll forfeit myself as hostage—for the continued safekeeping of my lady."

He paused, taking another deep breath "And you may do with me what you will. Ransom me to my uncle, Duncan MacKenzie, the Black Stag of Kintail. Or truss and toss me to your foul water horse. I care not. So long as my lady is left unmolested and in peace."

"Oh ho! Lord save us!" Ewan the Witty burst into laughter again, threw a look of feigned astonishment at his men. "I *knew* the man was besotted! And that raises the lady's value, I say!"

He tilted back his head, fixed Kenneth with a calculating stare. "Your coin and the golden lute—and we shall leave you be. Both of you!"

The golden lute?

Kenneth's heart plummeted. He spun toward Sir Lachlan. "What's the raving loon mean by that?"

"You know the tale," Sir Lachlan minded him. "He means the bejeweled lute some traveling bardess gave my Nessa. She told us about it one night not long after we arrived here. She used the lute to help the Lady Mariota escape Drumodyn's dungeon."

Kenneth's brows snapped together. Now he remembered. "But Nessa said she'd left the thing behind when they fled Assynt. This fool thinks we have it."

"Then let him think we do." Sir Lachlan slanted a glance out the window. "Anything to bide time. Tell him the lute is too precious and you must think before answering. Give him two hours. By then we will have finished all siege preparations and our other men will be in place at Dun Telve. With God's good mercy, we'll rout these fools."

"Well, MacKenzie?" Ewan the Witty's booming voice echoed around the tower room. "What is the lady worth to you?"

Kenneth blew out a hot breath. What was his lady's worth, the cateran dared ask.

More than a thousand golden lutes—and even the last breath in his body, Kenneth's heart roared.

He swallowed hard and steeled himself. "Sirrah, that lute is beyond price! All else, I will forfeit to you—but the lute . . ."

Letting his words tail off, he shook his head. "Nay, my

friend, I must think on it. Two hours, if you are willing? Then, I will answer you."

"Hah!" Ewan the Witty hooted a laugh. "A man after my heart, after all. Good, so be it. Two hours it is. But I warn you—not a moment longer."

Kenneth nodded, lifted his hand in token agreement. "Two hours."

Ewan the Witty raised his fist in return, then spurred back to his men. And so soon as the last one vanished into the trees, Kenneth slumped against the window arch and released the breath he'd been holding.

Two hours.

They seemed like a lifetime.

And if he used them well, they *would* be.

For himself and his heart's treasure, the woman he intended to make his wife.

Mariota tucked a plaid around her slumbering friend's knees and draped another across her shoulders. Such was the best she could do—the only succor she could offer without risking Nessa's sleep.

A blessedly deep-seeming sleep and one that filled Mariota with uneasy shame.

Especially with Nessa's snores tingeing the air with the fumes of potent Gascon wine.

The scatter of butter-less bannock crumbs littering the small table also jabbed at her, as did the half-eaten twist of dried venison and the remains of a large portion of salt herring. Anything but a shriveled stick of a woman, Nessa always overate when nervous.

But this time she'd indulged more than Mariota would have wished.

Even so, better to know her sprawled across the table, sleeping peaceably, her head cushioned on her arms, than to have Nessa full by her wits and insisting on accompanying her.

Or worse, attempting to prevent her from going.

Still, Mariota regretted the sore head that would surely plague her upon waking.

She suffered such an affliction already.

But *her* temple-throbbing malaise vanished with lightning speed when she caught his voice at the door!

Heart pounding, she swiped the remains of Nessa's feast into the food basket, covering it with a plaid in the same moment the door opened and her Keeper strode inside.

"Kenneth!" she cried, her knees watering at the sight of him. "I-I thought you were on the walls?"

"And so I was, but now I am here. If briefly." He pulled her into his arms and kissed her, a fiercely heated kiss that stunned and exhilarated her.

She flung her arms around his neck and kissed him back, her pulse leaping when he crushed her even tighter against him. The little storeroom vanished in a brilliant splintering of light, the very world around her seeming to spin wildly each time his tongue swept against hers.

She clung to him, almost dizzy, giddy with relief . . . until she remembered two little words.

If briefly.

At once, the world stopped spinning and she forced herself to break the kiss, pull away to stare at him. "What did you mean 'if briefly'? I thought the confrontation with Hugh's men was over?" she gasped, her heart thundering. "I heard the shouting and then it stopped. I thou—"

"A thinking time, lass. That is what this is—no more." He cupped her face in his hands, smoothed his thumbs over her cheeks. "I can stay but a moment—I must return to my men—but I wanted you to have this . . ."

He produced a wicked-looking dirk from beneath his plaid and slapped it onto the table. "I meant to give it to you earlier. That is why I went to the kitchens, but—"

"I do not want your dagger. I want you to tell me you aren't going to ride out and lead these men into a trap!" Mariota grabbed his arm, held tight. "I've told you—"

He touched his fingers to her mouth, silencing her. "The first part of ridding you of these blackguards was our victory, my lady. Do not diminish it by doubting we'll succeed at the next round."

"But—"

"I must return to the gatehouse," he said with a glance at Nessa. "When your friend wakens, mayhap the two of you can pass the time making plans for our wedding feast? I'd like it to be in the spring."

He tweaked her chin, smiled at her. "A big celebration with all of my family there and . . . yours."

"Oh, Kenneth!" Mariota reached for him, but a sudden rush of scalding tears blinded her and she grasped only air.

The Keeper of Cuidrach had gone, closing the door soundly behind him.

Dashing the tears from her cheeks, she glanced at the dirk, deciding to leave it for Nessa, then went straight to the far wall. She ran her fingers along the crack until the wall shifted and gave way, the secret door swiveling open with a shuddering groan and a cloud of stone dust.

Fine, gritty dust that made her nose twitch and her eyes burn, but so long as Nessa slept on and Cuillin didn't bestir himself too much, all would be well.

But the aging beast was already pushing to his feet. He lumbered across the room, leaned into her with all his bony weight.

"Ah, laddie." Mariota dropped to her knees and gathered him close, clinging to his neck. "Watch o'er yourself and my friend, you hear?" She pulled back with reluctance, a wrench she hadn't counted on. "I'll reward you with the best morsels of meat when I return."

If she returned, the dog's unexpected whimpers seemed to say, his liquid gaze going past her to the dark gap in the wall.

"I'll be back," she assured him, gave him another quick hug.

A fierce one borne of doubts and fears she refused to acknowledge.

But she had to go.

Now, before his whines wakened Nessa.

A thinking time, her Keeper had said.

A brief respite before a true assault began. A hopelessly one-sided attack she meant to prevent.

Just as she couldn't allow him to make good his doomed-to-failure plan of ambushing men who could instruct others in the art!

Whimpering old dogs or no.

And regardless of whether she suddenly felt as useful as a leaf in the wind. She'd simply make certain that leaf landed in the right place.

Determined to do just that, she lifted one of the rush-lights from its iron holder and stepped right through the opening in the wall. The door swung shut with surprising ease, but the cold dark of the passage hit her like a fist to the gut, its musty dankness rushing her, cloying as a shroud.

Debris cluttered the stone steps. Fetid bits of straw, centuries of decayed leaves, blown in through small openings and cracks in the downward-sloping wall. Refuse that squished and slid beneath her feet, giving her shudders.

But she clutched the rushlight and edged forward, one careful step at time until she reached the stair foot and the passage broadened into low-ceilinged circular room.

Several vaulted corridors stretched away into impene-trable darkness, their sloping floors slicked with damp, the rough-hewn walls streaked with glistening, black-green slime, the ceilings dripping thick swaths of cob-webs.

Three passageways. Each one unappealing as a naked blade pressed to her throat.

Mariota closed her eyes, willing her pulse to slow, her breath to steady. Then she listened, caught the drip of water, the distant lapping of waves, in the passage to her left.

Loch Hourn and the shore.

Not the way she needed to go.

Tilting her head, she listened deeper, hearing the absolute stillness in the middle passage. A thick, unmoving quiet, weighed down with centuries of disuse.

Emotion tightening her chest, she turned to the pas-sage to her right, imagined faint rustlings from somewhere within its depths . . . the kind of stirrings made by the slight currents of air.

Air she could almost feel against her cheek. A delicate, almost imperceptible breeze laced with the minutest trace of gorse, rich Highland earth and Caledonian pine.

The kind of pines that grew in a dark cluster not far from the great outcropping of rocks she'd glimpsed from her bedchamber window.

There, where she'd seen the fox.

And where her every instinct told her she'd find Hugh Alesone's men.

A certainty beyond all doubt when, after hurrying through a long, narrow passage, she came to the rotted remains of an ancient ironbound door.

Watery gray light streamed through gaps in the door's moldering wood and she instantly recognized the hollowed, cave-like inside of the outcropping beyond and the clatter of hooves and weaponry, the upraised voices and clumping feet of a gathering of men.

A large gathering of men.

Loud and angry.

And they'd be even more riled when they saw her. But it couldn't be helped, so she squeezed through the largest opening in the ruined door, then hitched up her skirts and scrambled out from the jumbled pile of rocks.

"The blessed saints—'tis herself!" Ewan the Witty's booming voice echoed off the swirling mist.

He grabbed her, his fierce grip righting her when she slithered on the mud-slicked ground. "The Bastard's own whore come to pay her respects!"

"Who would've guessed the likes of that?" another put in, eyeing her from beneath the dripping pine boughs.

"The lady and her shadow, a-falling o'er us now—after all our stumbling and groping through these God-accursed hills."

"Devil-damned is more like it." Ewan snatched the rushlight from her and tossed it into a dark-watered tarn where it disappeared with a *zish* and a plume of oily smoke.

"I'll own there's one scrawny-necked fool amongst us who ought to thank his Maker he did not send us false . . . this time," he snapped, addressing his men, but glaring at her from under shaggy, down-drawn brows. "I've had enough of that one and his fool red fox chasing us into bogs and brambles!"

A red fox?

Mariota bit back a gasp of surprise, disguising it with a cough.

"My being here has naught to do with Wee Finlay." She stood as straight as she could with Ewan's fingers digging into her arm, correctly guessing which man bore the big one's wrath. "And I know nothing of a fox."

She lifted her chin. "I came because your quarrel is not with those at Cuidrach, but with me. I will not see others suffer when I am the one you seek."

"Ho!" Ewan the Witty snorted. "Noble words for a murderess."

The others glowered and leered, one even reaching to pinch her breasts, much to the amusement of the rest.

Only Wee Finlay didn't laugh.

Small and stunted as Mariota remembered him, he stood with the horses at a nearby burnside, feeding them oats and watching as they cropped the tussocky grass.

He took a few steps forward, thrust out his chin.

"Whether she dirked Hugh or nay, she didn't steal your damnable lute. That was the fox, I'm telling you. The selfsame one that led us here."

Ewan patted his sword hilt. "Be glad the glen folk finally counted the alewife's ravishing as a good enough sacrifice for the Each Uisge," he charged, his eyes narrowing on the little man. "I swear I'd toss you to the beast myself were it otherwise—and I might yet!"

Mariota gasped, and the big man wheeled on her, seized her arm again.

"Do not think we've no need for you. Not after traipsing this far." He jerked his head, glowered at Kintail's great peaks rising so darkly out of the mist. "If you would hear the truth, after all this time and trouble, it matters nary a whit to me *who* rammed your blade into Hugh the Bastard's heart! 'Tis the lute I seek and naught else."

The words spoken, he thrust her toward another man and looked on with approval as that one hoisted her onto a waiting garron, then bound her hands.

"We all ken how many wenches spread their wares across Hugh's bed." He smirked, stepping close to smooth a hand down her thigh. "Truth be told, were I you, mayhap I'd have had done with him, too!"

"I did not kill Hugh Alesone." Mariota sat ramrod straight in the saddle, willed herself not to feel his fingers edging beneath her skirts. "But I can take you to the lute," she vowed, looking him in the eye. "Your man spoke true—I ne'er stole the lute. But I know where it is."

The immediate flare of greedy excitement in his eyes justified the lie, so Mariota drew a deep breath and braced herself for one more.

"It is still in Assynt . . . hidden."

Ewan the Witty's brows shot upward. "Say you?"

Mariota nodded.

But her stomach turned over at the doubt on his face, the way he'd sneered the two words.

She gripped the saddle horn to keep her fingers from trembling, sent a silent plea to the saints that he'd believe her.

Even a quarter of the journey back to Assynt would give Kenneth time to send a man for reinforcements from his uncle.

And so long as the supposed gleam of gold winked at her captors, they wouldn't dare harm her.

But as Ewan and his men continued to leer at her, she couldn't help but shudder, and pray she hadn't made a grave mistake.

Exactly two and a half hours later, Kenneth stopped pacing the parapet walk, unclenched his fists, and rammed an agitated hand through his hair. Wind whipped his plaid and his breath came harsh and uneven. But worst of all, a host of unwanted terrors looked him full in the face, each one daring him to challenge their existence.

And he couldn't.

Already, he'd stretched his patience longer than he had nerves and his gut told him that further waiting would be pointless.

The woods were empty, utterly still and unmoving.

Ewan the Witty and his men were gone.

And that could only mean one thing.

They had Mariota.

Heart in his throat, he wheeled around, his men's familiar faces and even the stone-slabbed paving of the wall-walk spinning before his eyes.

"No-o-o!" he cried, reaching the stair tower in three quick strides, bursting into its shadowy depths before Sir Lachlan or any of the others could catch him.

He took the downward-winding steps two at time, then raced into the hall, bumping into trestle tables, even tilting one over in his haste to reach the storeroom—a supposed haven whose door stood ajar. The sight filled him with tight, hot dread, a throbbing heat that cut off his breath.

All but sliding into the room, he collided with Jamie's broad back, his worst fears screaming to life. A horrible, ear-splitting wail the likes of which he hadn't known himself capable—and wasn't!

For the piercing cries weren't his own, but Cuillin's.

The old dog sat against the far wall, howling his heart out, his wails echoing around the little room . . . a room vacant of the one person Kenneth had hoped to find there.

He took a backward step, gripping the edge of the door for support. "She's gone," he said, the words a statement.

A truth confirmed when Jamie turned around, expelling his breath in a defeated sigh. Their eyes met and Kenneth flinched at the pallor of the younger man's face, the dark smudges of shock already visible beneath his eyes.

Kenneth's fingers tightened on the door. "It canna be . . ." He let the words tail off, feeling his blood chill.

Jamie raised shaking hands and grimaced. "I . . . I dinna ken how it is possible," he stammered, glancing at his dog. "On my soul, no one crossed the threshold and she sure as the Devil didna come out. I only heard Cuillin whimpering and thought he resented being locked in. But when his whines turned to howls, I opened the door and—"

"She was gone," Kenneth finished for him, and Jamie nodded.

He looked so miserable, Kenneth reached out and squeezed his arm. "She cannot have left this room," he said, but the absurdity of the denial only increased his disbelief, the scalding pain gripping his chest.

His gaze flicked to the window but he immediately dismissed the impossibility of the slit opening providing an escape—even a half-starved bairn couldn't wriggle through such a narrow space.

And the only person who'd been with her sat slumped at the little table, a disoriented look on her face, her dark eyes bleary and bloodshot.

But he had no comfort for her.

Not with the reason for her grogginess so apparent— an empty wine flagon stood near her elbow, and another lay tipped on its side by her feet.

Most telling of all, only one cup appeared used.

The second looked suspiciously untouched.

Kenneth's frown darkened, some deep, long-forgotten *something* nibbling at the fringes of his memory.

"Dear saints, where is my lady?" Nessa pressed trembling hands to her temples and searched the men's faces. "Pray tell me you took her away?"

Took her away.

Kenneth stared at her, his heart stopping.

"Nessa, you are an angel on earth!" He leaned down to

kiss her mussed hair, threw an arm around her shoulders and hugged her. "You just gave us the answer."

Or rather his ill-famed father had—however unwittingly.

Like a dark cloud from the past, one of that scoundrel's most notorious deeds rose from the dredges of Kenneth's mind—an oft-heard tale of how his father had used a secret passage cut beneath Eilean Creag Castle to sneak into the Lady Linnet's bedchamber and spirit her away.

Kidnap her right out from under the Black Stag's nose!

Clear as day, Kenneth saw Duncan MacKenzie at Eilean Creag's high table recounting his horror upon learning his lady wife had been seized—and as clearly, he recognized what had happened here.

"Beshrew me—she's slipped out on her own!" The certainty of it near split his head. "Sakes, she somehow persuaded Nessa to drink more than was wise, then left through a secret passage!"

He whirled around, fair knocking Jamie aside to get a better view of the wailing dog. "*He* saw her go. Like as not through that very wall—"

He broke off abruptly as the vertical crack in the wall grew in clarity, its telltale seam making his pulse pound, his blood roar in his ears.

In especial when Cuillin began sniffing and scratching at the wall, the distress in the old dog's eyes leaving no doubts to where Kenneth's lady had gone.

"By the Rood, 'tis true!" He knelt beside the dog, wrapped an arm around him and squeezed. "What did she say . . . she would look after Cuillin? Hah! It would seem he looked after her."

Hope and purpose welling inside him, he pushed to his feet and ran his hands up and down the rough crack, prodding its seam with the dirk she'd left on the table.

"We can only pray we understood him in time," Jamie said, putting his own hands to the wall.

And Kenneth agreed.

Anything else was unacceptable.

Chapter Sixteen

✦

"By the Powers of Heaven—it is so!"

For a seemingly endless moment, Kenneth stared into the depths of the secret passage, his entire body tensing with instinctive, elemental dread. The neck opening of his tunic choked him and he swallowed hard, both believing and disbelieving the evidence of his lady's escape.

The fears making his heart stand still.

Images flashed across his mind—her warmth and softness, her passion. Memories that stretched from the very first moment he'd glimpsed her silhouetted in the tower window to the last time he'd seen her and how her green-gold eyes had lit with joy when he'd walked into this very storeroom and she'd thought the siege was over, the danger passed.

How it'd torn him to pieces to tell her she'd guessed wrong.

He drew a sharp breath, closed his eyes.

She might be Archibald Macnicol's daughter, but she

wasn't a warrior, couldn't wield steel against stiff-necked, hard-bitten men.

Seasoned fighters who lived by blood and sword.

Men without scruple, by their style.

And she hadn't even taken the dirk he'd given her.

"May the Fiend flay the bastards," he seethed, his fingers tightening on that dirk now, fury gripping his vitals.

Rage swept him, but he had no breath for further speech. He saw only the yawning darkness before him, felt his world tipping into the empty, gaping void.

Behind him, Nessa gave a choked cry and Cuillin's howls turned to sharp, excited barks. Somewhere outside, the other castle dogs took up his barking. And somewhere inside Kenneth, whatever warmth had existed in his life vanished as if it'd never been.

He clenched his jaw against the cold. Saints, not even battling fierce North Sea storms had chilled him more. But so soon as the first great shudder struck him, he knew what had happened, recognized the truth with soul-ripping clarity.

With his lady's disappearance, the sun had ceased to shine.

And he'd been plunged into icy darkness.

He stiffened, could almost feel ice coating his skin, freezing the blood in his veins. Somehow his fingers still pressed the cold stone of the angled wall and he caught a whiff of his lady's scent lingering in the opening. Anything but comforting, that one slight trace of her undid him so thoroughly, he scarce noticed Jamie loom up beside him, torch in hand.

Hot and smoking, the torch flames danced in the chill air blowing up from the passage and Kenneth blinked, the unexpected flare of light jarring him to his senses just as Jamie pushed past into the stairwell.

"O-o-oh, nay, lad." Kenneth shot out a hand, catching him before he could plunge down the steps. "She may have gone that way, but she won't be down there now."

He was certain of it.

But Jamie looked unconvinced.

Lowering his torch, he opened and shut his mouth twice before he found words. "She could be lost. Braw men have entered such passages . . . never to return. My own father's castle has such a hellish maze. She—"

"Is in the hands of that loose-in-the-tongue stot who came chapping at our gates," Kenneth finished for him.

He was already striding for the door. "Come—we must ride now. That will serve us better than stumbling around below ground. We find those bastards, we have my lady."

"Aye, that will be the way of it." Sir Lachlan pushed through the men thronging the great hall. "Those varlets would ne'er have left otherwise."

He glanced round, looking pleased when others nodded. "I'd advise we leave a token guard here, send a swift rider to Eilean Creag for reinforcements and another to Dun Telve to gather the men in wait there. The rest of us ride at once, let not a sod of earth unturned until—"

He broke off, waved aside the young squire offering him a brimming wine cup. He looked at Kenneth, his face draining of all color. "Holy saints!" he swore, his eyes mirroring Kenneth's horror. "There *is* something that would have kept them here! The promise of—"

"My coin and the lute." Kenneth snatched the wine

from the gog-eyed squire and downed it in one deep, quenching gulp. He tossed the cup onto the rushes, every fearing dream he'd e'er suffered gloating at him from the shadows. "Those knaves were in a ferment at the first hint of such riches. They'll have questioned Mariota and I'll wager she's vowed she can take them to both."

The hall fell silent.

Everywhere, men froze. They exchanged glances, their dark expressions and the number of hands dropping to sword hilts, more telling than words.

"Split me—that means they ken you lied." Jamie leaned back against a trestle table, looking as if he needed its support, but he pushed away as quickly, his eyes widening. "And that is just the beginning! When they discover she's bluffing as well, they'll—"

"Aye, they will," Kenneth agreed, anger piercing him like a knife blade. "That, and more."

He flinched at every darkness lurking behind the word *more,* but forced himself to keep his voice level. "Dinna you worry, lad," he said, choosing his words as much for his own benefit as Jamie's. "We will find them before they can even think about doing aught to her. Meantime, I want you to ride to my uncle, have him send what men he can spare."

"Me?" Jamie blinked. "I can ride fast enough, and ken the way, but . . ." He tailed off, glancing at the other men. "I already failed the lady once," he blurted, looking miserable. "Had I but heard—"

"You did all anyone could have done," Kenneth argued, the young knight's ill ease minding him of his own doubts only some months ago in his uncle's hall.

Doubts Duncan MacKenzie swept aside by knighting

him there and then, the bold gesture securing Kenneth's place in the clan in a way no one could refute or deny.

Not even Kenneth.

He flushed now, remembering his surprise, his pleasure.

But Jamie already wore knight's spurs and he carried his own blade, a weapon he swung with greater skill than any other man in the hall.

He only needed a boost of confidence.

And of a sudden, Kenneth knew exactly how to give it to him.

Whipping back his plaid, he yanked free his new battle-ax and offered it to Jamie. But when the young man only stared at the weapon's gleaming blade, Kenneth stepped closer and slid the long, smooth haft beneath Jamie's belt.

There was a moment's silence. Then Kenneth gave him a gruff nod and others began roaring approval. Looking down at the weapon, Jamie flushed with a blend of pride and astonishment.

"I canna accept this," he said, his voice thick with emotion.

"Och, to be sure and you can. And dinna make such round eyes—yon ax is far more useful in your hands." Kenneth lifted his voice above the raucous acclaim rising around them. "Duncan MacKenzie might wager his soul on such a piece of wickedness, but I find the thing damned unwieldy—as any man present will attest!"

"Aye, laddie," a deep voice boomed from the back of the hall, "the Black Stag would be proud to see you carry his ax!"

" 'Tis true." Kenneth raised a hand when Jamie tried to argue. "Why do you think my uncle urged me to take you as one of my men? Many were the nights he praised your skill at swordery—and with a battle-ax!"

But Jamie only shook his head, looking stunned. "Still . . . he gave it to you, wanted you—"

"He wanted to know me well armed, and I am. But I do better with my own good fists and a dirk." Kenneth patted his sword hilt, gave Jamie a pained smile. "Sakes, lad, I count my blessings that I can swing this blade with some accuracy. I do not need a Viking's ax hampering me as well!"

"But—"

"No buts. Mayhap after some years of lording it here, I'll feel more at ease with a knight's weapons. This night, I prefer to rely on my wits!" The words spoken, he grabbed Jamie's arm and pulled him through the jostling crowd. "Just remember what matters most—my lady. And dinna stop until you reach Eilean Creag. We need my uncle's men."

His men parted for them, clearing space as they passed. And when they reached the far side of the hall, the door swung wide. Outside, men hastened to unbar the gates and saddled horses already stood at the ready.

"Off with you now!" Kenneth nigh pushed the young knight into the bailey.

Jamie threw him one last wild-eyed look, then took off running.

"Godspeed," Kenneth called, but Jamie was already halfway across the courtyard, making straight for one of Cuidrach's fastest horses.

"I'll reach Duncan by nightfall," he cried, swinging up into the saddle. "Those wretches will be damned forever and aye before the morrow ends!"

And with that, he spurred toward the gates and was gone before any shouts of encouragement could reach him.

Well pleased, Kenneth released his pent-up breath and turned back to his men.

Damned forever and aye, indeed!

Jamie's last words rang in his ears. And good words they were. A fitting fate for the blackguards who held his lady; a stirring battle cry that fired his blood.

Naught else needed to be said—or could be said, so tight was his throat. So he wrenched free his sword and held it aloft, knowing his men would understand.

And they did.

As one, they poured into the bailey, ready to ride.

More than eager himself, Kenneth sheathed his sword and tore after them, his confidence soaring as he vaulted onto his stallion's back.

To be sure, young Jamie had the rights of it. As did his men if the glint in their eyes was anything to go on.

Within hours, his lady would be back in his arms.

The saints only knew what would come of him if they were wrong.

"A bannock, my lady?"

Ignoring Ewan the Witty's offer, Mariota stepped from the shelter of a great Caledonian pine and smoothed her skirts with as much dignity as she could muster. Faith, for a man of such uncommon height and girth, the lout crept about on feet as silent as cat's paws.

A skill he'd deftly used to her disadvantage . . . and embarrassment.

Well aware of it, he stood near a clump of wet heather,

broadsword at his hip, his plaid tossed arrogantly over his shoulder. And most galling of all, his whole demeanor struck her as prickly proud.

Disturbingly intimate.

"I have hung higher-born ladies than you," he boasted, his face hardening. "And for far less sins than yours."

"You needn't remind me," Mariota returned. "'Tis well enough I ken the style of you."

His brow darkened. "By God and the Virgin! You dare speak to me thusly! You, a murderess!"

The tops of Mariota's ears began to burn. She drew a breath, choosing to ignore his outburst. "How long have you been standing there?"

Lurking at the wood's edge.

Leering at her.

He shrugged, his rage seemingly forgotten. "Cautious men live longer than careless ones." He drew himself to his full height, oozed self-congratulation. "Nor are they likely to lose what they've gained. And it's not just that— at times, they're even treated to the most unexpected . . . delights."

Mortification froze Mariota's tongue. She knew exactly what kind of delight he meant and the knowledge made her face flame.

Saints of mercy, he'd been there the whole time!

Watching her.

"You swore no one would follow me," she protested, her cheeks so hot she wondered they didn't ignite.

Ewan folded his arms, looking amused. "I said *no one* would follow you—I did not say I would not . . . trail along."

A crackling silence spun out between them, its tension

making Mariota's temples throb. She could only stare at him, indignation sweeping her. "I see," she finally managed. "See that you are a knave of such wickedness you ought ne'er to have been born!"

"Och, he's a craven cur, to be sure," one of his men chuckled, "e're preying on women, bairns, and dotards!"

But Ewan ignored both Mariota's slur and his man's jest, only flicked a few rain splatters off his plaid. And grinned.

Hot gall rose in Mariota's throat and she glanced aside, caught a small red squirrel peering at her from a moss-grown stone rising from a patch of late-blooming bell heather. Not that she minded the wee creature's regard, but she would have sworn his round, black eyes held sympathy.

But then he darted away, disappearing into the dead bracken, the mists sliding down the braes. And leaving nothing behind but the wet wind whistling through the trees and Ewan's sharp, unnerving stare.

The letch that clung so thickly to him she could almost taste his lust.

Shuddering, she shook out her skirts again—leastways so good as was possible with tied hands.

Still needing to exhibit her disdain, she squared her shoulders and straightened her back. That much she could do. She simply would *not* let her composure crack, wouldn't let him see any more of her ill ease than he already had.

Even if nothing was going as she'd hoped.

For truth, they could have been anywhere—or nowhere.

Nigh on Kintail's boundaries, or mayhap not farther

than a few leagues from Cuidrach's walls. On such a chill, gray day with so much drifting mist, it was impossible to tell. Not even full noon had brought a lift in the dark, roiling clouds, the curtains of fog cloaking the glens.

But wherever they were, she had a sinking feeling they'd been riding in circles and *he* wasn't letting her out of his sight.

Not even to tend her most private cares.

Holding his gaze, she kept her chin lifted, refused to shrink from him. Hugh Alesone had once praised Ewan the Witty as a man of uncommon talents and she now believed one of them must be the ability to ferret out a foe's weakness—as he was proving now, catching her at her most vulnerable and then increasing her misery by waving his fool bannock at her.

As if he knew she hadn't eaten since yestereve.

"Well?" He stepped closer, cocked a brow. "Dinna tell me you aren't hungry?"

Mariota stiffened, resisting the urge to bite his fingers when he thrust the moldy bit of sustenance beneath her nose. "I would sooner break bread with the Devil," she snapped, then cringed when her empty stomach betrayed her with a loud rumbling growl.

The men milling about sniggered.

Scattered laughter spread through the small clearing, quickly becoming coarse and ribald. But Ewan only rocked back on his heels, pinned her with a piercing stare.

His mouth curved in a mocking smile. "Do not press your high-flung ways, lady. If you shun our food, we might see ourselves forced to offer you *other* forms of nourishment."

"Hech—I'd rather feed on *her.* A bite o' tender thigh . . . a savory taste o' fine and slippery female heat!" The bull-necked speaker emphasized his desire by rubbing his crotch. "O-o-oh, aye, Ewan, give us a peek at her sweetness and I'll show the lot of you what a Highlander's tongue can do!"

"As if we dinna ken!" someone quipped from deep in the mist.

Raucous laughter underscored the general agreement as men came closer, heated anticipation on their bearded faces.

"Highlanders' tongues. Hah!" Ewan whirled on the crotch-rubber. "*Your* Highland tongue can be ripped right out of your mouth if you dare." He glared at the man, raised fingers to probe the bluish swelling at his left eye. "I dinna doubt *that part of her* has teeth just as wicked as the swing of her fist. Not that she'll be taking any more swipes at us."

His lips twisting, he tossed aside the bannock. "So-o-o! Have your look, my friends. But no more tarse-pulling . . . leastways, not yet." The warning spoken, he reached for Mariota's skirts. "And come no closer—"

"Drop my skirts at once or I'll do more than blacken your eye, you bastard!" Mariota stood rigid, glaring at him.

"Oh-ho!" A bold-faced man thrust his hand beneath his plaid—despite Ewan's harsh words. "Och, aye," he called, his hand already pumping, "having her drop those skirts would be a far sight better than just airing 'em!"

But Ewan the Witty paid the man no heed. Instead, his brows snapped together in a fierce frown.

"So I'm a bastard, eh? And the word hissed with such

scorn." He looked round at his men, feigning astonishment. "And here we'd thought you favored such churls? Men of tainted birth?"

Mariota pressed her lips together, refusing to be goaded.

Ewan tightened his grip on her skirts and jerked higher. "As for what you'll *do*, were I to set one finger to you, I'd have you writhing with need so fast you'd forget both of your baseborn lovers!"

"You, sirrah, are a dead man." Mariota let her eyes blaze and gave him a scorching look. "And you couldn't stir me if you had till the end of all ages to try."

Her fury smoldering, she drew herself up and squared her shoulders. "Indeed," she said, her voice measured and cold, "I doubt you could rouse any woman."

"Say you?" Angry color flooded Ewan's face and his eyes glittered, his lips thinning as if he'd bit into something bitter. "Be glad I am not so hungry for cat meat just now, Mariota of Dunach."

He stepped closer, leaning in until his hot breath almost gagged her. "When I am, you may be sure I'll show you how demanding a dead man can be—even if I think having you will be about as pleasurable as licking brine from a stinging nettle!"

"Try it and I'll ne'er take you to the golden lute." Mariota fixed him with a haughty stare. "It is hidden where no man shall find it—"

"In Assynt?" Ewan slid a glance at his men and spat into the heather. "Can it be that no man shall find it because it is no longer there?"

Mariota swallowed.

Truth was, she had no idea where the lute was.

Worse, she'd never even seen the thing! And the flash of cold anger in Ewan's eyes gave her the sickening impression that he knew it.

"I told you it's in Assynt," she said all the same—only to be rewarded by another upward tug on her skirts. Cold, damp air swirled across her thighs, chilling her even as fear heated the back of her neck. "It is—"

"Perhaps there where the Keeper of Cuidrach hoards his siller?" Ewan swelled his chest. "His well-stuffed coin bags?"

Mariota gasped.

Hugh's man smiled . . . a wicked smile full of glowering menace.

"O-o-oh, aye, you heard aright." He sneered at her. "You wagered poorly. We already ken the lute is hereabouts somewhere. Your own Keeper swore to surrender it to us—along with his fortune."

"He wouldn't have." Mariota shook her head. The heat at her nape slid around and down to spread through her chest, the hot pressure stealing her breath. "Ne'er would he have bargained with you."

"Ah, but he did—and for you!" This time Ewan shook his head. "The man is a fool, besotted beyond reason," he said, knotting her skirts so her legs remained exposed.

Satisfied, he stepped back and flipped his fingers in derision. "You've ensorcelled him. Why else would he offer up the entirety of his coin, the lute, and even his own sweet life to spare yours?"

His life? Mariota blinked, the tightness in her chest almost stopping her heart.

Her mouth went dry. "I do not believe you."

She couldn't.

Yet even as denial churned inside her, clawing at her innards and watering her knees, words Kenneth had said to her only recently whirled through her mind and squeezed her heart with dread.

There is nothing I would not do to protect you.

He'd even sworn he'd climb the face of the precipitous cliff that had scarred him—and not just once, but repeatedly, if doing so would keep her safe.

Had even vowed to marry her—and like as not would, even after learning her deepest secrets.

Her Keeper was that kind of man.

And now she'd thrust him into the midst of a maelstrom—a nightmare that was anything but his own making.

Only hers.

She glanced aside lest Ewan the Witty see fear in her eyes, her pain and regret, but when she looked back at him she recognized the truth in his gloating.

She would pay dearly for her foolishness and her Keeper would be relieved of an even higher price.

Her blood chilling at the thought, she forced her voice to remain steady. "I cannot . . . will not believe you," she repeated, the slight change of wording doing little to comfort her.

Far from it, cold shivers spilled through her when Ewan's lip curled.

He shrugged. "And I believe neither of you," he said, his words confirming her fears. "Why do you think we've been riding in circles? We are waiting, my lady. Waiting until your knight comes. And he will, love-blind fool that he is. He'll rally his few men and ride out to rescue you. And then . . ."

He paused, clapped his hands in front of her face. "Then our long journey will prove worthwhile indeed." He stepped away from her and threw a triumphant look to his men. "We shall have enough spoil to live on for all our days, you for sport, and your fool Keeper to ransom to his uncle."

Mariota bristled, her distress giving way to anger. "A plague on you! He will not be led into a trap. None of his blood. That I promise you!"

"You, my lady, are not in a position to promise anything." He seized her braid and wound it tightly around his fist. "As for your latest bastard lover . . ." He paused, cast a glance at the nearby hills. "That one will soon come charging out of the mist and into our hands, whether it pleases you or nay."

Releasing her hair, he eyed her from beneath lowered brows. "Kith and kin mean everything to such a man— his lady even more. He'll have lost his reason upon discovering you gone. And a man in such a state is always . . . vulnerable."

He looked pleased by the notion. "But even if he has retained his wits, it matters not. Before the morrow's moonrise, we shall have him."

"Or he you," Mariota shot back, but he'd already turned, was striding away to disappear into the mists.

Frowning after him, she added, "He'll fall upon you with a fury to set the heather ablaze."

That she knew—even if the surety of it terrified her.

"And well he might, my lady."

Wee Finlay appeared at her elbow, flicked a wary glance at Ewan's retreating back. "Blood breeds true no matter what side of the pallet a man is born on," he said, low-voiced. "The MacKenzies are a fierce lot, not ones to shy from whipping out their steel."

Mariota tensed at his words. They sliced through her to the core, cleaving her heart. No one knew better than she how ill at ease her lord yet felt with a blade in his hand.

He'd told her often enough, seeming almost proud of his lack of a knight's usual upbringing. And she'd seen him at swording practice, knew his skills needed honing.

His honest humility was by no means . . . unfounded.

Mariota's throat closed. Able to swing a dashing blade or no, he was all she'd e'er dreamed a man should be. More. So much more that the mere thought of harm coming to him froze her heart.

Losing him would rip her soul, steal the warmth and light from her life in one vicious swoop. Leave her unable to breathe and doom her to walk blind through unending darkness.

Hugh the Bastard had ne'er touched her.

Not truly.

Now she loved.

Couldn't bear to lose the man whose name stood writ on her every indrawn breath, who held her happiness, her *life*, in the well-doing of his own.

She shuddered, blinking back the stinging heat blurring her vision.

"Och, dinna look so stricken," Wee Finlay said. "All is no yet lost and I have my doubts you've cause to fret."

He cast another glance in Ewan's direction, reached crooked fingers to undo the knot in her skirt. "See you, I may be a bit past my better days, but I . . . remember. The kind of passion that burned in your Keeper's eyes when he spoke of you can give men untold strength and courage, doesn't always addle their wits as some would have you believe."

Mariota swallowed. "Why are you doing this?"

"Would that I could do more." He tugged down her skirts, smoothed the folds until her legs were again covered. When he straightened, he gave her an apologetic smile. "It shames me that I cannot."

"You would help me?"

But rather than answer her, he glanced at her bound wrists and even in the misty, half-light, she would've sworn a tinge of color stained his cheeks. She was certain of it when he plucked at his plaid, indicated his scrawny shoulders, his less than impressive stature.

Indeed, even standing at his tallest, he barely reached her chin.

He *did* produce a cloth-wrapped beef rib and a wineskin from beneath his plaid and offered both to her, viands she greedily accepted, biting into the cold meat with gusto and gulping heartily each time he held the wineskin to her lips.

"Right enough, lass." He used the cloth from the beef rib to wipe her mouth, her chin. "I canna tarry, shouldn't be seen with you."

He took a step backward, gave her a twisted, embarrassed-looking smile. "Being one o' them isn't proof against Ewan's wrath. For truth, he's already vowed to toss me to the Each Uisge if I vex him."

Mariota studied him, wondered what held the little man to such a band of marauders—something she'd oft pondered at Drumodyn—for unlike her, he couldn't claim to have been dazzled by Hugh Alesone's high looks and golden tongue.

"Why?"

"There are some things a man just canna do—if he wants to sleep at night," he said, his face shadowing. "See you, I saw the alewife climb down from Hugh's tower window that night, knew there'd been more afoot than you admitted, knew—"

"I did not kill him," Mariota cut in, the denial sounding strange, thick, and choked. "And neither did Elizabeth Paterson. 'Twas Hugh's heart-pains."

She paused, lowering her voice. "All at Drumodyn knew he suffered them and that night . . . that night, I found him abed with the alewife. He saw me on the threshold and the shock must've caused him to have a seizure for he clutched his chest and . . . and died."

"But your lady's dirk? It was—"

"In his chest, I know." Mariota paused again, the painful memories making her own chest tighten. "Elizabeth Paterson used my shock to overwhelm me. She grabbed the dirk and thrust it into Hugh's heart, jeering that I'd be blamed for his death—and I was."

Wee Finlay looked at his feet, shook his head. "And I ne'er said anything . . ."

"You've helped me now, and I thank you," Mariota said, a surprising sense of peace settling over her.

She closed her eyes for a moment, pushing away the images branded onto her memory and drinking in the sounds of rushing wind and a nearby river, willing the familiar, well-loved sounds to soothe her.

She also caught the muffled roar of distant cataracts, the foaming, splashing run of rapids they'd passed earlier.

A sound that reminded her of approaching thunder, the pounding of her own blood in her ears.

The need for caution.

But when she opened her eyes, Finlay was still looking at the ground. His mouth tight, he was nudging a clump of deer grass with the worn toe of his boot and much to her surprise, she felt a wave of empathy.

A jolt of sympathy for the little man who seemed to want to be noble but lacked the courage to follow his heart.

Feeling for him, and for herself, Mariota drew a deep, shuddering breath, seeking strength from the expanse of moor and glens stretching away beyond the mist—even if she couldn't see much of them, only the day's gray pall.

The hills were there all the same.

She could feel them.

The crags and high places, the silver-shimmering lochs and deep, shadowy glens. Not just land, sea, and sky, but the whole of her existence, her *heart,* throbbed in tune with these great moody hills and she refused to believe they'd not protect her now.

Wouldn't wrap their beauty and wonder around her.

Their magic.

She cleared her throat, looked at the wizened little man beside her. "Sir Kenneth believes there is a special healing in these hills," she said, sure of it. "Mayhap you will now find yours. I hope it will be so."

He looked up at that, and the regret on his face made her wince. "There are dark places in my soul, lady. I dinna deserve your forgiveness." He spread his hands, appearing even more uncomfortable. "See you, yon blackguards were the only folk that would give such a hump-backed wretch as me a roof o'er my head—a sense of belonging. They tolerated me not for my muscle but for my sharp eyes and my ability to keep my mouth shut."

He spat then, dragging his sleeve over his mouth. "And *that* is something I've grown sore tired of, of late. I—"

"Finlay!" Ewan the Witty's voice cut through the mist. "Where did you last see that fool fox?"

The little man grimaced and started forward, but Mariota hurried after him. "Wait," she cried, blocking his path. "What fox does he mean?"

Finlay flushed and glanced up at the roiling clouds. "Och, the heavens only know," he said, speaking quickly. "And you'd ne'er believe me if I told you."

"Told her what?" Ewan joined them, glowered at the little man. "Since we've naught else to do in this Devil's cauldron, we might as well keep following the wee beastie." He clamped a meaty hand on Finlay's shoulder. "Now—which direction shall we ride?"

"To the east." Wee Finlay stiffened, stuck out his chin. "Through yon trees," he added, pointing to a stand of birches. "I saw the fox slinking through the bracken there not an hour past."

"The side-glen to the widow's cottage is beyond that birchwood." Ewan pulled on his beard and frowned. "One of the narrowest passes in these hills lies that way, too. A devil-damned gorge if e'er there was one. I wouldn't want—"

He jerked around at a great hallooing, the clatter and ruckus of a fast-approaching party of horsemen. He dropped his hand to his sword hilt, but released it as the riders burst into view.

His own scouting party and judging by their lathered

horses and the excitement on their faces, they bore good tidings.

Ewan the Witty gave a triumphant bark of laughter and waited until the first rider drew rein before him. "The bastard knight comes," the man blurted, flashing a grin. "A small party—not even so many as we'd expected."

"What you do not say!" Ewan hooted another laugh, took a silvered wine flask from his belt and offered it to the scout. "Where are they headed?"

The man took a long drink, handed the flask to another rider. "Toward the widow's cottage," he supplied, sounding breathless. "The narrow gorge we passed on the way to his keep—the one they call the Devil's Glen."

There was a moment of silence, then Ewan nodded. "So that is to be the way of it—a slaughtering of lambs."

"There is more." The first rider twisted in his saddle, glancing back to where a few more men were yet cantering into the clearing. "We—"

"Just a few men, you say?" Ewan cut him off, apparently unaware of the other men just drawing up. "How many compared to our own?"

"Not even a third."

"Then the latest Keeper of Cuidrach's brief reign will come to an abrupt end but a stone's throw from his own moldering walls." Ewan threw a leer at Mariota, snapped his hand into a tightly balled fist. "The fool should have waited, sent to his vaunted uncle for more men."

In that moment, he finally looked at the new arrivals, the stragglers making up the rear of the little scouting party. "By Glory!" he cried, his brows shooting upward.

"I tried to tell you," the first rider said, but Ewan the Witty wasn't looking at him.

Or listening.

Like one bespelled, he'd locked his gaze on the stragglers, took a few steps toward them, his brow crinkling as if he doubted what he saw.

But then he grinned.

Wee Finlay's face went ashen.

And Mariota's heart plummeted, her last flicker of hope extinguished.

Chapter Seventeen

❖

The Devil's Glen.

The name took new significance so soon as Kenneth reined in at the edge of the wood. His heart thumping, he peered through the mist toward the deep ravine that all in Kintail knew to be hell-spawned. Or, at the very least, ruled by the fey. Mayhap even held under the spell of an enchanted slumber.

A place where anything could happen . . . and did.

He shuddered, tightening his grip on the reins, wariness making his body so tense he would have sworn he'd been cast into stone.

Almost believing it, he swallowed and sent a prayer to the saints. The Devil's Glen had been known to do worse to men.

Empty and inhospitable, dark and shadowy even in summer with the sun only breaching its steep-sided walls at fullest noon, the treacherous defile daunted the best of men, had proved itself as fierce and merciless as the most formidable Highland warrior, when wronged. And as unforgiving as the horned Dark One of its name, when not respected.

Only fools tread there.

Or men ridden by desperation.

The need to retrieve what was their own.

Kenneth frowned, smoothed a hand over his mouth and chin. The gorge truly was as menacing as legend declared. Threads of white-foaming cataracts plunged down its stony, gorse-covered flanks and a rapid, raging torrent claimed most of its narrow, rocky floor.

But it wasn't empty.

Not this chill, gray afternoon. More than the usual drifting mist-wraiths filled the Devil's Glen and the defile's black silence had given way to the hollow drumming of horses' hooves on stone and gravel, the creak of leather, the clank of mail and weaponry, the sound of men's voices.

Many men's voices, and uncaring if they were heard.

Sir Lachlan nudged his steed closer to Kenneth's. "She is there," he said, lifting an arm to point through the mist. "She's mounted, but caught up in the very middle of the dastards. Do you see her?"

Kenneth shook his head. "I see naught but mist and men. More than I can count." So many, their number took his breath. "Guidsakes, they would lure us to our death."

Lachlan did not dispute him. He rolled his shoulders, gave Kenneth a taut smile. "If need be—so be it."

But Kenneth scarce heard him.

He was leaning forward, straining to see through the mist—and to recall every tale about battle tactics and warfare that his uncle had e'er shared with him.

God willing, he'd remember enough—and put it to proper use!

He tightened his hands on the reins, thinking hard, even as his heart relived every precious moment he'd shared with his lady.

Woo her gently is what he'd planned to be doing this ill-starred day, not sitting on the edge of hell, praying the saints he'd see her again.

He frowned, the irony of it stinging like an adder bite.

But see her again he would. And more. There wasn't a force under the heavens that would stop him. Least of all a swaggering braggart named Ewan the Witty and his fool pack of caterans.

And not in his Kintail.

"Lachlan—where did you see her? How deeply into the gorge?"

"In the middle," Sir Lachlan repeated, "but I've lost sight of her."

Kenneth turned in the saddle, gave his friend a hard look. "I ken that gorge—it has no room to maneuver. 'Tis true yon caterans are greater in number, but we might best them yet if Jamie reached Duncan so swiftly as he vowed, and joins us with equal haste."

But so far, nothing but chill wind stirred the woods around them. And, much as he resisted admitting, Jamie and the hoped for reinforcements should've arrived some while ago. Kenneth frowned, rubbed the back of his neck.

"If naught happens soon, we'll use a tactic my uncle learned from the late Good King Robert Bruce's warring days," he decided, scanning the mist-cloaked gorge again. "We'll form a tight arrow formation with ourselves at the apex and cut right through the bastards, snatching up my lady as we pass, then pounding on straight out of the ravine. Our momentum and the surprise of such a move should give us the advantage . . ."

He trailed off and glanced at the seasoned garrison captain, knowing a flood of relief when Sir Lachlan nodded approval.

" 'Tis a well-used stratagem, but one that might work," that one agreed, his gaze on the gorge. "It's also our only option unless Jamie returns anon and we challenge them face on. We—"

"Heigh-ho, my lord! There is your lady!" One of Kenneth's men kneed his garron up beside them, gesticulated wildly. "In the middle of the gorge, just as Sir Lachlan said."

Kenneth swung back around and stared into the Devil's Glen, his heart slamming against his ribs when he spotted her, horsed and well guarded, a strapping, auburn-haired Highlander holding her mount's reins.

"The blessed saints!" Kenneth's eyes flew wide, his breath catching. "That's Jamie! They've got the lad— have him tied to Mariota's horse!"

"Och, it canna be." Sir Lachlan leaned forward, stared. "Ne'er in a thousand . . . God keep and preserve us, it *is* Jamie."

"And that means there'll be no men riding in from Eilean Creag," someone said from behind them. "No reinforcements will be coming," the man added unnecessarily, his voice flat. Grim.

Kenneth drew back his shoulders, inhaling deeply. "Then, by God, we shall help ourselves—and succeed." He looked round at his men and dared them to suggest otherwise. "We can do naught else."

* * *

"Lady, there is naught I wouldn't have done to reach Duncan."

Jamie turned guilt-ridden eyes on Mariota, jerked at the rope binding his hands, tying him to her mount's saddle. "I swear it on my mother's soul. Ne'er did I mean for this to happen. They took my sword," he said, his voice thick with broken pride. "And the new battle-ax Kenneth gave me. Even the dagger I keep in my boot! They—"

"They were more than a score of men to your one."

Mariota tilted her head. "You dare not forget that, Jamie. And from the looks of some of them when they returned with you, anyone can see you gave them a fierce fight. Kenneth will be proud of you."

She paused, mustering a smile. "For certes, I am."

Jamie pressed his lips together, pangs of conscience clearly bothering him. He looked away, swallowed audibly. "You speak as if we'll see Kenneth again."

Alive.

He left the word unspoken but it hovered between them, an unspeakable threat Mariota refused to acknowledge. Anything else would bring her to her knees, leave her bleeding on the edge of a bleak void she had no desire to traverse.

"We will see him again," she owned. "Both of us. That, I vow!"

Jamie blinked and flushed, slid a glance at the granite-faced men surrounding them, the countless drawn swords and iron-headed maces, the naked steel gleaming dully in the gray, watery light. "I would that I had your faith, my lady."

"You have courage—more than many battle-hardened

men twice your age." She started to say more, but Jamie wasn't listening.

"Saints of mercy!" He stared past her, neither his outburst nor the stunned look on his face needing translation.

"Kenneth!" Mariota's heart stilled. "Praise be!" she cried, a strange mix of relief, joy, and fear sweeping her as she caught sight of the man who was her very heart, breath, and soul.

Heat flashed through her, liquid and golden. She began to melt, the sweet, molten warmth she'd ne'er again hoped to feel spreading through her, making her heart pound and her breath catch, even as dread closed her throat, making it impossible for her to cry out again, to do more than stare.

And pray.

Heedless of her fears, her Keeper and his men surged forward, into the Devil's Glen. Then, seeing her, his face lit as if illuminated by all the heavens' stars and he thrust his sword into the air, let out a triumphant war-like *whoop,* his men's shouts no less enthusiastic.

"Cuidrach N' Righ!" they yelled in unison, the MacKenzie battle cry ripping through the gorge. *"Save the king!"*

Chaos erupted all around them.

A confusion of sound, all clashing swords and shouting, the thunderous pounding of fast-approaching horses, the clatter and din loud in Mariota's ears. Nearer by, men who'd been milling about ran for mounts and those not yet brandishing naked blades, drew their steel, swung around to face the threat barreling through the ravine's entrance.

"Dear saints!" she gasped, watching in horror as Ewan

the Witty grinned, raised his two-handed war brand and raced to join the men lowering spears to halt Kenneth's momentum.

Others burst from behind the whin bushes and outcropping rocks flanking the ravine, maces held high and swords swinging. They stormed forward, quickly forming a crescent-shaped front, the yelling, steel-weaving lot of them undaunted by Kenneth's furious charge.

But still he pounded on, murderous rage on his face and shouting his slogan, his sword now lowered before him like a jousting lance, its gleaming tip already dripping red—as were more than a few swords of the men riding with him.

Yet they dug in their spurs, kicking their beasts to ever greater speed as they thundered onward, even as some fell, disappearing beneath racing, flailing hooves, the slashing, smiting blades of Ewan and his men.

Blackguards they plowed down in swathes, but for each one cut down or trampled, five more rose to replace him.

Shouts, jeers, and the clash of steel filled the Devil's Glen, the cacophony deafening, the stench of fresh, spilled blood and panicked, sweat-lathered horses already thick in the air.

"O-o-oh, here is folly!" Mariota's stomach clenched, her heart seizing. The warmth that had spooled through her moments ago, slid from her like a cloak turned to ice.

She whirled to Jamie, unable to watch. "He's run mad—they'll all be skewered!"

"And us with them!" the young knight cried, his eyes round. "God save us, lady—I am no yet ready to die! Not by my own ax!"

Jerking round, Mariota saw the reason for his white-faced horror.

Wee Finlay had gone crazy-mad, too!

Mariota screamed as the little man raced toward them, Jamie's own new battle-ax clutched in his hand.

Disbelief lamed her—not that she'd be able to run if she could. "Finlay, no! Dinna do this!"

But he kept coming, his mouth pressed tight, his face set with deadly purpose as he raised the ax and let it whistle down, slicing the rope tying Jamie to Mariota's horse.

Half-winded, he thrust the ax into Jamie's hands, seized a dirk from his belt and began cutting the binds at Jamie's wrists.

He threw an apologetic glance at Mariota. "I'm cutting him loose first so his hands are free to protect you until your Keeper fights his way through yon men," he panted, giving her one of his twisted, guilt-ridden smiles.

And then Jamie was free, vaulting up behind her. "I'll not be forgetting you," he called to Wee Finlay as he took the reins.

"Tchah! Get you gone—now!" Wee Finlay stepped back, waved them away. "Make haste—"

He got no further.

Ewan the Witty's arcing blade silenced him, one flashing stroke and Finlay went down in a spray of blood, toppling full length onto the boggy, rock-strewn ground.

"No-o-o!" Mariota cried, horror squeezing her heart.

"You murdering whoreson!" Jamie struggled to control Mariota's panicked, sidling horse.

"Good riddance!" Ewan glared at the little man's crumpled body, wheeled round to glower at Jamie.

"Come here, you flame-topped varlet!" he jeered, wind-milling his blade. "I'll send you to join the wee bastard—be you so eager to die!"

" 'Tis you who shall die," Jamie roared, raising his ax.

Ewan laughed. "Say your prayers, laddie, your hour is upon yo—"

"Cuidach N' Righ!"

Ear-splitting loud, the battle cry rent the air, other-worldly in its eerie, thunderous echo, the dread slogan shook the gorge, turning heads, chilling blood and drawing eyes, upward.

Everywhere men froze.

Some dropped jaws . . . and weapons.

Others crossed themselves or whimpered for their mothers.

All stared in stunned wonder at the two men standing on the crest of ravine—one older but magnificently fierce-looking, the younger, *huge* in stature, and glowing with strength and vigor.

Truth tell, they both . . . glowed.

Garbed in full and chiefly Highland dress, their bright tartan plaids, mailed shirts, and flashy Celtic jewelry shone like molten gold—and the ground where they stood shimmered as if the sun itself had descended onto the ridge.

And of all the men who saw them, only the MacKenzies recognized the two and cheered, their joy complete when Ranald the Redoubtable and Cormac the Cowherd bent as one and lifted a huge boulder, hurled it down onto their gaping, stricken foes.

And just as the boulder came crashing into the Devil's Glen, old Ranald and Cormac joined hands, raised their arms above their heads in bold salute . . . and vanished.

"Holy Saint Columba!" Kenneth swung round to stare at Sir Lachlan. "Did you see that?"

But his garrison captain had no time to answer; *other* Highland warriors were cresting the opposite ridge, men no less fearsome and led by an older lairdly-looking man of equally impressive build and magnificence as Ranald the Redoubtable, but nowise . . . luminous.

Or centuries dead!

Hot fury blazing in their eyes, these Highlanders, too, sent a barrage of rocks hurtling onto Ewan and his men, then tore down the steep-sided ravine in such endless number that Kenneth whooped with joy and arced his blade with even greater vigor, taking out two of Ewan's sword-swinging churls before he could even raise his own battle cry to join the newcomers' exultant shouting.

"By the Rood!" Sir Lachlan gave a great shout beside him, his own sword slashing endlessly.

"A Macnicol! A Macnicol!" The newcomers roared their slogan, the clash of their steel loud as their voices as they surged into the gorge, felling and smiting.

"'Tis old Archibald!" one of Kenneth's men cried, awe in his voice. "I recognize him."

But Kenneth only flashed a glance at the curly-bearded warrior laird, for the battle still raged—even if some might now only call it a skirmish.

The field already won.

So long as his lady was yet safe!

Indeed, amidst the turmoil and fierce, hand-to-hand fighting still going on in places, he saw Archibald Macnicol swing down from his garron and shove his way through the melee, straight toward his daughter.

"Lass!" the puissant old warrior cried, his booming

voice filling the gorge, the urgency and *love* in that one word sealing the day's fate.

"Hold you fast, lassie!" the man shouted again, running now. "Remember your blood!"

Kenneth leapt down from his horse and ran, too.

So fast as he could with the bed of the ravine now clogged with fallen boulders, and dead and wounded men, those few still on their feet and fighting.

"By God, lass, show the bastard you're a Macnicol," a younger man running near Kenneth shouted then—a great stirk of an auburn-haired warrior who could've been Archibald himself, but younger.

"Aye, a Macnicol lass, and soon-to-be wife to a MacKenzie!" Kenneth called, and the young man threw a quick look at him, flung out an arm and gave him a comradely whack on the shoulder as they ran.

"Donald," the young man panted, without breaking stride, "her brother. Her *favorite* brother!"

Soon-to-be-wife.

Her brother?

Mariota heard the beloved voices through a red haze of terror and stared into the madness, half fearing one of Ewan the Witty's sword swipes had felled her and she'd wakened in some strange netherworld where her most secret dreams might seem reality, only to be wrest from her before she could reach for them.

Clutch them to her heart and never let them go.

"Lass!" Her father's voice came again, reaching her through the mist, and her Keeper's.

"Drop your blade, Ewan!" Kenneth roared, so near her heart split with joy.

" 'Tis over, man!" he shouted again. "Have done, lest

you wish to meet your Maker without a chance to plead your mercy!"

Over?

Mariota blinked, tried to hear above the pounding of blood in her ears, struggled to see through the swirling mist, the hot tears near blinding her.

Jamie still held her crushed against him, and he still brandished his ax with lightning flourishes, holding off Ewan the Witty's every approach. But young Jamie was wearying, the strain of one-handedly fending off the other's attack while holding her secure, taking its toll.

And still she saw nothing.

Not what she longed to see . . . *needed* to see.

Only Ewan the Witty's sneering grin and flashing steel, Jamie's ceaseless parries, and the red haze that threatened to blot all she held dear.

But then, without warning, those she loved most appeared out of the mist.

Her Keeper, her father, her brother Donald, and countless others.

They surged forward in a mad whirl of steel-weaving menace, swords, dirks, and maces flashing, her father's famed battle-ax gleaming the brightest, the look in his eye as he lunged at Ewan the Witty nigh as deadly.

Too stunned to cry out, Mariota stared as her father raised his arm, took aim. But before his ax found its mark, Kenneth slashed at Ewan with his blade and that one's arm went limp and his sword dropped to the ground.

"Such fury . . . for a whore," Ewan bellowed, still on his feet, glaring round.

"Vengeance for the lady who shall be my wife," Kenneth returned, unbuckling his sword belt, thrusting it into the hands of a startled-looking Donald. "And—"

"And for Finlay," his lady cried, her tear-filled gaze going to the bloodied body of the little man lying nearby. "He freed us," she said, swiping a hand beneath her eyes. "Then Jamie . . . Jamie—" she broke off, unable to finish.

Having heard enough, Kenneth flexed his fingers and shoved up the sleeves of his tunic. "You—to the death," he challenged Ewan. "Fists or dirks? If you are man enough to take me on without a yard of steel in your hand?"

Ewan spat, glanced at his fallen blade—and whipped a sparkling, bejeweled dirk from his belt the instant Kenneth followed his gaze.

Lunging, he made to ram the dagger into Kenneth's gut, but Kenneth only smiled, clamped an iron grip around the other's wrist before that one had a chance to splutter.

"One of the first lessons a man learns in seaport taverns," Kenneth said, seizing the dirk and driving it home, "is to expect a feint. In especial, from a bastard of your ilk."

"You are the bastard," Ewan wheezed, his eyes already glazing, his knees buckling. "I'll—"

"You'll ne'er harass an innocent woman again," Kenneth finished for him as he fell. "And 'tis apt you met your end on *that* dagger," he added, and heard his lady's gasp, knew he'd guessed correctly.

He hoped the appropriateness of Ewan's ending might help lay her ghosts.

From the corner of his eye, he caught Jamie helping her dismount, saw her fierce-looking father and her brother gather her in their arms, heard the choked sobs and joyous cries of a reunion long overdue.

"Lass, lass." The old warrior crushed her against him, cradling her like a bairn, stroking her hair. "Can you e'er forgive a stubborn old man?"

"Forgive *you*? Do you even need to ask?" Mariota's voice broke on a sob, her heart so full, the swelling heat in her throat so constricting she could only stare at the beloved faces through a blur of tears.

"Do you not ken I ne'er stopped loving you? But you—" She broke off, smoothed back his gray-shot hair. "Whate'er moved you to be here, I would know how you are faring? I'd heard you were so ill—"

"Ill?" Archibald stepped back, planted his hands on his hips. "Do I look ailing?"

And he didn't—much to her surprise, and delight. "But—"

"Languishing away o'er losing you is all that wore me down," he said, looking anything but feeble. "That, and mayhap life being far too peaceful in the north of late."

Kenneth watched them, his own throat thick with emotion, but his feet suddenly too heavy to carry him forward.

Nay, not his feet . . . his doubts.

Every last one of them surfaced now, rising up like wraiths from the bloodied ground to twine around his legs and hold him in place.

But so magnificent, so *lairdly* did Archibald Macnicol strike him, the older man's sheer power of presence seemed to humble every man gathered round, his authority even taming the Devil's Glen itself, leaving it only another mist-hung ravine, freed of menace and threat.

Frowning, Kenneth slid a glance at the opposite hill crest, sought reassurance, but Ranald and Cormac were gone, their hill-shaking battle cry only an echo in Kenneth's heart.

Archibald Macnicol's booming voice was real, though, and the old chief raised it now, bade Jamie to hold out his battle-ax. "To be notched," he explained, eyeing the young knight from beneath shaggy, beetled brows.

"A notch for helping to safeguard my daughter!" he decried, using the head of his own many-notched ax to mark the haft of Jamie's. "May it be the first o' many!" he added, lifting his voice above the cheers of the men standing near.

Cheers and . . . assorted babble.

Murmurs of speculation that included Kenneth's name.

And hearing the whispers, Kenneth stood straighter, took closer measure of the aging chieftain who carried a reputation as far-famed as his uncle.

But the old warrior felt his stare and turned, surprising Kenneth with the wetness of his cheeks, the *welcome* lighting his hawk-like eyes.

"So you are the man who would make my daughter an honest woman at last?" he boomed, striding forward to clasp Kenneth by the shoulders. "Well met, well met— 'tis long I've waited to see her wed and happy!"

Kenneth swallowed, held the older man's appraising stare. "Ewan the Witty spoke true," he said in a rush, amazed his tongue let him form the words. "I am indeed a bastard, sir. But—" He broke away from Archibald's grip to gather Mariota into his arms. "—I shall be the most blessed bastard in these hills if I might marry my lady with your blessing?"

Archibald Macnicol threw back his head and laughed. "My blessing? Ho—did you no hear me just now? I've longed for this day. Burn to bounce my grandbabes on my knee! Och, aye, you have my blessings, son. I ne'er thought to see the lass wed, to know her happy and with a good, *deserving* man."

But at her father's words, Mariota stiffened in Kenneth's arms, and the joy spinning inside her stilled, replaced by a cold fear that stopped her heart.

How fitting that her past would claim her now—at the very moment when her happiness should be bright enough to light the heavens.

She pulled back from Kenneth's arms, touched a hand to his cheek. "I must tell you—I should have sooner, but was afraid," she began, the words bitter gall on her tongue, "I am not widowed, was ne'er married. The Bastard of Drumodyn was—"

"A man unworthy of Mariota Macnicol," Kenneth finished for her, pulling her back into his arms, kissing her full on the lips, a deep, claiming kiss.

And made all the more potent for the rousing acclaim it drew from his men—and Archibald Macnicol's.

"I've known the truth for weeks now," he murmured against her ear. "It matters naught, lass. How could it? Loving you as I do?"

"You . . . you do know how much I love you, too?"

"Your kiss gave it away, lass. The very first one." He winked at her, smoothed back her hair. "That and . . . certain other things!"

Mariota blushed and clung to him, her world suddenly filled with light . . . incredible joy. She bit her lip, looked around the Devil's Glen at the shambles surrounding them.

"Then it is over?" she asked, no longer trying to stem her tears. "Truly over?"

"No, sweetness," he assured her, uncaring that his own eyes were more damp than was good for a man, " 'tis far from over. Our life together is only beginning."

Mariota drew a great, tremulous breath.

"I can scarce believe it," she said, her heart bursting. "You still want me to be your lady?"

Kenneth smiled, shook his head. "My lady *wife*," he corrected.

"You are certain?"

"Ne'er more so," he assured her.

She sniffed, dashed a tear from her cheek. "For always?"

And the Keeper of Cuidrach nodded. "Oh, aye, minx. For so long as there is a tomorrow and beyond."

Epilogue

❖

OUTSIDE CUIDRACH CASTLE'S WALLS, SOME MONTHS LATER . . .

It was a day touched by magic.

Singularly beautiful, its glory echoed from the hills, the brilliance of its bright spring sky softened by wisps of snowy-white clouds. The waters of Loch Hourn shimmered in the sun and ringing cheer filled the air as joy lit the faces of everyone moving about the gaily-festooned pavilions or claiming a place at lavishly decked trestle tables.

Even Cuidrach's stalwart sentinel, the grim-faced Bastard Stone, appeared well-pleased.

Beneficent.

And to the clansmen and friends gathered to celebrate Kenneth and Mariota's nuptials with hail and good wishes, it was a wedding feast the likes of which many had ne'er experienced and certainly wouldn't have expected to enjoy on the grassy, sun-kissed cliffs behind Cuidrach Castle, once a lonely ruin, now fully restored to its one-time grandeur and strength.

Its ghosts reconciled and at peace.

Indeed, to the happy carousers feasting beneath the slanting Highland sun, the cold wet winds of winter and Cuidrach's own gloomier past now seemed but a distant memory.

Relics of better-forgotten yesterdays with no place in Cuidrach's triumphant future.

Truth tell, a more vital, real-seeming attraction proved the splendid sixteen-oared longship riding the swells not far from the gold-burnished sands of Loch Hourn's curving shore.

Eye-catching and sleek, the galley drew many *ooohs* and *aaahs* from the men amongst the guests. And most impressive of all, the single-masted greyhound of the sea boasted a high prow carved to resemble a magnificent rearing stag—an unmistakable gesture of kinship from Duncan MacKenzie.

A token of the Black Stag of Kintail's irrefutable regard.

His forever warning to any fool crazed enough to doubt the Keeper of Cuidrach's authority.

His—and his lady wife's—place in the clan.

Just as the promise of a second galley, still being built in Scotland's far north, assured the goodwill of Archibald Macnicol and his sons.

Their boundless love.

A treasure Mariota now knew she'd possessed all along—just as she'd spent the last weeks reassuring a certain stubborn graybeard that he'd ne'er lost hers.

Nor would.

Not in a thousand lifetimes.

Her throat thickening, she blinked, poked at a wrinkle in the fine linen covering the bridal table—until a delighted female laugh drew her gaze to Nessa and Sir Lachlan. Wed only a fortnight ago, they looked a world apart from the other revelers and her own joy welled just watching them.

Feeling more blessed than she would have e'er believed, she gave in to the emotion flooding her and looked at her own beloved, wondered if it were possible to die of such all-consuming happiness.

Such endless, soaring bliss.

"Heigh-ho, my lady, you do glow this day. And you make the fairest bride I've e'er set eyes upon." Cuidrach's new seneschal gave her a jaunty smile. "The Keeper can be proud to have you," he owned, setting down a platter of cheese and sweetmeats. "He could not have done better."

"Nay, Finlay, I could not have done better." Mariota returned the little man's smile, her heart warming upon seeing how well *he* was doing.

How remarkably fast he'd recovered from a sword swipe that should have felled him.

She opened her mouth to say so, but before she could, her father gave a great hoot and slapped his hand on the table. "Ha—yon fox!" he cried, his gaze latching onto Cuillin and the old dog's new friend, Devorgilla of Doon's pet fox. "I have seen that wily creature before!"

He looked around the table, his expression incredulous. "On the journey here it was, I say you!"

"And so you may." Beside him, Devorgilla helped herself to a handful of honeyed almonds, tossed a few to her little friend and the dog. "Somerled ne'er tires of roaming the land."

Looking skeptical, the puissant old warrior harrumphed,

reached for his wine cup. "And I suppose the wee beastie ne'er fails to return to your hearth?"

Devorgilla's eyes twinkled. "Ach, to be sure, and that is the way of it."

Archibald frowned. "Just dinna tell me he was guiding us here?" He fixed a suspicious stare on the black-garbed old woman.

"You do not believe that he did?" the crone evaded. "There are many wonders in this world," she said, looking at Mariota and Kenneth. "Ne'er doubt them—marvels though they may seem."

Reaching out a gnarled hand, she tapped a finger to the bridal table's centerpiece, a fine golden lute.

Her gift to the happy twain.

"'Tis a special heirloom, this," she explained, a touch of satisfaction in her voice. "If my choice was wise, it will e'er mind those needing comfort that life's brightest joys can only be savored after the darkest of nights."

As if to prove it, the lute glowed at her touch—its gold turning bright and luminous.

"See you," she finished, crooking another smile, "wonders abound—leastways for those with the faith to believe. But of all the world's magic, the most wondrous of all is a heart that loves true."

And Mariota couldn't have agreed more.

Her eyes misting, she felt sweetest, golden warmth fill *her* heart, knew the wonder, the power, of truest, purest love. It surrounded her now, was there on the faces smiling back at her, not few amongst them as damp-eyed as her own.

Even if some like Duncan MacKenzie and her father, now deep in conversation with Devorgilla and a tall, scar-

faced Sassunach named Sir Marmaduke, tried to disguise
it behind grunts and gruff stares.

Others didn't.

Across the grass, on a large space cleared for dancing,
young Jamie and her favorite brother, Donald, paid hefty
court to Gunna of the Glen, their good-natured attempts
to outdo the other in winning the fair widow's favor not
quite the kind of love now filling Mariota's heart, but a
joyous sort, indeed.

And the very kind she intended to enjoy later, after the
feasting.

At the thought, her blood quickened and she almost
wished the celebrations over.

Instead she sighed and smiled.

Too many friends and kinsmen had journeyed great
distances to share the day, so for the now, she contented
herself with reaching for her Keeper's hand, lacing her
fingers with his.

"You are content?" he asked, squeezing her hand.

"I have ne'er been happier . . . ever." She swallowed,
felt her eyes begin to burn again. "My joy could not be
more perfect. Though . . ."

"Though . . . *what*?"

Kenneth watched her, suddenly wary when her gaze
slid to his uncle and that one's quiet, wine-sipping friend.
Her brow furrowed and there was something not quite
right about the way she narrowed her eyes on the two
men.

"I must say," she mused, her tone unsettling him even
more, "the day might have been more complete if you'd
invited that great paladin friend of yours—*Sir Duncan
Strongbow.*"

At the name, Sir Marmaduke Strongbow and Duncan MacKenzie swiveled their heads her way, their brows raised in mutual question.

Mariota smiled, lifted her wine cup in silent salute.

Kenneth flushed. "You guessed."

"Only just now," Mariota admitted, the knowledge making her heart thump even more. "But I would like to know why?"

Looking uncomfortable, her Keeper shifted on the trestle bench. "You truly do not know?"

Mariota let go of his hand, traced the wrinkle in the tablecloth. "Mayhap I would hear the words?"

Kenneth blew out a breath. Frowning now, he hooked his fingers beneath her chin and lifted her face, brushed his lips quickly over hers. "I have told you already, lass— I love you."

He looked round at the others, not at all surprised to find them staring.

Gawking.

And, to a man, looking like dim-witted, fool-grinning loons.

The smiles, sniffles, and snorts, he could take, but the gawking pushed him past his limits.

"By the Rood—aye, you heard a'right! I love the woman!" he snapped, reaching for her again, dragging her against him for another kiss.

A rough-edged, claiming one this time.

Deep and ravenous—much to his guests' approval.

"And," he declared, raking kith and kin with a hot-eyed stare, "lest any present suffer doubts, I made up the name Sir Duncan Strongbow because I could not bear to lose my lady to another—was willing to do anything to keep her. Everyone here will know that a man named thusly could ne'er prove a threat!"

He turned back to her then, his dark eyes blazing, but with passion. "You are not wroth, are you?"

"O-o-oh, nay, I am anything but angry," she breathed, wondering he couldn't see her elation, the *love* crashing through her.

She flicked a glance at Cuidrach's towers, namely their bedchamber window. "But since you asked, I might have to think of a few ways for you to make it up to me."

Kenneth arched a brow. "Say you?"

"Indeed. So long as you would not mind?"

"Mind?"

The Keeper of Cuidrach smiled.

"Sweet lass, it shall be my pleasure," he said, kissing her again. "My entire pleasure."

About the Author

SUE-ELLEN WELFONDER is a dedicated medievalist of Scottish descent who spent fifteen years living abroad, and still makes annual research trips to Great Britain. She is an active member of the Romance Writers of America and her own clan, the MacFie Society of North America. Her first novel, *Devil in a Kilt,* was one of *Romantic Times*'s top picks. It won *RT*'s Reviewers' Choice Award for Best First Historical Romance of 2001. Sue-Ellen Welfonder is married and lives with her husband, Manfred, and their Jack Russell Terrier, Em, in Florida.

Chapter One

✦

CUIDRACH CASTLE
AUTUMN 1347

Across miles of darkling hills and empty moorland, thick with bracken and winter-browned heather, Clan MacKenzie's Cuidrach Castle loomed above the silent waters of Loch Hourn, the stronghold's proud towers and its great sentinel, the Bastard Stone, silhouetted against a cold, frosty sky.

A chill night, icy stars glittered in the heavens and knifing winds whistled past the windows, rattling shutters and making those within glad for the leaping flames of the great hall's well-burning log fire and the eager-to-please squires circulating with trays of hot, spiced wine and steaming mounds of fresh-baked meat pasties. Men crowded benches drawn close to the hearth, jesting and jostling amongst themselves, their rich masculine laughter rising to the ceiling rafters, bawdy good cheer ringing in every ear.

Only one of Cuidrach's residents shunned the comforts and warmth of the hall this night, seeking instead the privacy of a tiny storeroom filled with wine casks, blessed torchlight, and James Macpherson's mounting frustration.

Holding back an oath that would surely curl the Devil's own toes, Young James of the Heather, sometimes teasingly called Jamie the Small, glared at the tiny red bead of blood on his thumb.

It was the fifth such jab wound he'd inflicted on himself in under an hour. And, he suspected, most likely not the last. Not if he meant to complete his task.

Sighing, he licked the blood off his finger and then shoved his stool closer to the best-burning wall torch. Mayhap with brighter light, he'd have a better chance of restitching the let-out seams of his new linen tunic.

It was a birthday gift from his liege-laird's lady and the finest tunic he'd e'er possessed. Softer than rose petals and with a bold Nordic design embroidered around the neck opening, just looking at it brought a flush of pleasure to his cheeks, and his heart thumped if he thought about the long hours Lady Mariota had spent crafting such a gift for him.

A gift he was determined to wear to his birthday revelries later that night.

He would, too. If only the tunic weren't so tight across the shoulders, the sleeves a mite too short. And his fool fingers so damnably clumsy.

Frowning, Jamie picked up his needle and set to work again. Truth be told, there was nothing wrong with the tunic . . . it was him.

Always had been him. *He was simply too big.*

And, he decided a short while later, his hearing was a bit too sharp. Leastways keen enough to note the sudden silence pressing against the closed storeroom door. He tilted his head, listening. His instincts hadn't lied: gone indeed were the muffled bursts of laughter and ribald song, the occasional barks of the castle dogs, the high-pitched skirls of female delight. Utter stillness held Cuidrach's great hall in a firm grip, the strange hush smothering all sound.

A deep kind of quiet that didn't smell well, even held sinister significance—if he were to trust the way the fine hairs on his nape were lifting. Or the cold chill spilling down his spine.

Curious, he set aside the unfinished tunic and his needle and stood. But before he could cross the tiny store-room, the door swung open. His liege-laird, Sir Kenneth MacKenzie, stood in the doorway, flanked by Sir Lachlan, the Cuidrach garrison captain, and a travel-stained man Jamie had never seen.

The stranger's rain-dampened cloak hung about his shoulders and his wind-tangled hair bespoke a hard ride. But it was more than the man's muddied boots and bleary-eyed fatigue that made Jamie's mouth run dry.

It was the look on the stranger's face.

The undeniable impression of strain and pity that poured off him and filled the little storeroom until Jamie thought he might choke on its rankness, especially when he caught the same wary sadness mirrored in Sir Kenneth's and Sir Lachlan's eyes.

Jamie froze. "What is it?" he asked, his gaze moving from face to face. "Tell me straight away for I can see that something dire has happened."

"Aye, lad, I'm afraid that is so. Would that I could make it otherwise, but . . ." Kenneth glanced at the stranger, cleared his throat. "See you, this man comes from Carnach in the north of Kintail. Alan Mor Matheson of Fairmaiden Castle sent him. He brings ill tidings. Your father—"

"Of a mercy!" Jamie stared at them. "Dinna tell me he is dead?"

None of the three men said a word, but the tautness of their grim-set expressions said . . . everything.

Jamie blinked, a wave of black dizziness washing over him. Sakes, even the floor seemed to dip and heave beneath his feet. It couldn't be true. Naught could have struck down his indomitable father. Munro Macpherson was honed from coldest iron, had steel running in his veins. And after a lifetime of the man's indifference, Jamie shouldn't care what fate befell him.

But he did, more than he would've believed. So much so that the roar of his own blood in his ears kept him from hearing what Kenneth was saying. He could only see the other man's mouth moving, the sad way Sir Lachlan and the courier shook their heads.

Jamie swallowed, pressed cold fingers against his temples. "Tell me that again, sir. I-I didna hear you."

"I said your father is not dead, though he is faring poorly, has taken to his bed. That's why Laird Matheson sent his man to us." Kenneth came forward, gripped Jamie's arms. "And there has been a tragedy, aye."

Jamie's heart stopped. He could scarce speak. Breaking away from Kenneth's grasp, he searched the men's faces. "If not my father, then who? One of my brothers?"

The three men exchanged glances.

Telling glances.

And so damning they filled Jamie with more dread

than if someone had leveled a sword at his throat. For one sickening moment, the faces of his nine brothers flashed before his eyes and he thought he was going to faint. But before he could, Sir Lachlan unfastened the hip flask at his belt, thrust the flagon into Jamie's hand.

"Drink this," he urged, his face grim. "All of it if you can."

And Jamie did, gulping down the fiery *uisge-beatha* so quickly the strong Highland spirits burned his throat and watered his eyes.

The last soft-burning droplets still on his tongue, he squared his shoulders and prepared for the worst. "Tell me true," he entreated, his fingers clenching around the flask. "Which one of my brothers is dead?"

"It grieves me to tell you, lad." Kenneth drew a long breath, slid another glance at the courier. " 'Tis not one of your brothers, but all of them. They drowned in the swollen waters of the Garbh Uisge when the footbridge collapsed beneath them."

"Christ God, no-o-o!" Shock and horror slammed into Jamie, crashing over him in hot and cold waves as an eerie silence swelled anew, its damning weight blotting all sound but a high-pitched buzzing in his ears and the keening wind.

A low, unearthly moan he only recognized as his own when lancing pain closed his throat and the wailing ceased.

And as soon as it did, he staggered backward, sagged against the stacked wine casks, disbelief laming him. His knees began to tremble and his vision blurred, his entire world contracting to a whirling black void.

A spinning darkness made all the more terrifying

because it taunted him with glimpses of his brothers' faces, cold and gray in death, but also as they'd been in life.

Neill, the oldest, with auburn hair bright as Jamie's own and the same hazel eyes. Confident and proud, he was the most hot-tempered of Jamie's brothers. After Neill, came Kendrick, the most dashing with his roguish grin and easy wit, with his ability to create a stir amongst the ladies simply by entering a room.

Then there was Hamish, the dreamer. A secret romantic, good-natured, quiet, and most content when left alone to ponder great chivalric myths and tales of ancient Gaelic heroism. And six others, all dear to him, brothers who'd been his lifeblood in the years his father had shunned him.

His heart's joy and only solace right up to the day he'd struck out across the heater, found a new home and purpose as squire to Duncan MacKenzie, the Black Stag of Kintail, his liege-laird's uncle.

And now his brothers were gone.

Jamie closed his eyes and swallowed. He couldn't believe it. He wouldn't be able to accept the loss so long as he had breath in his body. But when he opened his eyes and looked into the troubled faces of the three men standing just inside the storeroom's threshold, he knew it was true.

Still, he tried to deny it.

"It canna be. My brothers knew every clump of heather, every peat bog and lochan, every stone and hill face of our land," he said, willing the room to stop spinning. "They crossed that footbridge every day, would have known if it was near to collapsing."

The courier shrugged, looked uncomfortable. "'Tis thought the recurrent rains of late weakened the wood. The planks were aged and warped, some of them rotted. My pardon, sir, but you've not been to Baldreagan in years. The bridge truly was in need of repair."

Jamie struggled against the pain, gave the courier a long, probing look. "You are certain they are dead? All nine? There can be no mistake?"

"Nay, son, I am sorry." The man shook his head, his words squelching Jamie's last shimmer of hope. "I saw the bodies with my own eyes, was there when they were pulled from the river."

Jamie nodded, unable to speak.

The words tore a hole in his heart, stirred up images he couldn't bear. With great effort, he pushed away from the wine casks and moved to the storeroom's narrow-slit window, welcomed the blast of chill air, the heavy scent of rain on the raw, wet wind.

He curled his fingers around his sword belt, held tight as he looked out on the night mist, the dark ring of pines crouching so near to Cuidrach's walls. Swallowing hard, he fixed his gaze on the silent hills, willed their peace to soothe him. But this night, the beauty of Kintail failed him.

Indeed, he doubted that even the sweetest stretch of heather could calm him. He wondered how moments ago his only concern had been restitching his birthday tunic, and now . . . He tightened his grip on his belt, let out a long, unsteady breath just as Cuillin, his aged dog, nudged his leg, whimpering until he reached down to stroke the beast's shaggy head.

In return, Cuillin looked up at him with concern-filled

eyes, thumped his scraggly tail on the floor rushes. Neill had given him the dog, Jamie recalled, a shudder ripping through him at the memory. But as soon as the tremor passed, he turned back to the room, his decision made.

He cleared his throat. "I've ne'er been one to thrust myself into places where I am not welcome," he began, standing as straight as he could, "but I need to ride to Baldreagan, whether my presence suits my father or no. I must pay my respects to my brothers. 'Tis a debt I owe them."

To his surprise, the courier's mouth quirked in an awkward smile. " 'Tis glad I am to hear you say that," he said, stepping forward. "See you, as it happens, I've brought more than ill tidings."

He paused, puffed his chest a bit. "Truth be told, I have something that might prove of great interest to you."

Jamie cocked a brow, said nothing.

Undaunted, the courier fished aside his cloak, withdrew a rolled parchment tied with colorful string and sealed with wax. "Something that might give a lift to your aching heart. See here, I've a letter from—"

"My father?" Jamie asked, incredulous.

The courier shook his head. "Och, goodness, nay. Your da is in no form to be dashing off letters. 'Tis from my liege, Laird Matheson. But he sends it in your father's name—and out of his own wish to do well by you."

Jamie eyed the letter, suspicion making him wary. "My father and Alan Mor were e'er at odds. It is one thing for Matheson, as our nearest neighbor, to send word of my brothers' deaths if my father was unable. But to pen a letter in my da's name? And out of courtesy to me? Nay, I canna believe it."

"On my soul, it is true." The courier held out the parchment. "Much has changed in the years you've been away. As the letter will prove. You might even be pleasantly surprised."

Jamie bit back an oath, not wanting to take out his pain on a hapless courier. "I'd say this day has brought enough surprises." He looked down, nudged the floor rushes with the toe of his boot. "I'm not sure I wish to be privy to any more."

But he took the parchment, ran his thumb over the seal. "Though I will admit to being . . . curious."

"Then read the letter," Kenneth urged him. "What the man says makes sense, Jamie. Now might be a good time to mend the breach with your sire, put the past behind you."

I have tried to do that the whole of my life, Jamie almost blurted out. Instead, he found himself breaking the wax seal, unrolling the parchment. He stepped close to a wall torch, scanned the squiggly lines of ink, an odd mix of astonishment and dismay welling inside him.

A brief flare of anger, too. That he should be welcomed home only now, under such grievous circumstances. As for the rest . . . he looked up from the parchment, ran a quick hand through his hair.

He started to speak, but the words caught in his throat, trapped there by the irony of his plight. If Alan Mor weren't playing some nefarious game, everything he'd e'er wanted now lay within his reach.

If he did what was asked of him.

Seemingly in high favor for the first time in his life, he turned to the courier, tried not to frown. "You know what is in here?" And when the man nodded he continued, "Is it true that my father and Alan Mor have entered into an alliance? One they meant to seal with the marriage of my brother Neill and Alan Mor's eldest daughter?"

The man bobbed his head again. " 'Tis the God's truth, aye. So sure as I'm standing here." He accepted the ale cup Sir Lachlan offered him, took a sip before he went on. "Your father is in sore need, asks daily if you've arrived. He's failing by the day, won't even set foot outside his bedchamber. 'Tis hoped your return will revive him."

Pausing, the man stepped closer, laid a conspiratorial hand on Jamie's arm. "That, and seeing the alliance between the clans upheld."

"Through my marriage to this . . . Aveline?"

"Tchach, lad, which other lass would you have?" The courier drew himself up, looked mildly affronted. "Poor Sorcha is heartbroken o'er the loss of her Neill, and too old for you by years. The other daughters are already wed. It has to be Aveline—she's the youngest. And still a maid."

Jamie eyed the man askance, would've sworn he could feel an iron yoke settling on his shoulders.

It scarce mattered to him if Aveline Matheson was tender of years. And the state of her maidenhood concerned him even less.

He remembered the lassies of Fairmaiden Castle but, regrettably, not by name. If memory served, there wasn't a one amongst the brood he'd care to meet on a moonless night. And with surety nary a one he'd wish to bed.

One nearly equaled him in height and build. Another sported a mustache some men would envy. And one e'er smelled of onions. Truth be told, he couldn't recall a single redeeming feature amongst the lot of them. Binding himself to such a female would prove the surest and quickest route to misery.

But he did want to see his father, help him if he could.

Jamie sighed, felt the yoke tightening around his neck. "I ne'er thought to see my father again in this life. For certes, not because he claims to need me. As for taking one of the Matheson's daughters to wife—"

"Och, but Aveline is more than pleasing. And spirited." The courier stepped in front of him, blocking the way when Jamie would have paced back to the window. "She brings a healthy marriage portion, too. Prime grazing lands for your da's cattle. I say you, you willna be sorry. I swear it on the souls of my sons."

"I will think on it," Jamie offered, doing his best to hide his discomfiture.

"Why don't you hie yourself into the hall to get a meal and some sleep?" Kenneth clamped a hand on the courier's elbow, steering him to the door. "Jamie will give you his decision on the morrow."

Turning back to Jamie, he arched a raven brow. "For someone who spent his life yearning to win his father's favor, tell me why you lost all color upon hearing of the man's sudden need for you? Surely you aren't troubled by this talk of a desired marriage?"

Jamie folded his arms over his chest, felt heat creeping up the back of his neck. Damn him for a chivalrous fool, but he couldn't bring himself to voice his misgivings and admit he'd rather have his tender parts shrivel and fall off before he'd find himself obliged to bed one of Alan Mor's daughters.

If he even could!

"Ach, dinna look so glum." Sir Lachlan took the letter, glanced at it. "There is nothing writ here that binds you," he said, looking up from the parchment. "You needn't do aught you find displeasing."

And that was Jamie's problem.

Returning home, even now, *would* please him. So much, his heart nearly burst at the thought. And once there, he'd be hard-pressed to disappoint his father.

Or Aveline Matheson.

If indeed such an alliance required his compliance. Truth was, he lived by a strict code of honor, one that forbade him to shame an innocent maid—even if sparing her feelings came at the cost of his own.

Heaving a sigh, he snatched up his birthday tunic and donned it, unfinished seams or no. "We all ken I shall wed the lass if my da wishes it," he said, moving to the door. "I'll ride for Baldreagan at first light, and visit Alan Mor so soon as I've seen my father."

His intentions stated, he stepped into the great hall, paused to appreciate its smoky, torch-lit warmth. The comfort of kith and kin, a crackling hearth fire. Everyday pleasures his brothers would never again enjoy. Indeed, compared to their fate, his own struck him as more than palatable.

So long as Aveline wasn't the sister almost his own size, he'd find some way to tolerate her.

Or so he hoped.

THE DISH

Where authors give you the inside scoop!

♥ ♥ ♥ ♥ ♥ ♥ ♥ ♥ ♥ ♥ ♥ ♥ ♥ ♥ ♥ ♥

From the desk of Sue-Ellen Welfonder

Some characters wrap themselves around an author's heart and hold fast, claiming their place and beguiling, until the author agrees to write their book.

Kenneth MacKenzie, the hero of **UNTIL THE KNIGHT COMES** (on sale now), is such a character. Indeed, he has haunted me since my very first book, **DEVIL IN A KILT**, winner of the 2001 *Romantic Times* award for Best First Historical Romance. Kenneth's father was the villain in that book and, although he was quite dastardly, he also possessed a certain undeniable charm. So much so that I always regretted not being able to redeem him. But I could give him a bastard son, a hero just as dashing as his roguish father but worthy of becoming the Keeper of Cuidrach, the proud inheritance Clan MacKenzie reserves for the most valiant amongst the clan's by-blows.

Darkly seductive, Kenneth first appeared in my previous book, **ONLY FOR A KNIGHT**, but this one is his. Now he must claim his birthright, Cuidrach Castle and the Legacy of the Bastard Stone. And although he is well able to do this and more, he is not at all prepared to have his heart claimed by the enticing and mysterious woman who so unexpectedly greets him when he arrives at his supposedly deserted keep. Together, they must face a maze of secrets, betrayals, and a very determined enemy before they can surrender to the redeeming power of love.

Readers wishing for a peek at Kenneth's world might enjoy visiting my Web site at www.welfonder.com to see photos of Kintail and even the famed Bastard Stone. I happened across just such an unusual sea cliff while visiting Scotland during the writing of this book. Seeing it warmed my heart and convinced me that Kenneth and Mariota would indeed find their happy ending.

With all good wishes,

Sue-Ellen Welfonder

www.welfonder.com

♥ ♥ ♥ ♥ ♥ ♥ ♥ ♥ ♥ ♥ ♥ ♥ ♥ ♥ ♥ ♥

From the desk of Michelle Rowen

Angels and demons and talking rats. Oh my!

The best part about writing a paranormal romance novel is that *anything is possible.* If I get an idea for a book and think "This is a little weird. I haven't seen anything like this before," that's actually a *good* thing.

On the surface these stories may appear different and otherworldly, even bizarre . . . but I think the reason for the genre's immense popularity is that it acts as a mirror to our own lives, reflecting themes that are sometimes easier to look at if presented in a more fantastical manner.

My fallen angel in **ANGEL WITH ATTITUDE** (on sale now) isn't *just* a fallen angel: She's a girl who simply wants to go back home. She doesn't understand what happened, and will do anything in her power to make everything okay again. My demon isn't just a demon: He's the good-looking bad boy who's way too easy to fall for. Underneath his tough, snarky exterior, though, is a man who hates his existence, but is afraid to make a change (the devil you know vs. the devil you don't—only in this case it's *literal*). He knows he's living a lie, but he needs somebody to restore his faith in himself, humanity, and . . . *sigh* . . . love.

Together they discover that appearances are not always what they seem; that there are no easy answers in life; that the most difficult journey isn't always one of distance, but one we take within ourselves; and that having a witch girlfriend who thinks you're cheating on her is a good way to get yourself turned into a rat.

However, that last one's really just common sense.

Happy Reading!

Michelle Rowen

www.michellerowen.com